D0372984

Welles [...] chamber and yanked open the heavy door

Dr. Theophilus Algernon Tanner was gone in a puff of smoke, vanished in the fog, taken away a second time as if he had never existed.

"He's away, Director Welles," a technician stated. "We're showing a ninety-eight percent probability of a successful matter transfer via temporal annex."

"Do you think he made it, sir?" Chan asked.

"I don't care whether he makes it in one piece or not."

"Then what's the point, sir?"

"Peace of mind. And I'll tell you this much. I hope Tanner made it. Hell, yes, I hope he made it, the arrogant son of a bitch, and wherever he is, I hope he's choking on the whatever future hell he's trapped."

Other titles in the Deathlands saga:

Pilgrimage to Hell
Red Holocaust
Neutron Solstice
Crater Lake
Homeward Bound
Pony Soldiers
Dectra Chain
Ice and Fire
Red Equinox
Northstar Rising
Time Nomads
Latitude Zero
Seedling
Dark Carnival
Chill Factor
Moon Fate
Fury's Pilgrims
Shockscape
Deep Empire
Cold Asylum
Twilight Children
Rider, Reaper
Road Wars
Trader Redux
Genesis Echo
Shadowfall
Ground Zero
Emerald Fire
Bloodlines
Crossways
Keepers of the Sun
Circle Thrice
Eclipse at Noon
Stoneface
Bitter Fruit
Skydark
Demons of Eden
The Mars Arena
Watersleep
Nightmare Passage
Way of the Wolf

A GOLD EAGLE BOOK FROM
WORLDWIDE®

TORONTO • NEW YORK • LONDON
AMSTERDAM • PARIS • SYDNEY • HAMBURG
STOCKHOLM • ATHENS • TOKYO • MILAN
MADRID • WARSAW • BUDAPEST • AUCKLAND

This one's for Richard P. "Rick" Law, my seldom seen Yankee brother-in-law, a great bear of a man with the necessary combat knowledge and the survival wherewithal to feel right at home stomping around in the world of Deathlands. But be warned, Rick—next time we take the wives out on the town, *you're* picking up the tab.

First edition October 1998

ISBN 0-373-62543-X

DARK EMBLEM

Printed in U.S.A.

"I have broken the rainbow
against my heart...
I have blown the clouds of rose color and blood color
I have drowned my dreams."

—Luis Muñoz Marin
First elected Governor of Puerto Rico

"All things are taken from us, and become portions and parcels of the dreadful past."

—Alfred, Lord Tennyson

THE DEATHLANDS SAGA

This world is their legacy, a world born in the violent nuclear spasm of 2001 that was the bitter outcome of a struggle for global dominance.

There is no real escape from this shockscape where life always hangs in the balance, vulnerable to newly demonic nature, barbarism, lawlessness.

But they are the warrior survivalists, and they endure—in the way of the lion, the hawk and the tiger, true to nature's heart despite its ruination.

Ryan Cawdor: The privileged son of an East Coast baron. Acquainted with betrayal from a tender age, he is a master of the hard realities.
Krysty Wroth: Harmony ville's own Titian-haired beauty, a woman with the strength of tempered steel. Her premonitions and Gaia powers have been fostered by her Mother Sonja.
J. B. Dix, the Armorer: Weapons master and Ryan's close ally, he, too, honed his skills traversing the Deathlands with the legendary Trader.
Doctor Theophilus Tanner: Torn from his family and a gentler life in 1896, Doc has been thrown into a future he couldn't have imagined.
Dr. Mildred Wyeth: Her father was killed by the Ku Klux Klan, but her fate is not much lighter. Restored from predark cryogenic suspension, she brings twentieth-century healing skills to a nightmare.
Jak Lauren: A true child of the wastelands, reared on adversity, loss and danger, the albino teenager is a fierce fighter and loyal friend.
Dean Cawdor: Ryan's young son by Sharona accepts the only world he knows, and yet he is the seedling bearing the promise of tomorrow.

In a world where all was lost, they are humanity's last hope....

Prologue

The Beginning:
Omaha, Nebraska,
November, 1896

Dr. Theophilus Algernon Tanner was a most striking man—not handsome, but fascinating all the same in the most abstract sense of the word. His countenance came equipped with a head of prematurely gray hair that flowed down to his shoulders, a mouthful of strong, white teeth and a long, thin face with inquisitive bright blue eyes set below an imposingly high forehead. Tall and lanky, his very being vibrated with that special inner glow that marked men of potential greatness.

Dr. Tanner was one of those gifted few who seemed to literally shoot off sparks while thinking, and that was most of the time, since his mind was always working.

Indeed, his most attractive attribute lay below the surface. Tanner's most notable feature was the brilliant brain encased in his skull, a mass of tissue containing more education and raw knowledge than any ten of his academic contemporaries. He held two degrees by the age of twenty-five—a doctorate of science from Harvard, and a doctorate of philosophy from Oxford University in England, along with dozens of other diplomas, honors, awards and accolades. He'd given up framing and hanging them long ago, choosing to let the proof of his many accomplishments rest unattended within a wooden cedar chest in his attic.

A vain man could have covered four walls with the prizes of his profession, but Tanner wasn't a vain man.

Pompous at times, but never vain. He was much too practical for vanity.

Emily Chandler considered herself lucky to have caught him, and she loved her man with all her heart and soul. The woman was gorgeous, a vision in subtle beauty. The skin of her heart-shaped face was creamy white, her flawless complexion the perfect backdrop for her dark eyes and long auburn hair.

And she was always smiling, a small hidden grin that played on her lips as if she were finding joy from her own private amusements. To the average man of the period, she might have come across as threatening, her shining intelligence inescapable despite her feminine beauty.

Seen from afar while exiting a Harvard campus library one spring afternoon by a yearning Theo Tanner, she was utterly desirable. When the good Mr. Tanner had opportunity to address a gathering of female students a few weeks later, he gleefully said he opposed the idea that women should ever be allowed to vote in order to raise her ire and gain her attentions.

He found having her spend many late hours trying to persuade him of his folly to be a much easier way of meeting her than going right up and asking her to accompany him out to dinner or a show. During his younger days of intense study and teaching, he was a gangly twenty-year-old intent on mastering the universe.

One hour with Emily Chandler and he knew he had at last found something he coveted even more than knowledge, for Theo Tanner had never been in love before. He'd never made the time for romance, spending his years striving forward to better himself, to understand the world and its surroundings, to read, to seek, to know. His quest for knowledge was tempered with caution, hence his twin majors of study and expertise.

Now, at the age of twenty-eight, he was perched on the cusp of true happiness. In four more years, he'd be present at the turn of the century, and he was only beginning to guess at the marvels the future would bring. Still, daring to venture beyond the mortal coils of the known into the great unknown was the mission of any worthy scientist, but having the proper moral code to know what to do with your discoveries was another matter.

That was why he had double-majored, taking his second degree in philosophy, staying up all hours of the night and always reading, learning, cramming his already-stuffed mind with even more information. He was constantly talking out loud to himself, a habit from childhood he'd never managed to break, or repeating the words he was reading over and over, ingraining them in his memory for future use, whether on exams or in the real world. Once he learned something, Theo Tanner didn't forget.

The family made a point of taking a daily walk, either before he left to go to his morning classes, or after Tanner returned home in the afternoon from the university. The air was good for the children, and allowed the family a chance to exercise and share pleasantries with their fellow citizens as they strolled the sidewalks surrounding their cozy two-story home. In these early months of winter, Emily would bundle up young Jolyon and place him inside the carriage, while Tanner assisted Rachel in buttoning her coat and wrapping the child's long red scarf around her delicate neck.

Then the front door would be thrown open, and away the family would go.

Tanner was wearing his long overcoat with small golden buttons, belted snugly at his waist. A high collar and a cravat were held in place by a gleaming diamond pin. He carried a handsome ebony walking stick with a gold-plated tip and handle to match the buttons of his coat.

His right arm was linked around Emily's slender limb. She wore her own long overcoat, which came down to her knees and fastened up primly and warmly to her neck. On her head was a wide-brimmed hat with a long cluster of white and gray feathers bobbed on the left.

"I say, Theophilus, hold up!"

A stout man in a worn black wide hat and matching cloak was racing up behind them, calling out Tanner's name repeatedly as he came closer, the leather soles of his shoes slapping down on the wooden sidewalk.

"Hello, Jonathan," Tanner replied easily as the man in the hat and cloak came thudding to a stop. "Glad to see you out bettering your body this brisk morning."

"Better? My body? Huh. Don't believe so. Whew!" the man gasped back in reply, striving to catch his wind from the sprint.

"I hope you are well, Mr. Nolan," Emily added.

"Never better, dear Emily," Jonathan Nolan replied, and tipped his hat to Rachel. "Good morning to you, Miss Rachel."

"H'lo," the young girl said, embarrassed at the direct attention. She turned shyly and averted her eyes to look across the street. A horse-drawn carriage clattered up and came to a stop at the curb. Rachel loved horses and she admired the creature as it waited patiently for the passenger in the carriage to step down, pay the driver's fare, and then depart.

"What can we do for you, Jonathan?" Tanner asked. "Working on another scientific article for your newspaper? I would be glad to proof it for you this evening at home after our supper. Anything for a man trying to enlighten his readers. No time right now, I am afraid—unless you want to loan me a copy to take along."

"No, no article this time, actually, but as always you shall be the first I contact for a quote or to check facts," the overweight man replied. "I just came from Martin's Books and he mentioned the book you ordered had arrived—a first edition of Houseman's *A Shropshire Lad.*"

Tanner looked puzzled. "I must confess, Jonathan, that while I have long coveted such a volume, I had placed no such order. Martin must be in error."

"No, Theo, he is not." Emily sighed. "I placed the order. I know you frequent Pages Bookstore, and I tried another in the hopes of avoiding your discovery of my surprise. The book was to have been for Christmas."

Nolan blushed with embarrassment. "Dash it all, I am terribly sorry. I can—"

A shrill scream cut him off, and it took a few seconds before Tanner realized the sound was coming from his daughter. A second after his realization, the child gripped his hand with bone-crushing force. Jolyon, his sleep disrupted, also began to wail from the confines of the carriage.

"Rachel, what is it, child? What?" Tanner thundered, kneeling to reach eye level with the girl. Her eyes were still looking out upon the empty street, the horse and carriage now long gone. He peered out, his eyes searching for what had upset her so, but saw nothing out of the ordinary.

Nothing at all.

Tanner canceled his classes at the university for the day, choosing to stay at home with his daughter. He didn't press Rachel for an explanation, instead waiting for the girl to speak to him when she was ready. The day passed slowly, with Tanner trying to concentrate on a book but failing miserably. Finally, much later that night, as he tucked his older child into bed, the youngster at last described what had frightened her on the sidewalk.

"I saw something, Father. In the air." Even at her young age, Rachel was her father's child, and her choice and usage of words were precise.

"Saw what, dear Child? A bird? Bat? Flying squirrel? What?" Tanner asked, offering up suggestions, none of which seemed to be correct.

"The air looked odd," Rachel continued. "Like it was hot. And there was an eye in the middle of it."

Tanner mused over that revelation for a moment.

"An eye belonging to whom?" he finally asked.

Rachel was evasive. "A big eye, Father. I think it was looking at me from heaven."

Even as his mind tried to process what his little girl was telling him, Tanner spoke in calm tones, slipping easily into the patented parental know-it-all mode. "Then, Child, if the eye was from heaven, there is no reason for you to be frightened. After all, logic dictates there is no reason for you to be scared if God is looking down at us."

The explanation seemed to placate the girl. "You think so, Father?"

"I do," Tanner said firmly.

"Very well, then, Father," Rachel replied sleepily, her memory of the magical eye apparently already vanishing into the depths of her young mind after Tanner's reassurances. "Good night."

"Good night, Child," he replied and kissed her softly on the forehead.

"So?" Emily asked when her husband joined her in their own bed.

"We have no cause for fear, my dear one," Tanner remarked as he pulled the heavy down comforter over his body, and quickly explained Rachel's biblically tinged interpretation of what she'd seen hovering in the air.

"That is sweet," Emily said, snuggling closer to his shoulder. "We must be truly blessed if God is watching us."

"Aye, indeed," Tanner said sleepily as he placed a comforting arm around his wife. "Blessed."

So why did his daughter's story nag at him so? Rachel wasn't prone to childish lies or exaggeration. Like her mother, she was quite direct and forthcoming. He found his parental concern battling his scientific curiosity, and determined he'd return tomorrow to the same spot and spend some time observing the area of air that had disturbed his child, thereby satiating both. For while Tanner was a man always fascinated by the unknown, he was a father even more interested in the well-being of his children.

THE FRIGHT YOUNG RACHEL had suffered cast a pall over the family's usual walks, and with Emily's agreement to stay behind and watch over the children, Theo Tanner had chosen to make these daily excursions alone, always stopping at the same corner where the mysterious organ of sight had previously levitated. He would loiter there for hours, waiting. Each day, he waited longer, making his trips during the same time span in hopes of glimpsing the oculus, yet nothing happened. No shimmering of light, no blinking of an unearthly eyeball, no haze hanging in the air before his own astonished eyes—nothing.

A week passed without further incident, and Tanner decided he was ready to try the usual daily family outing again. This time, he chose an afternoon for the walk. The air was brisk, yet warm for the climate and time of year. Emily took extra care in bundling up the baby, nonetheless, before placing little Jolyon into the carriage. Tanner placed his hand in Rachel's and down the front steps everyone went. Down and to the right, past the rainbow of color inside Bowman's Flower Shop, the sinfully good aromas emanating from Elliot's Bakery, the Boyd and Hurst and Felts' residences. Turn right again and there was the empty lot with the sign promising a new business establishment soon courtesy of one Mr. Wesley Keith Johnson, Esq., although naught had changed in the past two years since he'd staked and claimed the property.

Across the way was Pages Bookstore, a small and intimate affair, and the Bluebird Restaurant where he'd consumed many a fine cup of dark bitter coffee. And so on and on, another block, another, and again to the right—more buildings, more homes, more passersby known and unknown, most of whom couldn't resist smiling at the sight of the baby being pushed along. The sound of the baby-carriage wheels was steady on the wooden sidewalk while Rachel skipped along, excited to be out with her mother and father in the late afternoon.

He'd planned to avoid the corner where Rachel had seen the enigmatic eye, but habit was a hard master to disobey, and since they had fallen into their traditional routine without thinking, soon they were at the same spot once more. As they waited to cross the street, Tanner felt his little girl grip his hand even more tightly.

"We should stop at market for potatoes, Theo. I'll add them to the stew tonight," Emily remarked. "I should have brought the shopping basket along."

Her husband didn't reply. His attention was on the spot where Rachel had seen the eye and devil take it all, but was there a strange shimmering hanging there in space and time? A sort of quivering of the air, like the haze of heat on a summer meadow in the midst of a hot July day at noon? Yet, there was no heat in the brisk Nebraska air—only a queer dryness—a lack of moisture that seemed to be spreading in his mouth and nasal passages.

"I say...I feel a most definite chill coming on," Tanner muttered, stomping his feet and vigorously rubbing his hands together.

Emily's brow furrowed beneath the bangs of her auburn hair. "Nonsense, Theo, it is a beautiful afternoon. Are you coming down with an illness? Those students of yours. There is no telling what types of germs they bring into the classrooms on a daily basis."

Tanner smiled at his wife, showing off his beautiful array of teeth, only to discover his intended gesture of reassurance had created the exact opposite effect.

"Your teeth, Theo, they are chattering," his beloved wife said, a hint of worry coloring her gentle voice.

He reached up and felt his lower jaw. "Hmm. So they are, so they are," he murmured. Again, he glanced over at the street, but the odd warping of the air was gone. He was torn between asking if Rachel had seen anything and dismissing it immediately, in order to keep from upsetting the girl yet again.

"My delicate constitution seems to have caught a cold," he finally announced. "Yes, I do not feel all that well, I am afraid."

"What is wrong, Father?" Rachel asked, peering at her father with the intent gaze of a child.

"Nothing, dear little one," Tanner lied. "Nothing at all."

Rachel turned as white as an eggshell. "You saw it, Father! You saw it! You saw it, did you not?"

Tanner nodded. "Aye, perhaps I did see... something—"

"More eyes from heaven?" Emily asked in a teasing tone, but before she could add another word she was interrupted by a sound unlike any that she had ever heard in her twenty-seven years; a sound that she would never be able to forget, or rid her memory of. A sound that would take up residence in her dreams; a sucking noise that was cut off by a loud, pithy pop. And then, before the waiting Tanner family, a temporal doorway was torn open, renting the very fabric of time and space.

This was no wooden door in a frame of the type familiar to the denizens of this particular point in time, nor was it a fanciful air lock of the future, nor even a magic portal. This doorway was something else, something more precise, with accurate angles and deliberate calibrated measurements, hanging suspended in what Dr. Theophilus Algernon Tanner had always understood to be three-dimensional space.

What floated within the angles was a darker kind of geometry. This was a gateway via a fourth unknown dimension.

Later, long after the shock had faded, Tanner would find this route to be one of an infinite number along the currents and eddies swirling within the invisible dimension of time-no time.

"The eye! God's eye! God's eye! Look, Father! Do you see it? Do you see?" Rachel screamed, a loud piercing sound that stabbed at Tanner's wildly pounding heart even as the scientist in his brain looked upon the sight with detached fascination. A mix of dread and fear combined with his wondering about what exactly the eye was, and what the eye had wrought.

The sun still hung in the sky, but the color of the

world changed from light to dark as the door swung open and gave a great cosmic inhalation. The world was now a reverse negative, white on black with an absence of color, the atmosphere thick and cloying.

And damn it all, but a fog bank had somehow rolled in through the mysterious conduit, obscuring the corner from sight, obscuring those trapped within the swirling mist from even clearly seeing one another, much less the angular obscenity that had appeared in their midst.

Terror in her throat, Emily reached down and pulled her baby from the confines of the carriage, clutching little Jolyon to her breast. Minus her grip on the handle and the baby's weight, the carriage skittered away, pulled by the suction. Her new hat flew from her head and instantly vanished in the mist. "Theo!" she screamed. "Where are you?"

Rachel was on her feet, her hair and clothing whipping around her frail body by seemingly gale-force winds. The red scarf she wore plumed from her neck like a signal flare. "Father!" she called, but the screaming of mother and daughter was blocked, torn away, by the rift hanging near the sidewalk.

And Tanner...he was somehow suspended in midair, his frock coat flowing behind him like a cape, his shoulder-length hair streaming from his skull, each fine fiber standing up and out, crackling with static electricity.

"Thunder and damnation," he said in an unsteady voice.

Struggling to keep her footing in the maelstrom,

Emily reached out and felt her fingers brush Tanner's hand. "I love you," he managed to yell above the unholy sound coming from the doorway, and then he vanished into nothingness.

Rachel Tanner wasn't as lucky. Buffeted by the unholy winds, doomed by her very proximity to the gateway, her young body was ripped apart by the sudden closing of the rift matrix and, as it fell inward upon itself, she perished before her mother's frightened gaze.

Her fragile corpse was shredded into wet hunks of meat. Arms, legs, fingers, toes, flesh, bone and blood spun in the air, intermingled with the mist and the bits of the blue dress the child had been wearing. The red scarf coiled like a serpent, rearing and striking at an invisible foe.

Emily vomited, one arm going to her heaving stomach in a reflex action, loosening her grip on Jolyon and before she could react, the winds tore her other child, her baby boy, away from her, leaving nothing behind but a dismembered torso dressed in blood-soaked pajamas, a lifeless carcass that fell with a wet plop once the rift collapsed fully upon itself, sucking back the unexplained mist and vanishing as quickly as it had come. The ghastly remnants of Rachel Tanner fell like rain upon her mother, who had stumbled and landed on her knees, her chest heaving with racking sobs.

Witnesses saw the mist, heard the sounds, viewed the aftermath.

One moment, a family of four was on a stroll.

The next, a lone woman remained, dressed in a tattered dress and scarf, surrounded by the gore of her murdered children and the stink of voided flesh. Her husband had vanished, spirited away by and into the very air itself.

As to be expected, Emily Tanner never was quite the same after that dark day.

"The eye," she whispered over and over. "The eye, the eye, Satan's unblinking eye."

On the strength of her spouse's estate and reputation, along with her parents' consent, she was institutionalized for a time, sedated, studied and pitied. Outlandish theories abounded about what she'd endured on that Omaha street corner, but there was no explaining the mishap using the science of the late nineteenth century.

A few suggested sorcery, which had always been the explanation given to advanced science by those who could not begin to understand what they had seen from a limited point of reference or experience.

As for Dr. Theophilus Algernon Tanner, he was on his way to a new destination. "An ideal subject," one report said, due to his intellect and where he happened to have fallen in the time stream. "The perfect candidate," read another communiqué in choosing him as guinea pig. The final decision had termed him "the logical choice, ideally suited in body and spirit and, more importantly, mind."

Out of all the other men, women and children, the madmen and the brilliant, the young and the old, the weak of mind and strong of spirit, out of all of those alive in the United States of America during that November month of 1896, Tanner had been the one chosen.

Chosen to make a pilgrimage—a pilgrimage to hell.

Chapter One

"Wherever you want to lead, Ryan..." J. B. Dix had said long days ago, and as Ryan Cawdor now regained his senses, grateful this latest mat-trans journey hadn't invoked the nightmares that usually came during the fantastic quantum journeys, he found himself dwelling on the words.

What had brought the words to mind was the color of the walls surrounding him—armaglass walls of milky, colorless gray.

"Fireblast," Ryan muttered. Unless his memory was starting to slip, the walls of the chamber he was now resting within were exactly the same as the mat-trans unit beneath that stickie-infested pesthole hospital in Carolina.

The light in the hexagonal-shaped chamber seemed to be impossibly bright and his head was pounding, as if an unknown assailant had shoved a lighted candle into the open eye socket of his face and twisted down, driving the flame both into the frontal lobe of his brain and the optic nerve of his remaining good eye.

The white-hot light had begun to slowly fade into a more reasonable wattage. Through the spots dancing in front of his vision, Ryan was able to make out the forms of his companions, all six of them in various prone positions on the polished floor around him.

"Looks like we're calling North Carolina home again," Mildred Wyeth commented.

"Not much changed," Jak Lauren agreed.

Since they knew the area, and not a great deal of time had passed since their last visit to the complex, a quick recce soon found the group out of the chamber and into a small white anteroom located outside the armaglass door. As before, an ordinary desk with a computer and monitor rested directly across from the observation window of the gateway. Everyone kept their hardware ready as they crossed the room to another door, which they knew to be made of painted wood with a simple bronze doorknob. There were no high-tech locking systems or security keypads. No apparent locks of any kind.

Maintaining a triple red alert, they then entered the mat-trans control room, which was also still intact. Ryan held up a hand and all paused, listening and waiting. Things appeared to be quiet and safe.

"We got two choices," Ryan stated.

No one replied. They knew the options: try Carolina's hospitality again or take the risk of another gateway jump. Neither was particularly appealing.

"Any of you feel strongly about picking one over the other?" he asked.

"Your call," Jak said with a shrug.

"Doesn't matter to me," J.B. agreed.

"For now, let's check the rest of the area. Make sure we don't have any company."

Ryan, on point, took a moment to glance back. They were good friends, every last one of them.

No, more than friends. Dean was his biological son and Krysty his soul mate, but the others were just as important in the tangled web that was his life.

They were family—more so than Ryan's blood kin back in the mountains of West Virginia. Most of the relatives who shared the Cawdor name were long chilled, dead and buried. His murderous brother, Harvey, had cowardly challenged a young Ryan and taken his left eye, leaving the disfigured and maimed boy for dead. His adulteress stepmother, Rachel, who'd seen to the death of Ryan's father, Lord Cawdor, had then, in an act of taboo lust, slept with the insane Harvey. His nephew Jabez had seen the power and station of the Cawdor name as a direct route to the domination of others and the rape of helpless young women and children.

Ryan had claimed Harvey, and had seen to chilling his mad brother personally, while Doc Tanner's weapon had taken Lady Rachel. Krysty had killed Jabez with her bare hands after he'd attempted to sodomize her. When the bloody combat was over, Ryan had left his nephew Nathan, who'd been sired by his murdered older brother, Morgan, in charge.

Nathan Freeman dropped the surname Cawdor during his subsequent banishment, a banishment Ryan himself had shared for many long years. Ryan had come home for his reckoning and cleaned house, later finding Nathan and installing him as the new baron of Front Royal.

The raven-haired savior of Front Royal had no desire to rule a ville. He merely wanted his name cleared and his father's memory respectfully restored. With the diseased darkness of Harvey Cawdor vanquished, both of the one-eyed warrior's wishes were now a reality.

His fingertips traced the deep scar that lined the right side of his face as he walked through the hallways of the hidden hospital complex. Every time he looked in the mirror at his rugged features, Harvey's handiwork was there, twin disfigurements looking back at him: one stretching from forehead to cheek, and the other hidden away—a ruin of an eye socket still open and raw, which Ryan kept covered with a scuffed leather patch.

The final encounter with Harvey and his madness seemed as recent as yesterday, Ryan mused as he shrugged his broad shoulders. The movement made the long white scarf around his neck shift, and he reached up automatically to adjust it. Both ends of the scarf were weighted—a simple measure of extra security that had saved his life numerous times when opponents believed him to be weaponless.

The last time the companions had been at this particular juncture of the Deathlands, there had been some concern among the group about heading north across land on foot. They were close to the old state-line boundary, and could pass through the forests of Virginia to the state's western cousin to personally check up on the status of the surviving members of the House of Cawdor.

Ryan had been privy to rumors that the status quo he'd left behind years ago was no longer in place. He honestly wasn't sure why he even cared, since he'd chosen to reject his heritage of wealth and finery to find his own individual path.

Still, ammunition was at an all-time low for the group's array of blasters, and most of their jack had been previously exhausted in Freedom. While they'd been able to replenish some hardware along the way since then, their scavenging there hadn't been nearly enough. No, a long road trip across two states was the last thing wanted or needed. Front Royal would have to wait until they'd found a secure spot to rest up in, and he already knew this stretch of Carolina with the high mutant population wasn't going to be their safe haven.

Chapter Two

The odor came wafting in like a runaway pack of screamwings as the group stepped out in the hall that led to the stairwell. The strong smell of the fire muties had lighted in a previous attack became stronger, along with the rancid smell of the corpses Ryan and his friends had chilled days earlier. The stench of the hallway of death where the dead stickies were scattered was foul, making them all glad they weren't staying in the secret complex.

As they walked, J.B. took out a small drawstring pouch from one of the many pockets that lined the inside of his well-worn leather jacket. From the denim blue sack came a long thin black cheroot, crudely rolled. The Armorer took a moment to sniff the tobacco stick with a deep sigh.

"Where in the hell did you get that?" the African-American woman following J.B. demanded.

"What?"

Mildred Wyeth gave an exaggerated point with her right index finger at the cheroot J.B. was holding. "That."

"Had them tucked away. I forgot about picking up a sack at the tobacco shop in the Freedom Mall," the Armorer replied after sticking the cigar into the corner of his mouth. "Kind of funny. Us being back here jogged my memory. North Carolina's tobacco country, remember?"

"I've tried to forget," she retorted. "Smoking's a filthy habit. Public smoking was banned in many places during the 1990s. One of the few good things to come out of that final era."

"That was a long time ago. Lot's changed since then," J.B. replied as he took out a silver-plated Zippo lighter and flicked it open with a quick flip of the wrist. He held the bright yellow flame to the tip of the cheroot and sucked in the smoke deeply with a contented moan.

"Haven't seen you puffing on one of those in a long while," Ryan said, glad the smoke from the cheroot was behind him, blowing in the opposite direction.

"Want one?" J.B. asked.

"No, thanks," Ryan replied. "I know of a hundred better ways to kill myself."

The Armorer shrugged and went back to enjoying his smoke.

J.B. was Ryan's oldest friend. They had been brought together on the legendary Trader's once-thriving caravan of war wags years earlier, and soon found their personalities and talents to perfectly complement each other. While Ryan was the Trader's designated war captain, J.B. and his love of weapons made him the perfect lieutenant.

Weaponsmith, Armorer, Master Blaster, Gunsmith—he wore the designations with quiet pride and calm efficiency. A living, breathing cache of knowledge of all forms of weaponry and how they could be used most effectively, J.B. used his eidetic memory to keep himself and his companions safe and whole. His mastery of guns and their specs was invaluable to anyone attempting to traverse Deathlands.

He was still learning, but it was the rare weapon indeed he hadn't read about or held in his own hands. Traveling with the Trader had provided him the opportunity to spend time in every backwater town and ville Deathlands had to offer, and in all of them a new blaster could be traded for or, at the very least, handed over for a closer look in exchange for his own.

Those had been days of wonder for J.B., instilling in his heart a wanderlust he'd never been able to shake. There was always something new around the corner, and even with no guarantees of it being friend or foe he wanted to see what the world had to offer for himself.

Under five foot nine, with a slim build that gave no indication of the wiry muscularity beneath his clothes, J.B. was approximately forty years old. His actual age was unknown to his friends, and even to the Armorer himself, since his family hadn't believed in celebrating birthdays. He wore a multipocketed brown leather jacket, dark trousers that were also lined with more pockets, heavy combat boots and a battered, well-traveled fedora.

Perched on his nose was the new pair of wire-rimmed glasses, obtained back in Freedom, along with darker news concerning his deteriorating vision—news from the mall optician the Armorer had chosen to share with no one until he became a potential liability.

The doctor had called the disease glaucoma, and the current sad state of what passed for eye care in the ruin of Deathlands offered no cure or treatment. "A matter of time," he told J.B. with a sigh. "Only a matter of time."

When that day came, when his pale gray eyes no longer could be trusted, J.B. had already decided he would take care of cutting his own losses.

But for now, his vision was clear, even if the new frames pinched like a vise. He groaned, and removed them to temporarily relieve the aching pressure.

At a first glance, J.B. looked like a runty man, unhealthy and malnourished. His complexion was sallow and dank, and from close-up faint acne scars from his teen years could be seen on his cheeks and forehead.

In another time, J.B. Dix would have been seen as a man of no consequence.

Looks could be deceiving.

The compact man was a walking arsenal, capable of massive amounts of carnage when he chose to unleash his full capacity. The obvious signs were in the mini-Uzi hung low over one shoulder, the trigger at waist level for easy use, or in the Smith & Wesson M-4000 scattergun he carried in his left hand, an extremely deadly weapon that didn't fire ordinary rounds, but instead held eight Remington 12-gauge cartridges, each with twenty fléchettes, or even in the fighting knife sheathed at his hip. But his clothing and boots also contained a wealth of hidden equipment: fuses of varying lengths and a tight ball of plas-ex, coils of wire and packets of shiny lock picks, an invaluable folding minisextant, and spare ammo and blades.

J.B. took another puff from his concise cigar. "Yeah, I don't come across these as often as I'd like. Nothing like a good smoke."

"Or a good case of lung cancer," Mildred muttered.

The woman behind J.B. was his companion and lover, Dr. Mildred Wyeth, a time traveler from the period before the nukecaust that ended the civilized world. Like the Armorer, Mildred was a prized companion. Intelligent, compassionate and an astute judge of character, she was a trained physician and former pioneer in the field of cryonics and cryogenics.

The woman had suffered an adverse reaction to anesthesia during a minor operation and had been preserved using the very same cryonic processes she had helped to develop. Mildred had remained on ice until Ryan and the others had found her sleeping in her silver coffin. In a series of tense hours, they had managed to restore her to life successfully.

A doctor of another kind entirely followed Mildred Wyeth.

Peering from behind the stocky black woman was

the weathered face of Doc Tanner. A lifetime of hard sights was etched into his skin—and his eyes. Doc gripped his ebony walking cane tightly. The silver lion-head handle of the stick was serene, impassively keeping the secret of the honed blade of Toledo steel housed hidden inside the body of the cane.

A most unusual handblaster was holstered at the man's hip. In the holster was an ornately tooled Le Mat, a unique weapon dating back to the early days of the Civil War. Engraved in flowing script and decorated with twenty-four-carat gold as a commemorative tribute to the great Confederate solider James Ewell Brown Stuart—or Jeb Stuart, as his friends and folks in Virginia referred to him—the massive handcannon weighed in at over three and a half pounds.

The blaster was a quick way to check how weary Doc was getting. After a long day or particularly intense event, the heavy gun added a noticeable lurch to his step.

At the moment, Doc Tanner was lurching like a drunken barmaid, but he gave no complaint.

The gun had two barrels and an adjustable hammer, firing a single .63-caliber round like a shotgun, and nine .44-caliber rounds in revolver mode. Finding ammo for the grapefruit scattergun round was extremely difficult, but the old man refused to give up the sometimes clumsy blaster for a more modern weapon.

"Once a man is set in his ways, there is no reason to change unless absolutely, positively necessary,"

Doc often intoned. "And I have no intention of attempting to reinvent myself now."

Doc was a living link to the past that stretched back even farther than Mildred Wyeth's. The old man had been born in South Strafford, Vermont, on February 14, 1868. Twenty-eight years later, he'd been time-trawled via a modified matter-transfer chronal unit to the year 1998, an unwitting subject in an experiment of the future. Two years after that, at the flash point of the millennium in the year 2000, he'd been thrust forward more than a hundred years into the unknown, the future, the after-the-holocaust world of Deathlands.

Doc stumbled, the heavy blaster weighing heavily on his thin frame. He used his swordstick to break his fall, even as a steadying hand came from behind courtesy of Krysty Wroth.

"My thanks, Child," Doc said absently. "This rubble-strewed hall is hell on two-legged locomotion."

"Don't mention it," she replied easily. She was ready to fall asleep on her feet herself, so she could only imagine how Doc was feeling. Even her usually sentient red hair was drooping, hiding the fact that besides being a stunningly beautiful woman, Krysty was also a mutant. Her abilities were masked, not overt like the sucker-lined hands and tongues of the stickies or the crumbling flesh of the scalies.

Powers of the mind. That's what the tall redhead possessed, the knack of being able to sense the presence of other intelligent life-forms and also, if said life-forms were friend or foe. She was able to smell trouble when it was coming toward them, able to know good from evil, right from wrong, black from white.

She also had power deep from within. Taught by Mother Sonja, back during her childhood in Harmony to call upon and wield the near-mystic force of Gaia, the Earth Mother, Krysty could channel the very energy of the planet itself using her body as a vessel.

Such an act infused her with incredible strength, along with heightened awareness, but only for a short time. While the world seemed to slow to a crawl to her enhanced eyes, she would move at triple speed. Immersion within Gaia's forces took a terrific toll on her physical and mental well-being. Remaining in the trance too long, she would ultimately lose her soul, and her earthly shell would literally burn out.

The price she paid for summoning this power was dreadful and always left her exhausted and drained for hours—sometimes days—after the fury of the Earth Mother had raced through her. In the aftermath, she was as weak and helpless as a newborn.

A striking beauty, Krysty possessed flawlessly pale alabaster skin. When combined with the sparkling emerald of her eyes and the passionate fire of her long red hair, it added to her already considerable presence.

Dean Cawdor was behind Krysty. Like his father, the youth shared the same dark complexion and black, curly hair. In many ways, he was a perfect

Ryan Cawdor in miniature. Perhaps he wouldn't be as tall as Ryan or possess his imposing presence, but he shared his sire's innate intelligence and sense of morality and fair play.

Ryan had committed some ruthless acts in his younger days and done some things he knew would assure him of his own private chamber in whatever purgatory he eventually ended up serving after his death, but that was yesterday, this was now, and he was doing his damnedest to live free and in the present.

A combination of Krysty's and Dean's influence had seen to that.

The back of the line of friends creeping down the rubble-strewed hallways was brought up by a man even smaller than J. B. Dix. Not even a man, really, if manhood was determined by chronological age. The youth was sixteen years old, five feet four inches tall, and might've weighed one hundred and ten pounds soaking wet. His face was shockingly white—not flesh tone, but ghost pale, with numerous scars on the chin and cheeks.

At first glance, no one saw the scars. They were too busy peering at Jak's eyes, which were a blood-red crimson, twin rubies set in a grim visage, fringed by bangs of pure white hair. The long mane cascaded across his narrow shoulders like a waterfall.

Hidden on his person, Jak had several leaf-bladed throwing knives, their hilts taped for perfect balance. The style of leather and camou-canvas jacket he'd favored and worn for so long had tiny shards of razored steel sewn into the lining and sleeves, strategically torn in the most easy-to-reach places.

The young albino didn't need to worry about using a blaster when he had access to his knives, but a heavy, well-used and well-maintained Colt Python was fastened to one of his skinny legs. Just in case.

So many weapons—a necessary evil in the Deathlands. Ryan didn't share J.B.'s burning fascination with hardware. His own personal arsenal was simple and neat. A 9 mm SIG-Sauer P-226 pistol was at his side, holstered and safe. The blaster held fifteen full-metal-jacketed bullets and came with a built-in baffle silencer. Over one shoulder, Ryan had looped his walnut-stocked Steyr SSG-70 bolt-action rifle, which fired ten 7.62 mm rounds and came with a laser image-enhancer and a Starlite night scope.

Ryan also had two bladed weapons, a large eighteen-inch panga strapped to his left hip, and a flensing knife hidden away at the small of his back. Various auto-loads and other clips of ammunition, along with a talent for the archaic art of hand-to-hand combat, made Ryan a dangerous two-legged killing machine.

Unlike many of the other hardmen of the Deathlands, Ryan Cawdor was also a thinking man, with a capacity for compassion, if allowed by his foes to grant such gifts.

Rarely was he given such an option.

"We going up?" Dean asked, looking into the dimness of the open stairwell.

"Yeah," his father replied. "Krysty, grab that torch over there."

The woman complied, hefting the canvas-tipped piece of wood into the air. "Still got some life in it, I think," she said. "Must've been left behind when those stickies were down here before."

J.B. stubbed out the end of the cigar and placed it in a pocket, then used the lighter to ignite the end of the stick, proving the crusty torch indeed still worked.

"Okay, let's go."

Ryan took the point, followed by the others. Krysty was close to Ryan and J.B., shining the light up into the dark for a long span of minutes, until a new presence joined them unexpectedly on the winding staircase.

"Fressssh meat!" a wet voice snarled as Krysty's left arm was bent painfully back and the makeshift torch was snatched from her hand. Red embers flew as the lighted head of the stolen torch was shoved into a cloth bag, and instantly the world of the hospital stairwell went black.

Doc cried out briefly in the darkness, then was lost in the new images that seemed to swirl out of the night of forgetfulness and come alive in his mind, taking him back to another time.

Chicago, Illinois Redoubt, 1998

AS A SLENDER YOUNG MAN Theophilus Algernon Tanner had spent many a lazy summer afternoon swimming in the nearby Connecticut River to escape the surprisingly damnable Vermont heat. The summer of his twelfth birthday was humid and sticky and made one almost yearn for the subzero cold snaps of the long winter months. Never much for active sport or physical activity, the boy did enjoy spending hours in the water, sometimes practicing a clumsy dog paddle, other times just content to float gently on his back, his face directed upward at the cloud-filled skies.

Theo rarely paid attention to the sky. His eyes were usually closed, his keen young mind lost in thought and as adrift as his lanky preteen body. Since the river was quite still at the point where Theo liked to relax and play, he was able to idly doze in this floating position, cooled by the water from the back while warmed from the front by the sun overhead.

But this day the water suddenly sucked him down, holding him helpless beneath the surface by an unexpected undertow. Young Theo's eyes popped open in shock, horrified and confused to discover the blue sky above had been replaced by a swirling mass of dim blue and brown, and in his ears was a terrible roaring as his eardrums were assaulted by the onrush of water now enveloping his helplessly prone body.

He scrambled madly, trying to pull himself back to the world above. His arms pumped and his legs kicked and still he stayed in place, almost as if he were being held down by some elemental water demon who'd claimed him as a sacrifice to the river gods.

Then the grip was loosened, and the boy was able to thrust himself free of the water and into the air, where his lungs gratefully sucked in life-giving oxygen in between bouts of coughing up the stomachful of the Connecticut River he'd swallowed.

"Look here, Mark! We done come upon Algae Tanner!" a tenor voice said, cracking slightly on the word "upon" in a betrayal of the end of adolescence and the beginning of maturity, not that his actions were any indication of impending adulthood.

"Right where you'd expect to find him," a slower speaker replied, his words coming out in a nasal tone.

"What do you mean?" the tenor asked, setting up the joke.

"Floating on the water, just like any old kind of pond scum."

Bullies. Even as an adult he would still remember their names. One had been dubbed Merlin by his parents; the other a more pedestrian Albert.

With his keen intellect, slight build and strange hair color (even as a teen the sandy brown had already started to transform into the eventual gray he would possess as an adult), Theo was used to being the butt of humor from the less gifted, and while he never took such pranks meekly, he wasn't the type to dwell upon concepts of revenge.

As a result, he'd spent much of his youth isolated. Luckily he hadn't minded solitude. In fact, he'd grown fond of keeping his own council.

Isolated. Yet he could still hear snippets of conversation swirling around him, like the blue water and brown silt of the Connecticut River of his youth...

"Any diseases we should be worried about?" Theo didn't know that voice.

"Negative. Cryo sleep kept him on ice. Nothing to fear, at least, nothing from his era. Still, I hope everyone in this operating room has had his shots."

Laughter. Bullies again? Theo didn't know.

"No, I'd say he'd be the one we should be concerned with. There are bugs floating in the air our guest has never had the joy of breathing."

"Blood pressure's high. Pulse rate's racing overtime."

"That's to be expected. Keep an eye on the lower numbers. If they go up another ten points, let me know. They should be dropping soon."

"Negative on the drop, sir. Top and bottom are climbing to the rafters."

"Dammit. He's going into cardiac arrest. We need the cart!"

"Can we contain him?" a new voice, smooth, polished, asked.

"I don't know."

"I said, can we contain him?" It was no longer a question, but a blunt statement of fact, an order phrased in the form of a query.

"I'm trying. We're trying."

"This is the first successful trawl of a human subject, a subject we chose most carefully. This is no unthinking fool plucked randomly off the street. We have plans for this man."

"So what if he dies, anyway? We can always start over."

"Meaning?"

"Look, you muddle-headed dolt," a voice said with exasperation, "what we are dealing with here is time travel, pure and simple. Correct?"

"Time travel of a sort, yes."

"So if this goes south, we go back a day or an hour or a week and we activate the mat-trans and bring the quantum interphase on-line with the trawling guide and use the same coordinates to lock onto his form. Then we bring him here again. Tanner's still there in Omaha, alive, back in past time. We fetch him a little earlier and there's no problem, okay? Try and think."

"I *am* thinking, and let me correct you on your misguided understanding of time trawling. There are no second chances. The variables are too great to allow us to make another attempt, no matter how much earlier we go back within the time line."

The conversation had lost some of the urgency, growing more complicated and outlandish. Deciding he'd like to have a look at just who was parceling out the commentary on his fate, Tanner opened his eyes and saw he was surrounded by phantoms. Ghosts. Figures of white in white, as viewed from behind a distorting pane of glass. And that damnable breathing, his own breath, rasping in his ears like a blacksmith's bellows.

Never a religious man, Tanner suddenly found himself in the presence of what appeared to be angels, and their presence fascinated him as much as it terrified him, for while the part of his magnificent mind that dwelt with philosophy took solace, the coldly scientific section of his brain was frightened. Angels were something he couldn't even begin to comprehend or explain. He closed his eyes tightly.

Heaven or hell? He didn't feel the kiss of hellfire, but he was at a loss how it was supposed to feel, anyway.

Regardless, he decided it was time to face his fears, and so Dr. Theophilus Algernon Tanner opened his eyes once more and found his vision blurred with tears.

"He's awake again."

"About time."

A man leaned over into Tanner's field of vision, a portly man with a wide face and a well-groomed black mustache. The eyes peering down were so dark they appeared to be the same color as the man's jet-black hair.

The mouth beneath the mustache opened, casting forth a smell of garlic and tomato, as if the man had just eaten a particularly tangy salad and dressing.

"Hello, Theo. How do you feel?" he asked gently.

"Do not," the figure on the hospital bed rasped, the interior of his mouth dry. The corners of his mouth were spotted with dried blood where his lips had cracked from lack of moisture.

"I'm sorry?"

"Do not call me that," Tanner said, enunciating

each word as precisely as his dry mouth and throat would allow.

"Theo?" the man said, puzzled. He consulted a black notebook, not turning beyond the first page. "It's your name, isn't it?"

"Only...only my beloved Emily calls me that," Tanner stammered, wondering what had happened to his voice.

The man frowned as he flipped pages in the compact book. "Emily...Emily...help me here, somebody. Is she the wife? Mother? Child?"

"Wife...wife. My wife. What has happened to me? To her?" Tanner asked, struggling to come to terms with what his memory was telling him—*a great sucking sound and the eye of God opened and the wind and blood, so much blood before being lain to rest amongst the angels.*

Tanner's query was ignored as the man made a note in the book. "Wife. How could I have missed the wife?" he murmured before he spoke aloud again.

"You've been through a terrific strain, Dr. Tanner. To be frank, I'm amazed you survived."

"Survived what? What happened to me?"

"Something wonderful." A blond woman with an eager smile chirped. "You're the first!"

"It does not feel all that wonderful, my dear," Tanner said, running his tongue along the inside of his mouth. "It feels most horrible. Like I have been dead and resurrected."

"That's to be expected. My name is Herman

Welles. I'll be serving as your physician and your sounding board until you're fully acclimated to our program here."

Suddenly Tanner sat bolt upright in the hospital bed, nearly cracking his head on a slight overhang of electric lights mounted above the headboard. "Where is my wife? My children?" he cried in a shrill voice that fright caused to climb into the upper vocal register.

"Later," Welles responded. "For now, we are only concerned with you and your well-being."

"Hang my well-being, man!" Tanner thundered, his normal bass voice having returned to echo off the walls of the small room. "I need to see my wife and little Rachel and Jolyon!"

In his haste to get out of the bed, Tanner hadn't commented on the bank of high-tech medical equipment blinking to his left, or on the style of clothing Welles and the two other attendants in the room were wearing. An IV drip in one of his lean arms tore free in a spray of blood and solution as he made his way out of the hospital bed.

"Dr. Tanner, please!" the nurse said, lunging to grab the leaking IV.

"Are they all right?" he asked her fearfully. His bright blue eyes darted to and fro, examining his surroundings for the first time. The walls of the room were a neutral soothing mint-green color that matched his hospital gown and the linens on the bed.

Turning to the man who seemed to act as the leader of the small knot of people surrounding him,

Tanner asked, "I—I must be in some form of hospital or medical facility, though I admit the design is unfamiliar to me and quite strange. Was there an accident? Tell me, are my wife and children all right?"

"That depends on the definition. I could say yes, and be telling the truth depending on how closely you want to analyze my meaning."

Tanner grabbed Welles by the lapels of his lab coat and snarled into his face. "Double-talk! Babble! I have heard your kind before, sir, and I know enough to not waste my time on your attempts to stonewall. Enough of your mendacity!"

"Geez, he sure talks funny, doesn't he?" the blond nurse said.

Tanner spun and pointed a finger at her. "Ignoramus!"

The automatic door to the room slid open as the man in a hospital dressing gown approached, causing him to shrink back in surprise. In 1896, doors weren't known for opening by themselves. The shock of seeing the doors, combined with the presence of two large men standing in the hallway outside the door, was enough to keep him rooted in place.

"I feel positively light-headed," Tanner remarked in a casual tone, reaching out and holding on to the frame of the open door for support. Behind him, he smelled the breath of the man who had identified himself as Welles. As he turned to tell the overweight doctor to back off, Tanner felt a stinging sensation in his left buttock.

Tanner spun clumsily to face Welles, who was holding a syringe.

"You're much too active for a dead man, Dr. Tanner. I think you need some more bed rest."

"You bastard—" he managed to croak, before falling backward into the arms of the waiting security team.

"What do you think, Nurse?" Welles asked the blonde as they watched the security men gently place Tanner back in the hospital bed, only this time, strapping him down with an assortment of nylon belts.

"I don't know, Doctor. He seems awfully stubborn."

"He'd have to be, to survive the trawling process. Still, I wonder if we have indeed obtained our puppet—and if so, how many of his strings must we cut before he allows us control?"

Chapter Three

In the ebony night of the stairwell, Ryan and the others knew they were going to be forced to fight on instinct alone.

In the wink of an eye, Ryan had coaxed his mind to visualize his companions' positions. Unlike J.B., his memory wasn't as crisp as a photograph, but Ryan's powers of short-term observation were still formidable.

This was going to be dirty and intense. They were too close to one another to risk the use of blasters. One ricochet could injure the wrong party; one stray bullet could mean the unintentional chilling of a friend. The only advantage they had was obvious—their foes were at the same disadvantage in the raven black, for even the eerie catlike eyes of Jak Lauren needed some kind of ambient light to function in the dark.

The trusty panga leaped silently into Ryan's right hand, a quick movement of practiced skill.

Unseen by Ryan, J.B. pulled his own blade from its sheath, while Doc armed himself with the exposed steel of his lethal swordstick.

Two of Jak's customized leaf-bladed throwing knives were in his pale hands, one implement in the left and the other deadly cutter in the right, both now invisible in the darkness. When it came to combat in tight quarters, the albino was equally at home using his left or his right hand.

Ryan's keen ears caught a "thwipping" sound, followed by a scream and a wet gurgling. Jak had unleashed one of the knives, and yet again, Ryan was both impressed and astonished by the lithe albino's uncanny skill in a knife fight.

"Cut me cut me hurts hurts cut me—" Then the cry was cut off, terminated by a wheezing sound and the unmistakable sound of a body hitting solid ground.

Then, all was still, until a series of shots rang out, a burst of leaded death.

Knowing none of his people would have made such a stupid and costly mistake, Ryan lunged toward the white flash he'd spied from the barrel of the weapon, grateful the fool behind the long blaster hadn't thought of fitting the weapon with a flashhider for night firing.

Raising his own blaster from his side, Ryan followed through and squeezed off a bullet, a second round coughing with deadly authority, catching the figure in the dark.

Ryan stood, holding his breath, waiting, listening. After sixty seconds had passed, Krysty spoke.

"I think we're alone, lover."

Taking out his lighter, J.B. thumbed the sparking wheel and held the flame high, looking around at the carnage.

Ryan stood from his crouched position and warily walked up to the fallen bodies.

The first corpse spotted was tangled in the stairwell's guardrail, a mess of limp arms and legs, along with a steady dripping of crimson. J.B. looked up impassively from the slain figure.

"Mutie," the Armorer said tersely.

Using the light provided by the lighter, Jak had crossed and found the second one he'd taken out blindly with his throwing knife. "Mine too," the albino said. "Stickie."

"No surprise there. Rarely see norms runnin' with muties—old Lester being the exception," J.B. noted, referring to the scarred human leader who'd taken up with a local band of stickies and led them in a fatal assault against the norms of Freedom Mall.

"And you, Ryan," Krysty replied in a teasing tone, picking up the fallen extinguished torch and holding out the tip end to be relit by J.B.'s lighter.

Ryan glanced over at her in the faint light given off by the tiny flame, knowing she was referring to herself, to her own mutant traits, and he gave her a half smile in return. "Yeah," he replied. "And me."

Then he calmly observed the results of his shots in the flickering light. The first one had wormed into the front of the stickie's right shoulder and out the back in a spray of gruesome red. One of the creature's wide unblinking eyes was missing where the second one had struck home, boring its way through to the back of the head.

The stickie's hands—typical of the breed—were

open in death and ghastly, with long fingers ending in amazingly strong suckers. J.B. could attest to the power of the mutie's fingertips; he still had scabs on his face where he'd been attacked days earlier. The coin-sized facial wounds were nearly healed now, but for days after the injury the Armorer had been forced to keep bandages on his face.

Choosing not to wear a shirt, the dead mutie was bare-chested with the usual stickie trait of no apparent body hair. He wore a pair of tattered dress slacks that had already turned dark with blood from his wounds. Jak's kill was in similar shape, except the knife had caught the mutie in the throat, puncturing the carotid artery and causing a fountain of the pinkish stickie blood to spray. Some of the blood had peppered Doc, but the man hadn't bothered to make mention of the unwanted shower, since Jak's actions may have saved his life.

The albino retrieved his thrown weapon and wiped the blade clean on the stickie's clothing before returning the knife to an inner hiding place inside his camou jacket.

"Wonder what brought them down here, Dad?" Dean asked. "I thought all the stickies in this part of Carolina were out smashing through stuff at the mall."

"Could be they've started exploring now that they've burned down part of Freedom. Guess we'll never know for sure."

"Cowardly bastards. They've probably been hiding in the dark, waiting for a chance to jump someone," the boy said.

"Alas, I fear you are correct regarding our attackers, young Dean," Doc said softly. "Makes one wary, and sends one sliding backward into childhood, alone in bed at night and frightened of the hidden terrors of the night."

"Were you scared of the dark when you were a kid, Doc?"

"Of course not," Doc replied, then laid a finger alongside his nose and winked. "But my mother was an understanding parent and allowed me to keep a candle burning in the window all through my slumber—both for illumination for weary travelers, and for my own youthful peace of mind."

"These muties look like rouges—not part of Lester's band. Not smart or organized enough," J.B. said as he busily emptied the dropped Uzi of the clip of 9 mm bullets. The fighting in Freedom combined with other gun-battles had eaten into their supply of badly needed ammunition. "Triple-strange to see a stickie carrying a blaster, though. Usually they prefer to stick to using their hands."

"Was that a pun, J.B.?" Mildred asked in a voice tinged with mock amazement.

The Armorer looked back at her blankly. "Huh?"

"'Stick to using their hands?' Get it? 'Stick to? Hands? Stickies?'"

J.B. stared at the black woman. She finally gave up on him getting the joke. "Shit, John, I've said it before and I'll say it again. We've *got* to work on your sense of humor."

"Don't got one," the weapons specialist told her stoically.

"That's what I mean," Mildred retorted without missing a beat.

"Guess here in Carolina the local stickie population decided to change their habits, Lester or no Lester," Ryan said. "Running into these two answered any doubts I might've had about passing back through this part of the Deathlands. I do intend to get up to Front Royal, but not using this route. Too dangerous without enough ammunition. Even if these stickies are wolf-heads from Lester's mutie army, there're probably plenty more farther up in the hospital complex."

"So. We go back down?" Jak asked, rocking back and forth on his booted heels impatiently.

"Yeah," Ryan said thoughtfully. "Yeah, let's go back to the gateway. I'd just as soon get the hell out of this pit of a stairwell and on our way to another locale before we get any more surprises."

No one disagreed and they all fell in step with Ryan as he took the relighted torch from Krysty and led the way back down. At the bottom, the landing was well illuminated by the strip lighting shining through the hole from the chamber where the cryogenic complex and mat-trans unit were both housed. Ryan extinguished the torch and placed it back against the desk where they'd found it.

"My father always told me, put your tools back where you got them," Doc said in an approving tone.

From this side, the hole itself remained an inelegant affair, blown open previously by the wild-eyed Alvis Alton during his quest for hidden riches. Alvis's timing had proved to be both a blessing and a curse. He'd been able to assist Ryan and the others when they arrived in the hidden complex through the mat-trans unit, but at the same time he'd brought down a horde of stickies with the noise he created when he set off his explosives.

Back into the first hallway and nothing; past the silver doors leading to the cryo units, the inhabitants of the cylinder-like tombs within sealed away never to awaken again, their pods having failed at one time or another during their long sleep, causing irreparable brain damage to some, death to others.

From the trip taken mere moments before, J.B. knew that the seemingly daunting maze of rooms and hallways was actually laid out in a simple rectangle shape, and after passing the cryo lab a suite of empty hospital beds would be next on the agenda.

"Sure would be nice to grab some sleep in there, lover," Krysty remarked to Ryan as she stifled a yawn and looked at him with her eyes at half-mast while passing the beds. "Can't remember the last time I had a good night's sleep. There's a bed in there for each of us, and curtains for privacy. And they're large enough to share."

"I know. Too bad we can't risk it," Ryan replied. "I'm about to drop on my feet myself, but it's only a matter of time before another pack of stickies comes across this place. Like I said back on the stairs, I'd just as soon get the hell out of this pesthole and be on my way before that happens."

"Sometimes I wonder about the paths we've chosen," she said tiredly. "But I guess it beats the alternative."

"Anything beats the alternative."

"Want me to reopen it, Dad?" Dean asked as the group converged on their final destination back at the mat-trans control room.

"Go ahead, Dean."

The boy keyed in the universal code of three-five-two and the vanadium-steel door obediently slid upward, allowing them entry into the low-ceilinged room. Wider than tall, the control center for the mat-trans chamber remained as white as a Colorado snowfall. A crisscrossing of bold black lines gave the floor a neutral checkerboard pattern. A single desk also painted white held a comp unit, keyboard, mouse and wide-screen monitor station. It was the only furnishing in the room. A star-burst pattern ran across the nearly black screen.

The door, off to the far left, was made of painted wood with a simple bronze doorknob. They stepped through, feeling more secure now with the first vanadium steel door locked, and walked back into the hexagonal chamber.

This mat-trans chamber located beneath the hospital was the traditional shape, but a low ceiling tapered to a central point, and the taller members of the group had to duck crossing the center of the room. Groupings of mat-trans disks hung overhead, open to the world and close enough to reach up and touch. A smooth floor made of a clear substance held the series of lower mat-trans disks suspended and waiting, as if sealed in Lucite blocks.

Waiting until all were seated, Ryan closed the chamber door and quickly stepped across to take his place between Krysty and Dean. The gray gloominess of the walls increased as the mists from the top of the chamber began their descent, swirling in a mass of growing opaqueness that would soon obscure the room mere instants before unconsciousness would claim them all.

Once the mat-trans chamber was in full vibrant bloom, Ryan had to close his eye against the blinding light. For some unknown reason, this chamber was much brighter than the norm, with a piercing bank of white that slid past his eyelid and into the very core of his being. He ducked his head between his knees in an effort to shield his face from the brilliance of the white. The warmth of the light came from all sides, washing down from the ceiling and splashing up from the floor, caressing him in shimmering tones that seemed to be coming from inside, instead of outside his body.

The thickness of the fog increased and, when combined with the luminance of the chamber, made the haze much more apparent than usual.

Mildred snuck a peek before slamming her eyelids shut.

"'Purple haze, within my brain...acting funny, but I don't know why,'" Mildred sang softly while strumming an air guitar.

"What's with the movements?" J.B. whispered, his eyes squeezed tight to keep out the white light. His spectacles were tucked safely away inside one of the pockets of his leather jacket. "You keep poking me in the ribs with your elbow."

"I'm playing the guitar, J.B.," Mildred replied, her eyes closed. "Jimi Hendrix. *Purple Haze.* Before your time."

The Armorer considered this for a few seconds. "Oh. Okay."

Unlike most of the companions, all of whom subconsciously held their breath as the eldritch process of matter transfer began, Mildred always breathed deeply, taking the ion-charged atmosphere down into her lungs. She honestly believed it helped with the dispersal and recalibration of her individual molecules when they were broken down and reassembled on the other side, at their eventual destination.

Plus the deep breathing aided in calming her nerves. Matter transfer was almost routine now, but she still didn't like the process. Too many variables were involved to avoid the eventual happenstance of an error beyond their control, and when that happened, she could only pray it wouldn't be a fatal one.

"'Excuse me, while I kiss the sky,'" she sang, and then the white was replaced by darkness and blissful unconsciousness.

Chapter Four

Ryan was dreaming, adrift and helpless in the suspended state between living and dying that the mat-trans journey created within the souls of sentient, conscious beings. The only way the human mind could hope to effectively survive the experience of total molecular disassembly and reassembly was to reject the reality of what was happening during a jump and enter instead into a waking dream cobbled together of truth and fiction, past and regret.

In layman's terms, one could always count on a gateway journey to give a man triple-bad nightmares.

In Ryan's current case, he was running flat out, putting his back into it, arms pumping, legs straining, running, running, running. The air in that part of Front Royal tasted electric and sharp, and to his young eyes—young? eyes?—gave a dark and fearsome aura to everything in sight, alternating their colors between black and blue as a maze of storm clouds raced across the evening sky.

The drawbridge was up, so he had to stop before plunging headlong into the moat. His legs flew out from beneath him, and he fell hard to the cobbled surface of the road leading to the drawbridge. Gasping for breath, he quickly examined his lower extremities and gave particular care to his left kneecap, which had suffered the brunt of his sudden landing. The fabric of the trousers was torn away from the knee, revealing shredded flesh and blue blood.

Blue blood? the boy thought stupidly, looking at the bodily fluid in numb surprise. He might be royalty of a sort because of his father's position of power in this southeastern pocket of Deathlands, but unlike some of his relatives he rarely flaunted the elevated seat he currently held as a son of the late, great Lord Titus Cawdor.

And since when did he think of himself as a boy?

"There you go again, Ryan, showing off your so-called heritage," a voice said with a sneer. It was a familiar voice that had much of the cadence and timbre of his own, but pitched higher and dripping with thinly veiled envy and hate. "It's time I took a more active role in your future status as a member of the House of Cawdor."

Somehow, while Ryan had been examining his injuries, the drawbridge had managed to come whispering down without his noticing. Concentration was a good thing to possess, but shutting out his surroundings would be the death of him yet. He had already decided the wounds and bruises were superficial, but now they were completely forgotten as he took in the sight revealed by the dropped drawbridge.

Harvey Cawdor loomed before him in all of his terrible crooked glory.

"Hello, Brother. Time to die," Harvey said, and suddenly Ryan was a child again, a boy of fifteen, lost and injured in the cold, betrayed by the very blood he shared with his brother. There would be no pleading of familial ties for mercy in this battle challenge.

The same brother who'd overseen the murder of their father wasn't the sort to grow misty-eyed over family.

Harvey was grotesquely fat, poured into the finest silken robes his subjects could buy with a half-crown studded with jewels atop his lumpen potato head. Hanging at the sides of his jiggling hips were twin Colt pistols of shining metal in tooled holsters crafted by the finest leathersmiths in Deathlands and paid for with money smeared in blood.

But fat, evil Harvey hadn't drawn either of the small-caliber blasters.

In his right hand, he held a blade, double-edged with a sharp point.

Ryan felt his left eye start to throb, pulsating in time with his heartbeat, a pulse that was increasing in speed. His legs felt leaden, paralyzed with fear.

He knew he wasn't afraid of his brother. What terrified this younger Ryan was the knowledge of what Harvey was about to do. Despite the location being different, despite the circumstances in this mat-trans-induced dream being reconfigured from the fragments Ryan held in his adult memory, the outcome was going to be exactly the same.

"End of the road, you little bastard," Harvey said, leering confidently down at his younger sibling.

"Go ahead. Do it, you fat butcher," Ryan snarled, his lips curling from his teeth as he spoke.

The blade came up, then down, the needle point directed at Ryan's left eye.

It was the last thing the eye ever saw. After the eye burst and the boy felt wet blood and fluid run down his cheek, Harvey pulled the blade free and went for the other side of Ryan's face, trying to blind him but instead plunging into his right cheek and cutting down, peeling back the flesh from the bone and causing a jet of blue blood to spray outward, joining the other torrent from the ruined eye.

Blinded by blue, Ryan screamed. The sound was horrible and exposed, revealing to his corrupt brother just how much the injury and the betrayal had cost—in both body and still maturing soul. He screamed again in agony, hoping the pain might stop but knowing despite his efforts, the scars would remain with him to his dying day.

KRYSTY WAS DREAMING. She was singing a predark country tune in a dump of a jolt-and-alcohol bar made of dirty tar paper and aluminum siding, on the outskirts of the tiny ville known as Hazelwood, fifty or so miles outside of Harmony. Hazelwood was the kind of place a man loyal to his wife and family traveled to if he wanted an anonymous night out with the boys...or the girls. No questions asked.

The song was a classic about cheating hearts and being weak and she sang it well, but the watchers in the smoky audience sipping at their watery drinks weren't there for the music.

They were there to ogle Krysty.

Her current attire left nothing to the imagination.

She was completely nude from neck to knees. The only articles of clothing on her voluptuous body were a silly-looking shiny white cowboy hat with a silver star-burst pinned to the wide white brim perched precariously on top of her crimson hair, and her well-worn blue cowboy boots with the chiseled silver points on the toes, and the silver spread-wing falcons on the front.

"Shake it, honey," a voice called from the audience. "Show us you mean it!"

Krysty ignored the man's comment and kept singing, holding the old-style microphone to her lips in both hands. Behind her, a backup band consisting of an amplified electric guitar and a simple trap drum kit provided accompaniment. Vocals and music both came from a few old, black Vox amplifiers, powered by a portable gasoline generator that chugged contentedly to itself outside the bar.

Why she was singing this particular song, one her Uncle Tyas had a particular fondness for, made perfect sense to her. She knew all the lyrics and had always enjoyed the tune. Why she was nude was another matter entirely, and as she finished the last verse of the Hank Williams classic she decided she'd better get around to investigating her current situation.

"I never knew you had such a pretty voice," Ryan

Cawdor said from where he was sitting with the polished candy-apple sun-burst Les Paul electric guitar.

"I never knew you played guitar," Krysty retorted.

"I'll let you in on a secret—I don't," Ryan said with conviction, and gave her a saucy wink with his right blue eye.

"I don't play drums, either," J. B. Dix added, spinning the drumsticks between his fingers in an elaborate display of showmanship before bringing them down on the snare to snap off a rim shot, accenting his words.

Things were getting so silly, Krysty decided to play along for a moment. "Mind telling me what happened to my clothes?" she asked.

"You'll get them back after the last song set," Ryan told her with a leer on his lips. "Until then, you might as well go ahead and get busy—there's at least thirty guys in here waiting for a chance to hump you blue. After I have my turn."

The boldness of the statement caused Krysty to burst into disbelieving laughter. "Well, they're in for a triple-long wait. And so are you, asshole."

"You gonna let her get away with talking to you like that?" J.B. asked loudly from behind the drums. "Mildred tries giving me shit and I shut her up quick."

"How so?"

J.B. grinned and licked his lips. "I give her a mouthful."

Ryan, who was not Ryan, she knew that now,

turned back to face Krysty. "How's that sound, you curvy piece of ass? You hungry?" he asked lazily, patting his crotch. "Got something for you before you open up that pretty mouth to sing us another tune."

Angry, her face flushing as red as her now undulating hair, Krysty gave a series of retorts about what he could do with his manhood. After she'd run out of suggestions, the raven-haired man stood, still smiling, but the single eye narrowed and the long scar down the other side of his face pulsed with pent-up fury.

Krysty Wroth was so nonplussed by what happened next that she stood perfectly still and slack-jawed and allowed it to occur without protest.

Ryan Cawdor drew back his right arm and slapped her.

Her head snapped back, pulling her neck taut as she staggered, her boot heels leaving the ground as she fell off the slight incline of the elevated stage, falling bare-assed onto the grit of the earthen floor of the bar. A whoop of excitement went up from the watching crowd as Krysty struggled to get to her feet, but her progress was halted by the man who appeared to be her lover as he leaped from the stage and landed on top of her, pinning her arms to the ground up over her head.

Ryan (not Ryan) leaned in close, and she could smell the stink of his breath, a mix of gasoline and motor oil. A long tongue slithered out of his mouth, and he licked her from cheek to forehead. "Damn, you taste good," he said.

Pulling one of her arms free, Krysty went for the nearest part of her attacker's body with her fingers. As she tore at her tormentor's face, scratching long furrows into his cheeks with her fingernails, Krysty was surprised at the absence of blood. One of her nails broke, splitting down to the soft underside, but she didn't even notice the pain as she continued to struggle, concentrating on ripping new gashes into the countenance of the man who'd willingly offered up his life to save her own countless times. She felt her heart stop as a glint of polished blue steel peeked out, shining from underneath the epidermal layer.

Still no blood, only warm flesh that was starting to feel more and more like cold, alien rubber, or even discarded chewing gum as she continued to scrape at her attacker's face.

The worn eye patch fell away and behind it lurked not an empty eye socket, but a piercing narrow beam of blue light that started to grow in intensity even as she gaped in a mix of terror and curiosity. With a final effort of strength forced from her very soul, she pulled at the mask and tore away the outer shell.

Cort Strasser, a.k.a. Skullface, leaned over her, revealed before her disbelieving eyes.

"No way," she said in a whisper.

"Way," he snarled back, and his face, his words, were blue.

JAK WAS DREAMING. In his mind's eye he was sleeping next to Christina, his wife, who in so many ways was as much a child as Jak Lauren himself, despite her being the older of the pair. In the adjoining room, Jenny, their little girl, also slept. The family of three were in a ranch house, a sprawling mass of clay and wood located in the most desolate part of New Mexico the young man had been able to find.

They were at peace and until that moment, their night terrors had been held at bay.

The following day, there was much to be done, including beginning a lengthy repair job on the ranch house roof, but after growing up in the swamplands of Louisiana, Jak was no stranger to hard work and hot sun. He'd given up wandering Deathlands with Ryan Cawdor to settle down in an attempt to have what might be called a normal life. Jak owed the one-eyed man his life and felt a strong loyalty to him, but he also knew if he were to find peace he would have to abandon Ryan's companionship in exchange for love and family.

Jak knew that would entail a struggle, for such peace was hard to find for people of his heritage and skin color. Jak was an albino, and albinos weren't normal, nor considered of a kind with man. Albinos were marked as mutants, and while the mutant breeds might eventually lay claim to the remains of the civilized world, Jak wanted no part of such a plan.

Until Christina was stolen from his bed. Until Jenny was taken away.

The unspoken message left in their stead was, No Peace.

In Jenny's small bunk bed were rose petals. In his own, ashes and dust. Jak crushed them together and rubbed them down both sides of his stark white face, streaking his cheeks with long dusky lines of war paint mixed with his own tears and sweat. The albino had grown up listening to late-night talk of magic among the oldies in his community, and had heard many tales of the avenging dead and the terrible price paid for want of retribution.

Damn the price, he decided.

The fury sang in Jak's blood. Such an affront was to invite his full vengeance, and as he suited up in the formfitting lightweight battle armor he'd never worn before, advanced riot gear rescued from a locker deep underground in an already forgotten military redoubt, he knew it was only the beginning of a very long night.

He chose to abandon his more familiar fighting tools, his leaf-bladed throwing knives, his mighty Colt Python, deciding, instead, to rely on his wits and fighting skills, and the mysterious rune-inscribed midnight blue blade he kept hidden from prying eyes.

Christina had thought him silly for hanging on to the oversized weapon, which dated back thousands of predark years.

"You're too small a man, Jak, to hoist such a blade," she had said, unable to lift it herself using both hands. It fell to the well-worn boards of the front porch of their home with a muffled clatter.

"You say I'm small?" he retorted, reaching down and easily retrieving the weapon.

"No," she answered. "You're plenty big enough for me."

"Hate people call me small," he said, wiping away the stray particles of grit that had adhered to the surface of the sword when it dropped.

"I never said that and I never would say that," Christina said firmly. "But there's something dark and unholy and evil about that blade, and I wish you'd put it away."

"Okay," he had said and gave her an elfish smile. "Blade gone. Won't see it again."

Now she was gone, and the sword had reappeared.

The jewels encrusted in the hilt of the blade felt cool against his pale white hands as he hefted the weapon high over his head, cool and comforting, like they belonged there as part of him.

"No peace?" Jak whispered in a voice that was no longer his own. "So be it."

Alone in the world, he saddled his great steed and rode west, following the trail of the ones who'd taken his wife and child. It wasn't as hard as it might have seemed, since no care had been taken to cover their tracks. Even when Jak thought he was lost, the sword sheathed at his hip would act as a sullen guide, pulling him back on course, the deep blue of the metal attracted by some hidden magnet.

Once his horse was spooked by a hissing rattler and Jak fell from the saddle as the equine reared in fright. The armor he'd taken from the closet and now wore protected him from the impact of the fall as he landed heavily on the rocky sand. Transport was going to be another matter, since his steed ran past, frightened, leaving Jak alone with his thoughts.

(Not alone.)

A rattler slithered close, warily keeping the coils of its body out of reach of Jak's blade. The unmistakable chittering of the rattle at the end of the snake's tail provided accompaniment to the reptile's sinuous movements.

"What? Thought heard—"

(Not alone.)

"Hear you...in head," Jak said softly.

(Yes.)

"Where are they?"

(Not safe not yet no one is safe not yet.)

"Not safe?"

(No one, not even you.)

And the rattler started to grow in height and bulk, a combination of inflating and expanding, stretching and elongating, pulsating and reaching that raised it to a height of thirty feet.

(You die now, you die.)

"No. You do," Jak replied, and leaped to one side as the massive head of the reptile came striking down, incredibly fast. White fangs bit into tan sand and stone, and the entire landscape seemed to rock from the impact. Jak was once again sent tumbling, but this time he was expecting the fall and he quickly rolled and regained his footing.

The serpent, momentarily dazed by the missed strike, didn't bring up its huge head, but instead kept it close to the ground as undulating coils pushed it toward the waiting Jak. Hurtling like an air-to-surface missile, the head picked up speed and came directly for its intended target like a launched arrow from a bow, and again, the agile albino was able to sidestep the attack.

Even as he avoided being struck, Jak released his own offensive, bringing his sword above his head in preparation.

As he swung the sword down in an elegant reaching arc, the entire blade seemed to glow with a translucent blue, and before he could react to the appearance of the unexpected light the blue grew past the weapon and crawled up his arm and across his shoulder and up and down his body, coating him in blue, obscuring his sight, his mouth, his mind.

(No peace.)

"Peace," Jak said.

The oversized head of the rattler was sliced off neatly and a spray of blue blood squirted outward, lifeblood as blue rain pouring through the halo of blue light surrounding Jak, and he was frozen in place in the dark of the desert, alone and helpless.

Helpless in blue.

MILDRED WAS DREAMING. She was wearing a Greek toga or some sort of filmy outer garment that rippled around her body. She was adrift in blue. Ice blue. Icy cold. Her keen physician's mind reminded her that Greek for icy cold was *kryos,* the study of cryonics, the preservation of the living dead.

The only part of her body that seemed to be working was her eyes, so she looked around frantically, managing to catch a glimpse of herself in a mirror. Again, she was blue—lips, face, hair. All blue. Then, she heard a voice. Dr. Victoria Blue's voice. The voice of her colleague and friend. They were active in the cryo program together.

Mildred was confused. Why was Victoria looking down at her with a strained, sad smile?

"The cyst!" Mildred wanted to scream, and immediately she knew she was in for abdominal surgery on an ovarian cyst, or rather, what they believed to be a cyst. It was December 28 of the year 2000—on the cusp of the new year.

"We're losing her!" Victoria said. "There's no other way. The cryo process is experimental, but we'll have to make the attempt."

Mildred blinked, and the bedroom was gone, replaced by the neutral blue tones of a hospital ward. The walls were whipping past her, faster and faster. She tried to speak, but found her voice missing. She still couldn't move. She looked down her prone body and saw her bare feet at the bottom of the gurney. Mildred tried to wiggle her toes. They stayed frozen. Then, she noticed her feet and her toes were blue as the twin doors looming up in front of her parted like stage curtains, and she was inside, and through.

Then came the large tub, made of metal, fabric and naugahide.

Then the underwater pump and the distribution system.

Mildred recognized the system other cryo specialists had coined "Squid." After a person was placed inside the tub, a couple of hundred pounds of ice were added along with numerous buckets of water—then with a flip of the switch the squid would start circulating the water very rapidly around the body. The process dropped the temperature much more quickly than just packing a person in blocks of ice.

The IV lines already in her arm for the surgery on the cyst were now being used again, this time to assist in the cryo preparation process. That much Mildred recognized from the procedure she had carried out on others personally. An assortment of medications were being dumped into her bloodstream: first heparin to prevent blood clots; potassium chloride or phenobarbital of some kind; other chemicals to depress the brain metabolism so that the cells could stay alive in a less active state; something to keep the acidity level of the pH proper; calcium channel blockers to prevent calcium from traveling into the cells and starting a number of chemical reactions that typically do a lot of brain damage.

"God Almighty," Mildred thought, reeling, her heart pounding in terror as she recognized the procedure she was beginning to endure. Why was she still awake?

When the scalpel fell on her leg, the pain was excruciating. The clinical part of her doctor's mind noted her friends were doing a femoral bypass, opening up the femoral artery and vein in the leg and hooking up a pump to flush her entire vascular system. Victoria Blue was still with her, but new cast members were being added to the operating stage, one by one. First, a thoracic surgeon came in, leading a team of twelve with carts of instruments and med gear. The surgeon looked down and without any warning shoved a scalpel into her chest.

Bach was playing on the sound system in the room as he proceeded to do a textbook example of open-heart surgery while the paralyzed and helpless Mildred Wyeth watched herself be sliced open.

She knew why. The point was to get tight control of the circulation. This was to make sure if any clots developed around her heart, there was still control to get the fluid to the brain. She also knew what was coming next, as all of the water in her body was replaced with a glycerol-based mix of fluids to prevent damage from occurring during the freezing process.

For obviously, in cryo storage, any water or moisture turned to ice.

After the perfusion with glycerol was complete Mildred was lifted and placed in a chilled bath of silicone oil. The oil was pumped through dry ice, and once she was secure they left her, returning after her body had dropped to the temperature of the ice. She was placed in a special tank wrapped in a sleeping bag and in an aluminum pod for protection. Liquid nitrogen was sprayed in, and she dropped to minus 196 degrees C.

Then she was tucked away in a stainless-steel tank, vacuum insulated, and held in limbo, her mind still screaming, suspended at that temperature until science caught up someday.

But the subjects weren't supposed to be conscious, more alive than dead, seeing yet not dreaming. A single tear crept from her left eye and froze a shining trail on her cheek. If Mildred had been able to see her face, she knew the color of the tear would be blue.

DEAN WAS DREAMING. He was back in the bucking hold of a boat, caught in the center of a violent storm. He could look at the bulkheads, and he knew he'd been there before and something triple-bad was going to happen, but there wasn't a thing he could do about it except sit, wait and watch, hoping the events wouldn't follow their earlier pattern; that above, his father and J.B. would be able to steer clear of the danger, the coming danger that Krysty was now warning.

The redhead could feel it coming, she was saying, just like she'd said the first time.

"Something's wrong, something's bad wrong. Got to warn Ryan. There's danger."

Loud crashes of thunder kept drowning out Krysty's voice, but Dean could still read her lips, and he knew already what she was telling them.

Then came a final crash of thunder, and everyone in the crowded section was thrown back, and then heaved forward as the yacht yawed from the impact. And this time when the explosion went off and the front half of the nose of *The Patch* was nigh high-vaporized, bringing in a crushing flood of blue-black seawater, he didn't manage to scramble his way to the upper deck and safety.

This time, Mildred didn't grab a handful of the boy's shirttail and pull him upright.

This time, like Krysty, who'd been thrown off her booted feet and hurled into the thrashing waters, and like Jak, who'd been tossed forward down the narrow passageway and directly into the newly created hole in the bulkhead, Dean also went tumbling like a dropped bit of refuse into the ocean blue.

Dean took blank note of how one of the toe tips of Krysty's cowboy boots caught the light and flickered like a faraway star, a pale wink of blue and gone before he fell into deep oblivion.

J.B. WAS DREAMING. He was on an elevated mountain peak somewhere in Colorado, the air crisp in his lungs. When he exhaled, small clouds of steam puffed out. His glasses were slightly misted over with condensation from the heat of his body and the cool of the air, but when he reached to wipe them clean he was perplexed to find he wasn't wearing his specs.

The misty covering on his eyes that obscured his vision was coming from inside his own body. Triple-strange to overheat from the inside. He'd have to ask Mildred about that. He might be getting sick, and even the mildest of infections could prove fatal in the uninhabitable Deathlands.

"Hey, J.B.," Trader said.

The Armorer turned to take in the old man. The

Trader looked good. Damn good. Last time J.B. had seen his former mentor, the Trader was showing his age and then some. Now, he looked as healthy and robust as the day J.B. and he had first met, all those years ago outside J.B.'s boyhood home of Cripple Creek near the Rockies.

The Trader's grizzled salt-and-pepper hair stood on his scalp like an angry porcupine, and his big cigar was firmly clamped between his teeth. J.B. could smell the pungent scent of burning tobacco and that, too, helped assure him of his friend's identity, for the Trader had always smoked the same putrid weed.

The older man's red-brown complexion was visible under the days of stubble across his broad face. His powerful build was unstooped by disease or age, and his trusty Armalite rifle was slung over his shoulder in a casual manner, but ready to be unlimbered and fired in an instant if needed.

J.B. was glad to see him. "Hey, Trader," he said. "What brings you over?"

"Got something for you," Trader rumbled, his voice like a misfiring diesel engine. He reached into a coat pocket, his own long coat lined with even more hiding places than J.B.'s scuffed leather jacket. "Found them back on War Wag One. Thought you could use a pair."

He held out a small box covered in black felt about the size of the palm of his hand. The hinged lid was closed. A golden line where top met bottom glinted in the sunlight.

"Didn't have to do that," J.B. said warily. He wasn't a man who liked to owe favors, not even to the Trader.

"No, I didn't, but I did," Trader replied, his gruff voice colored with annoyance. "Now show some respect and say thank-you."

"Thanks. I think. What is it?" J.B. asked.

"Go ahead," Trader urged. "Open the box."

The Armorer reached out and took the package, holding it in his left hand while using a dirty fingernail of his right to flip open the top.

"Dark night!" he bellowed in shock. J.B. wasn't the sort to startle at a prank, but the Trader had certainly put a scare into him with the contents of the innocuous little box.

Inside the case were two human eyes, eyelids attached, severed at the optic nerves. One eye was light blue, the other nearly cobalt. Some stray drops of red had splattered on the interior pink lining of the box. Gory, yes, but what had elicited the bellow from J.B. was that both of the eyes shifted and peered up at him.

"Goddammit! What kind of shit are you trying to pull, Trader?" J.B. demanded in a loud voice. He looked up to find the larger man had miraculously vanished. He slammed the small container shut, locking away the dismembered eyeballs in their twin puddles of grue.

A small scrap of paper had fallen from the box when J.B. opened it. He leaned down and picked it up from the dirt.

"I'll be keeping an eye out for you," the message read.

J.B. wasn't amused.

"So," Trader said from behind, "you ready to fly?"

The Armorer turned to find the Trader standing next to a sky wag, a great wooden and canvas bird with biwings and single propeller. "You like her?" the older man asked, before going into a series of hacking coughs. He cleared his throat and hawked up a mouthful of blood and phlegm, spitting it off to one side.

"No way. Get up in that thing, hit a hell-wind and it'll dump you out on your ass," J.B. replied, walking away. "Thanks for the present."

"Good day for flying," Trader called back to J.B. "Not a cloud in the sky."

He was right. The sky was as open as a traveling gaudy's front door—and in J.B.'s mind, about as uninviting.

"Step in, we'll go for a spin," Trader said, appearing in front of the Armorer.

"You're no pilot," J.B. said, starting to back away.

"The hell you say!"

J.B. continued to back up, and pushed against something. He spun and damn if he wasn't seated in the plane now, the Trader in the second seat behind him with the controls.

And the sky went from sky blue to electric, crackling with lightning. The hell-winds J.B. had mentioned came sweeping in, the upper atmosphere of much of the world permanently damaged in the nuclear battle between the superpowers.

"Guess we'd better bail," Trader said mildly, standing in his seat and giving J.B. a two-fingered salute.

"Bail?"

The Trader pointed to his back. "Parachute. Insurance policy. That's predark slang for covering your ass."

The big man leaped out, clearing the plane. Even as the craft began to shudder in the bucking winds, uncontrolled, J.B. peered down and watched the chute open, jerking the Trader's hanging body in a spastic movement.

The Armorer reached into a pocket and took out a cigar, biting down hard on the end.

Hell of a way to die.

J.B. fell, plunging to his doom, surrounded by blue.

Chapter Five

Doc Tanner had started the mat-trans jump with a clear mind and a level head. As far as he could determine, he wasn't dreaming. If he had been awake, he would undoubtedly have remarked on this as being "most unusual." Traditionally during a mat-trans jaunt, Doc was cursed with Stygian nightmares of such dire calamities he could hardly withstand the mental assault. When he eventually returned to consciousness, his entire body always ached from thrashing on the floor of the chamber in semiremembered agony.

This time was different.

This time, he was happy to note, he slumbered peacefully.

Doc lay in a feather bed with a sweet-smelling pillow stuffed with fresh straw under his head and a second one gripped in his hands. A smiling crescent moon shone down on him through an open bedroom window, and a gentle summer breeze wafted over his slumbering form, cooling him as he slept.

Then he heard a voice. A woman's voice.

"Emily?" he asked.

"No, Krysty," came the reply.

For brief seconds, Doc was confused—was he in

bed with another woman? "Howling calamities!" he said in disbelief, fearing for his marriage.

"Right, Doc," Krysty replied, but he couldn't hear the words.

"You must speak up," he said impatiently. "I cannot hear you."

"Where's Lori?" the Titian-haired beauty yelled in reply, but again, even with raising her voice and calling out as loudly as possible, Doc could barely hear her voice. The words were faint, as if she were standing far, far away on a distant mountain peak and calling into a valley.

"What?" Doc answered, in a sane, calm, rational speaking voice. "What did you say?"

"Lori! Where is she?" Krysty was closer now. Doc could see her flushed face, smell her sweat. She had been running, or involved in some sort of physical activity. A guilty flash of lust crept through his loins, for after all, he was in his bedchamber and dressed only in a nightshirt, and one of the most ravishing and sexy women he'd ever laid eyes on was standing right next to his bed, wearing a skintight shirt and breathing heavily.

"Snap out of it, Doc. Your mind's wandering again."

"Um, my apologies."

"Where's Lori?" she asked again.

"I...I do not know, my dear," he replied lamely, feeling ashamed of himself for looking at Krysty in an unpure manner and eager to shift blame for his own feelings of guilt. "We—we got separated."

"Well, she's a big girl now. Hope she can look after herself!" Krysty cried, punching Doc easily in the shoulder with a left jab, and then she turned, her long hair fanning out behind as she ran away from the coming storm flashing softly on the horizon.

The bedroom was gone. No walls, no windows. No smiling cartoon moon looking down.

Doc was alone once more.

Doc was dreaming.

Yes, a dream. Despite his earlier beliefs to the contrary, that was the only answer. Yes. Logic dictated his conscious mind was sleeping while his unconscious plundered his brain, skirting the damaged areas marked Do Not Enter and Condemned and Warning! DANGER! for a change, and, instead, pulling out pieces of memory long in storage, kept there if needed, locked away if not.

Lori, young Lori. Despite the dream Krysty's assurances, Doc knew Lori wasn't a big girl. In fact, despite the strip-queen body and the mounds of antagonism she routinely spouted, she was even more immature than young Dean.

Dean had never met Lori. She had passed on before Doc made Ryan's son's acquaintance.

So.

Damn the philosophy lesson and the code he knew he was trying to make sense of—instead, he would try to deal with the stone-hard facts. Doc knew he was in the middle of a jump dream, his memories of the past unbottled and poured into his skull in a volatile mix courtesy of the blender provided by the frightening forces of the mat-trans experience.

Ignore it, he finally decided. Go back to sleep.

Doc closed his eyes and nodded his head and was surprised to find his eyelids weren't functioning—either that or he could see right through them, since he was looking down at his hands instead of the back of his eyelids.

"No, not mine," he whispered, for Doc was flabbergasted to find his hands were young again, and the veins were bold and purple and the muscles underneath the taut skin were pulsating within their fleshy outer covering, muscles that now enabled him to have a bold strong grip, as if modified with tensile cables of steel. The liver spots of artificial age thrust cruelly upon his weathered skin had vanished. His threadbare garments—trousers, shirt, coat—all were also whole and new. The felt of his black frock coat was brushed and unfrayed. The leather of his boots crinkled like new brown paper and shone like wet vinyl in the flickering flames.

Flames?

A tall stovepipe hat stood erect on his head, though Doc couldn't recall wearing such a chapeau more than once or twice, and even then, only because the headgear was a gift, and he'd never liked the thing, feeling that it made a mockery of him and goodness, but wasn't it terribly hot in this latest splotch of mind vomit.

The shock of returned youth fell away as Doc realized he was surrounded by fire.

"By the Three Kennedys!" he boomed, and the voice in his ears was like freshly thrown thunder. He'd have to speak loud and plain to be heard here; a chem storm was brewing, flashing pink lightning against the darkness of the night sky. The air smelled acidic and alien, like the laboratories of his college days.

And then, he knew. He remembered this place. It was Snakefish, California, a mere scrap of a once prosperous state decimated by the sub-launched nuclear missiles from Soviet submarines off the West Coast. It was the home of Baron Edgar Brennan, who'd either taken or been given the comical name of a long-dead folksy cowboy actor, according to Mildred Wyeth. The physician had heard of Edgar and his strange ville secondhand, since she was still in cryo sleep during the time of that adventure, but Doc had assured her she hadn't missed much.

Baron Brennan had set himself up in high style thanks to a hidden cache of gasoline…but he was an old man, and in a tale as ancient as the world, youth overtook age. His subjects in Snakefish had turned against him. Ultimately he died with his face in the dirt, shot in the back by a sawed-off shotgun, a double-barreled charge of death that nearly cut him in two, chilling him messily, if not instantly.

Way of the world. A baron fell, another rose to take his place. Like a well-swung scythe aimed at tall stalks of wheat in the field, if they were cut down, more would come back.

Patterns within patterns.

They—Ryan, Doc, J.B., Jak, Krysty, Lori and that other poor unfortunate, Rick Ginsburg—all of them were at the fuel refinery where the gasoline that kept the baron in power was processed. Three large storage tanks were sticking up tall against the backdrop of the mountains. A score of rocking-donkey pumps bobbed up and down in patient, unchanging motion, great metal monstrosities bringing up the thick crude and sending it into a long warehouse-like building where the actual refining and processing of the gas were accomplished.

There were several low walls but only one possible entrance into the complex.

Ryan had chosen this as the locale of their final stand against the new baron and his followers, using the site's allure to bring in their foes, even as they fled out the back. Behind them, a stream of refined gasoline was gaining speed, the oily stench of fuel hanging in the air. Jak had opened all of the main valves on the three oversized fuel containers, and now thousands of gallons of gas were flooding through the complex, along the roadway and toward their murderous pursuers.

The hot exhaust from one of their foes' chrome-and-leather-enhanced Harley-Davidson motorcycles ignited the released fuel into an explosion of cataclysmic proportions.

The wretched ville of Snakefish was burning. The worshippers of the giant sand serpents went up in flames, abandoned by their reptile god to twist in the heated wind.

Time to go. Smoke hung in the air, and Doc felt himself cough as he tried to take in a fresh breath. Thick black smoke billowed around him like a hot fog, an ashen blanket draped around his shoulders.

"Run, dammit!" The cry came out of the fire. Who had issued the order? Ryan? Yes, that was the voice of command the one-eyed leader wielded so well, motivating all of them past death again and again.

And there she was, running as fast as she could across the withered pavement, her blond hair shining like a beacon, glowing brighter in the light of the fires.

Lori Quint, a seventeen-year-old beauty with a body like a newborn colt, all legs and stumbling, running for her life, her high-heeled boots of tooled red leather slapping down on the road. Doc listened. He could hear the tiny silver spurs on her footwear jingle with their trademark thin clear sounds, a faint hint of merry music in the overheated air. For long months after the tragedy about to occur, he'd heard that very same faint jingle in his nightmares.

Nightmares such as this.

The jingle was coming up fast behind him, reaching out for him, begging him for help, each jingle whispering his name.

A seventeen year old, with a woman's body and the mind of a much younger girl.

Even as a man in his mid- to late-thirties, and truth be told that was his real biological age, Doc felt a twinge of cradle-robbing when enraptured in the throes of passion with Lori. He was a man who appeared and acted over sixty years old, and she wasn't his lover in appearance, but more of a daughter.

During his earlier lifetime in the late 1800s, one of Doc's wealthier friends from Oxford had arrived at the local men's club on a weekly basis with a new young woman on his crooked arm—his nieces, he called them with a nudge and a wink. "Theophilus! Come over here, you scowling brigand, and meet my niece!"

Doc had smiled, allowing his colleague to present his lie to everyone's amusement. It was harmless enough, since the man's wife had been dead seven years and his children now adults with their own love affairs to conduct.

It wasn't until after Lori was dead, her nubile frame engulfed and turned to ash by the firestorm, that Doc realized that though he grieved for her he hadn't loved the girl. Oh, he'd cared for her, and sought comfort in her arms, in her embrace, in their lovemaking. She'd made him feel alive once more, whispering his name, shuddering with pleasure at his touch...even as she'd later chisel away at his self-esteem by pointing out her own vitality against the damages of time inflicted on his body.

She'd taken the young Joshua Mote as her lover, allowing Doc and Ryan to catch her in the midst of a particularly randy bit of sex. She'd offered no explanation for her illicit affair, no apology to the man she'd wronged. A woman had needs, Doc knew that, but a woman should also have decency and compassion.

And his sexual equipment and plumbing worked just fine, thank you very much.

At that moment in time, his eyes filled with the sight of her betrayal, Doc had never missed his wife so much.

Lori Quint. She'd been headstrong, that one, with the unproved wisdom and brazenness of youth. One moment she was as valuable an ally as could be hoped for in Deathlands, quick to protect herself and her companions by firing off .22-caliber rounds from her pearl-handled PPK.

Other times, however, a darkness revealed itself behind her laughing eyes. She'd back-talk Ryan or pick verbal fights with Krysty. She'd ignore J.B.'s advice and Doc's pleading and plunge headlong without regard for what might be hiding around the corner.

Behind her, the yellow and orange and red petals of the onrush of fire opened like an expectant flower, but this was no inviting garden bud—this was a serpent of flame.

The tall blond girl was silhouetted against the towering wall of yellow-orange fire as it swept toward her, hot tongues of flame licking at her boot heels.

"My sweetness, my lovely fawn," Doc whispered, the pet names cruelly ironic as he watched them engulf the girl, watched helplessly as she fell, and melted, within the fringes of the inferno. Then he could watch no more as his eyes filled with tears of regret and loss.

So close.

How many had died?

First his beloved children, and then Emily, and now his newly found angel, Lori.

Next off, the entire world and almighty man and his loves and hates and accomplishments and regrets, all dead, all dead.

And as for the good Dr. Theophilus Algernon Tanner? Hell, ol' Doc just kept on living. Perhaps he'd still be doddering around at the end of time, perched on the arid edge of eternity, the tails of his faded frock coat flapping around his legs in the buffeting winds as the universe finally wound to a stop. What good was his regained youth now?

Doc stood above an ocean of time and was amused to discover that the color of temporal fluid and mass was a wickedly shimmering blue.

"Boo hoo, blue hue, toodle loo, to you," he whispered, reaching up with a hand. The age spots had returned. Doc smiled wistfully, pulled the string to the single blue bulb hanging from the ceiling overhead and turned out the light.

Chapter Six

Darkness.

"Without a doubt, that sucked," Mildred said, her voice broken and weak.

Ryan opened his eye. Above, the hexagonal configuration of metallic disks housed in the ceiling fixtures of yet another mat-trans unit shone down impassively on him, the massive amounts of energy sent surging through them mere seconds before now spent and fading away. Ignoring the sensation of nausea, Ryan turned his face to the wall and found himself looking at a new color of armaglass.

The jump had been successful. The dingy gray walls of the North Carolina redoubt were gone, left behind and forgotten.

"Takeoffs aren't the problem. It's the landings," J.B. stated, the jump dream still fresh in his mind as his own pained voice offered up a mirror of Mildred's.

"What color is this, anyway?" Ryan asked, gesturing toward the armaglass wall. He was sitting up now, trying to ease the pounding in his brain.

"Blue?" Mildred ventured.

J.B. nodded. "Yeah. Blue. Haven't seen this shade of blue before, though."

"I have. In dream," Jak said. The albino was already squatting on his feet, his ruby eyes scanning the walls and his comrades.

"He's right. Saw this shade of blue in my jump dream, too," Ryan replied, squinting his eye and looking at the armaglass.

"I used to wonder if they would ever run out of colors for the armaglass. As many colors of blue we've encountered, I guess they were starting to get desperate," Mildred said.

J.B. shrugged. "Either that, or some higher authority liked blue."

"I recall reading a survey long ago that blue was the most popular choice for favorite color," the physician mused.

"Well, there you go," J.B. answered, checking his weapons to make sure they'd come through safely. "I always liked blue myself."

"Other than seeing similar shades matching the armaglass in our dreams, either of you recognize this chamber?" Ryan asked impatiently.

"No."

"Sorry."

"Okay, then we're in new territory. Everybody awake?" Ryan asked, getting to his feet. He reached down and felt the butt of the SIG-Sauer still holstered and fastened down. He flicked back the strap, freeing the handblaster for when he needed it. His other rifle was still safely strapped around his body, tucked away at his back.

"Define awake, lover." The redhead was on her stomach, her arms tucked beneath her limber body.

"I'll take that as a yes, Krysty," he replied, kneeling to shake his son. "Dean, you feel okay?"

Dean, who was on his side, rolled over and looked up at his father. A small spot of saliva dotted one of his cheeks. "Sure. Dreamed I was back on *The Patch.* Fell in the drink. Drowned."

"I am delighted each and every one of you feels so giddy and free. I, on the other hand, feel like something tracked in on the bottom of a shoe. My left hipbone is killing me," Doc told them.

"Roll off that damned Le Mat and you'll be more apt to feel better," Mildred suggested.

"Alas, to roll requires strength I currently do not possess, my good Dr. Wyeth. Perhaps you might assist me?"

"Assist yourself. I've got my own jump sickness to deal with," she retorted, sitting up with her back against one of the blue armaglass walls. Her stomach was cramping, but it had been a while since she or any of the others had eaten, so she suspected her nausea was induced more by hunger than by aftereffects from the mat-trans journey.

"I'm going to take a look and see what's waiting outside the chamber," Ryan said. "Triple red alert for everybody. J.B., watch my back. The rest of you go ahead and get your blasters ready, just in case."

"My dear Ryan, I doubt I currently have the strength to even hold my own pistol aloft to shoot."

"You're excused, then, Doc. But try and keep

both eyes open. If the shit starts flying, I bet you'll find the energy to fight back."

"Well said," the old man answered, and got himself into a semierect seated position facing the chamber doorway.

Stepping lightly across the floor, with J.B. close at hand, Ryan stopped and readied himself before trying the handle of the heavy armaglass door. It lifted smoothly in his gloved grip and the door opened a crack.

Drawing his blaster and keeping it held at his side, Ryan's single blue eye peered out carefully. Outside the mat-trans, within his limited field of view, he spotted an array of digital displays and comp monitors. The comps were active, flickering in random patterns of frantic life and colored lights, the secret glowing dance that allowed each of the mat-trans units around the world to operate safely and securely. Their hard-drive bays glowing with tiny yellow dancing lights, their internal drives whirring away, all of the comps outside the chamber appeared to be in full working order.

"No anteroom," he said quietly to his waiting friends. "This mat-trans opens right into the control center. Comps everywhere."

"People?" J.B. asked.

Ryan shook his head no.

"Weird. I thought the engineers usually wanted a buffer zone between the unit and the control computers," Mildred replied, voicing her private opinion that while the mat-trans chambers were self-enclosed, nearly every one of the devices they'd encountered so far seemed to keep a smaller room and wall between master control and the units themselves. These smallish, buffer rooms seemed to offer a protective layer between the forces unleashed within the self-enclosed mat-trans unit and the software kept housed in the memories of the control comps, as well as serving as a simple waiting area before and after a jump.

Ryan slowly continued to take in what he could see from his protected vantage point inside the gateway. Along the far wall, behind twin desks of industrial metal with off-white terminal stations and monitor cabinets, he spied a long series of familiar-looking information storage and retrieval units, as tall as a man, chattering softly to themselves.

The unit data banks didn't hold his eye. The surface of the wall they were leaning against, however, did warrant a second look.

They were stone walls, with mortar slopped in the cracks instead of vanadium steel alloy, and Ryan thought they looked like the interiors of a castle or keep. He found himself scanning the corners, looking for the flames of burning torches. Instead, all he saw were the fluorescent strip lights used as illumination within a redoubt or a mat-trans gateway control area.

"I don't like the looks of this," Ryan said softly to his waiting friends, and before he could continue his thought, a new wrench was thrown into the gears of the situation.

"Are you coming out or not?" a commanding voice from outside the mat-trans chamber boomed.

Ryan almost fired a round from the barrel of the SIG-Sauer the moment he heard the unknown speaker, but his honed instincts told him to hold off until he could learn more and determine the situation. If he closed the mat-trans chamber door, the auto mechanism would initiate another jump, and multiple jumps were enough to make a person feel like walking death.

Three figures came out from one side of the mat-trans chamber, their presence previously hidden by one of the thick exterior armaglass walls. A single man, the leader, was now standing in front of Ryan and the partially opened door.

"I promise I won't bite," the man said with a grin, both hands held out, palms open and empty in the so-called universal gesture of friendship.

"I've heard that before," Ryan retorted.

"Yes, I imagine you have. Still, you have nothing to worry about from me."

"I'm not worried about you," the one-eyed man stated, keeping the bore of the SIG-Sauer leveled at the heads of the two sec men, who were on a higher plane than the shorter man standing in front of them.

"You mean my guards? They're here for me, not you," the mystery man said, nodding toward the imposing human presence on his left, then right. "Meet Garcia and Lopez."

The two sec men flanking the speaker were large specimens, heavily muscled and solid, each a few inches taller than Ryan's six feet two inches. They were dressed identically in sleeveless black T-shirts, olive green Army-issue trousers and what appeared to be regulation U.S. Army combat boots. Red headbands circled their heads.

There couldn't have been anyone more different from them than the third man standing between them.

Tall, lean and imposing, with long silver hair coming back off his forehead that gave him a dramatic widow's peak at the center of his hairline, the man looked like royalty, or what Ryan had always thought picture-book royalty should look like. The mystery man's face was long and narrow, with high cheekbones that added a cultured air of elegance to his overall appearance. His eyebrows were bushy and of a stiffer, darker gray than his hair, giving his flashing eyes a shielded, hooded look, like a human bird of prey.

However, it wasn't the fellow's face that gave Ryan pause. What worried him were the clothes the man was wearing. First and foremost, mental alarm bells went off when the one-eyed man spied the long white lab coat. Under the overcoat was a neatly pressed black dress shirt and dark charcoal-gray trousers. Against the fabric of the black shirt was a light gray necktie with a golden lion's head for a tie tack.

Ryan hadn't seen a necktie since he visited the Anthill.

There had been other encounters with men in formal attire, but after the chaos and the degradation of the hidden installation behind the rock faces of

Mount Rushmore, Ryan had decided once and for all that the presence of ties and business suits in Deathlands was never a good sign.

The man was smiling, apparently delighted at the arrival of his new visitors, but his inviting expression wasn't as open and inviting as it might have seemed, since he felt the need for guards. The menacing hulks of the twin sec men on either side of the greeter were the deterrents that kept Ryan's gun hand steady, and the muzzle of the SIG-Sauer lowered in a readied, but nonthreatening position. Ryan knew the armaglass of the chamber would protect him in the event of a gun battle, but he really didn't want to test it under such potentially disastrous conditions.

"How many of you are there inside the gateway?" the man asked.

"About a hundred," Ryan replied, causing Krysty and Dean to exchange grins as they listened from inside the mat-trans chamber. "Mebbe more. I'm lousy at math."

"Tracking comps out here put your number at—" he paused to step out of Ryan's line of sight to consult a monitor screen "—seven. Seven people."

"Dark night," J.B. murmured from his vantage point near Ryan. "We've stepped in it now."

"Not necessarily, John Barrymore," Doc whispered back. "These people seem to be friendly."

The Armorer gave Tanner a grim look of pity. "Doc, you of all people should know by now that nothing is ever what it seems in Deathlands."

The whitecoat outside the armaglass door continued to try to convince Ryan. "I assure you, I'm civilized. Won't you come out so we can compare notes?"

"Thanks, but no. Reckon I'm closing this door so we'll be on our way."

The man's voice became more excited. "Look, obviously you are aware of the existence of the matter-transfer units and their subsequent linked network. That ranks you and your people as being a cut above the average bloodthirsty grunts roaming the world today. We need to talk. We *have* to talk. Exchange information."

"Not interested. Later, pal, and don't forget to write," he said, repeating an expression he'd heard his own father use while Ryan was still a mere slip of a lad. As he spoke, he pulled the door closed on the chamber's counterbalanced hinges and it clicked true with a solid latching sound.

"What's the deal?" Krysty asked as Ryan strode into the chamber.

"Company. Some guy in a lab coat and a matching set of sec men. Get ready for another jump." he replied tersely, sitting on one of the hexagonal tiles in the floor.

"Oh, mercy," Doc whimpered, leaning back against the armaglass wall and sliding slowly into a seated position. "My head has already endured one bout of nausea. I do not think I can withstand another one of these soul-scrambling jaunts."

"Don't ready yourself for transport just yet, Doc," Mildred said, peering at the lack of activity from the array of silver disks mounted in the ceiling above. "We don't seem to be going anywhere."

The woman was right. None of the usual telltale prep signs were occurring—no mist, no whine, no glowing lights as the disks powered up.

"Sure you shut the door?" Mildred asked.

"Yeah, I'm sure. Fireblast," Ryan spit. "There must be an override outside the chamber."

"A logical assumption," Doc agreed. "Since the man outside seems to be aware of how these mystical conveyances operate."

There was a noise from outside the armaglass. Someone was knocking on the chamber door. Rap, rap, rap. Three times, then stop. Then three raps again.

"Look like we stay," Jak said morosely, one of his throwing knives already selected and waiting in his hand.

"Looks like," Ryan agreed, taking out the SIG-Sauer from his side holster once more and hefting the solid weight of the blaster in his right hand. While getting to his feet, his injured shoulder from previous adventures gave him a quick twinge of discomfort, as if to remind him that he still wasn't up to full fighting strength. "Everybody on their toes. You too, Doc."

"Gladly, sir. I would rather walk a country mile barefoot over broken glass than endure another mat-trans jump at the moment." Despite his bravado, Ryan noted the older man looked shaky as he stood erect, bracing himself ever so slightly on his walking stick.

Ryan opened the chamber door.

"Back so soon?" the man outside asked by way of greeting.

"Like we never left," Ryan replied.

The whitecoat gestured to the twin sec men. "As you can see, my friends here have lowered their weapons."

"Good for them. I'm keeping mine level until I know the playing field," Ryan said. "Tell them to keep the blasters down until we've all come out."

"They have ears. Your request is going to be met."

One by one Ryan's band of followers exited the gateway. Once the seventh member of the group, Doc Tanner, stepped gingerly off the bottom access step, the man who'd been patiently watching their progress held up his arms.

"Greetings," he said in a clipped tenor voice. "I am Dr. Silas Jamaisvous."

Staring at the whitecoat, Doc felt his mind slip away.

Dulce, New Mexico Redoubt, 1998

THE INTERVIEW ROOM was a lounge, used for breaks by various members of the duty staff within the massive Dulce redoubt when they didn't want to go to the full-service commissary, and as such the furnishings were simple. Vending machines and a small coffee machine lined one of the windowless walls.

Dr. Theophilus Tanner had been kept sedated during the move. He was unable to determine if he had been told the truth, or was being subjected to yet another mind game.

Such as the one now under way.

"I'm going to ask a battery of questions. Respond and—"

"I do not think so."

"What did you say?"

"I said, no."

"No?" Dr. Herman Welles looked across the table at the frowning man who'd uttered the single syllable.

"No," Tanner replied flatly, his blue eyes flat in their sockets like shards of gravel peeking out from beneath his brows. "I shall ask the questions for a change. I have endured enough of your inquiries. I have suffered through your physical tests. I have been kept in the dark long enough. I am not an idiot, nor am I easily confused or baffled by these futuristic trappings."

"I know. This is one of the reasons why you were chosen."

"So I have heard. If I am capable of comprehension, ergo, it is time I received some answers of my own."

Welles pondered this, tapping his ballpoint pen against the front of his teeth absentmindedly, then, much to Tanner's surprise, he nodded in agreement. "You're right, Dr. Tanner. Proceed."

Tanner folded his hands in front of him on the scuffed tabletop, covering a faded ring left in the plastic covering ages ago by a coffee cup.

"So, ask," Welles prodded.

Tanner held up a hand for silence. Then he spoke. "First, let us establish a few essential facts. I am Dr. Theophilus Algernon Tanner."

Welles agreed. "Yes."

"And you," Tanner added, pointing a bony finger at the corpulent figure seated across from him in a white lab coat, white shirt, black slacks and garish green tie, "you are Herman Welles."

"Correct. At least, that's what it says on my birth certificate."

"Such forms of identification can easily be faked," Tanner noted.

Welles shrugged. "The price we pay. You will have to take my word."

Tanner stood and crossed the room to the community coffeepot, pouring himself a foam cup of the steaming brew. "Coffee?" he asked.

"No, thanks."

Tanner returned to his chair and took a long pull from the cup before setting it down on the table, purposely placing it within the existing scorch mark. Welles watched silently, observing. While Tanner's back had been turned, the overweight man had taken out his pipe and now was busy tapping it against a glass ashtray on the tabletop, knocking out the previous bowl of tightly packed ashes.

Waiting until Welles had finished and relit the pipe, filling the small lounge with the smell of burning cherry, Tanner asked his next question. "Married?"

"No. Divorced. Six years now."

"Children?"

"None."

"How tragic for you. I have a wife, Emily—"

Welles cut in. "No, you don't."

Tanner pressed on. "And two children, a boy and a girl."

"Both deceased," Welles added.

Tanner continued to speak, his words overlapping Welles's voice. "I chose—*we* chose, Emily and I—chose their names, their most unusual names. Special names. Rachel after my wife's mother. Jolyon for one of my own family members who died in battle during the War Between The States."

Welles puffed on his pipe and sighed, consulting his notebook. "The names you give are correct, Doctor. However, they are names of the dead."

Tanner's placid facade collapsed. Welles suddenly found himself sitting across from a lion. His patient bared his fine white teeth and howled in wordless frustration and rage, slamming his hands on the table and sending the half-full coffee cup and ashtray crashing to the floor. "I am Dr. Theophilus Algernon Tanner! I have a wife! I have two children! I am a teacher, a scholar, a lecturer! By God, I am halfway through writing a book! Nonfiction! The finest minds of my generation consult with me on a daily basis!''

''Not any longer.'' Welles now stood, his own temper rising. His round face was reddening, and a sheen of sweat appeared on his brow. ''You, sir, are a curiosity. A living science experiment. A man without a frame of reference or a shred of comprehension.''

''You are incorrect, sir! I comprehend all!''

''Tanner, you are fucking Rip Van Winkle. Get used to it.'' And on that final pronouncement, Welles slammed closed the black notebook. Always with the damnable black notebook.

Tanner lunged forward, both arms outstretched to their full length, his wrists extended well past the cuffs of his hospital dressing gown. His rail-thin body skated lightly across the slick tabletop and right at the dumbfounded Welles.

''I have it!'' he crowed triumphantly as both of his long-fingered hands clamped down on Welles's notebook. Tanner snatched it boldly away, rolling, moving to one side on the table as Welles screeched in shock.

''Damn you, Tanner, give that back!'' Welles sputtered. ''Give it back or I'll—''

''Hush, Welles, before you cause me to fall in gales of laughter at your schoolboy predicament,'' Tanner soothed, his rich baritone taking the tone of a leisurely played bassoon. ''Like all bullies, you cannot handle having the tables turned. You shall have your precious book, full of the damnable lies of my life and times as filtered through your own corruptive sieve of an intellect! Shall we begin with the first page of our meeting?"

Keeping the table between them, Doc opened the book and began to read.

"'Patient appears confused, baffled, uncertain of his surroundings. Perhaps the decision in choosing subject was hasty, since he shows no signs of open-mindedness or creative thinking. He seems fixated on one subject, and one subject only—that being his family. His wife and children. This obsession must be circumvented before subject will be pliable enough for establishment of mission parameters.'"

"Tanner, you shouldn't be reading that," Welles warned.

"Subject. That's all I was to you then, and all I remain now," came back the response. "A subject. A test case. You could not even be bothered to write my name on these pages, nor the names of Emily or Rachel or dear little Jolyon. You could not even be bothered to remember the names of the lives you ruined, you despicable miscreant!"

"Now see here, Tanner, you settle down or I'll have to call in security."

"Call them, you elephantine pile of excrement! Show them all what an ineffectual dung heap you really are!" Tanner taunted as he happily tore one of the blue-lined pages from the book and crumpled it into a ball. He tossed the wadded paper and giggled darkly as it bounced off Welles's fat damp forehead with a plop, landing on the tabletop.

"That is one," he said, his voice starting to rise in timbre as he pulled out a second sheet of the notebook and began to crush it between long, elegant fingers. "I do hope you utilized one of those photocopying devices I have heard about to make a second, backup reproduction of your spurious observations and notes about me."

Pushed into a raging silence, Welles turned and ran to the lounge door, thumbing a wall communicator and screaming for a security team.

The goon squad wasn't long in coming, and the faceless men in their hooded white parkas and mirrored sunglasses made quick work subduing Tanner, who hadn't bothered to offer any resistance beyond gales of booming resonant laughter. One of them easily retrieved Welles's notebook from the smirking prisoner and handed it back stone-faced to the Chronos director.

"Your property, sir."

Welles snatched it from the guard and gave a dismissive wave of his hand. "Keep two on hand to subdue Tanner. The rest of you may go."

Now that Tanner was helpless and held by the summoned security men, Welles got closer and screamed in his face.

"Your wife is dead! Your children are dead! All you knew is dead! These are the facts! This is the future!"

"No, sir, it is not," Tanner replied. "Your future, perhaps. Not mine."

"Take him out of here," Welles ordered. "Take him out before I do something I'll regret."

EMILY TANNER WAS long dead, long buried. Her mortal remains had decayed into dust within the confines of the family vault, a great marble edifice, located high atop a steep hill among a smattering of trees—ancient trees with skeletal branches reaching for heaven, and settling instead for their positions of anguish, arms held high in sympathetic agony surrounding the burial chambers.

Her husband knew this to be true, once the future year he'd been trawled into was revealed and his mind had wrapped itself around the inescapable truth that he had indeed traveled one-hundred-plus years in the span of a single heart-bursting moment.

He looked down at the photograph and wished more than ever to be at her side, alive or dead.

"I wish to go to Deadwood," Tanner said.

"Uh-uh. No way. You know the rules. If the powers that be find I snuck you photos of the family tomb, they'd have both our asses."

"How did you happen to come upon said photographs, dear Allan?"

Allan Harvey grinned mischievously, his wide black face crinkling inward in a maze of smile lines. He liked Tanner. The burly security man had spoken with the refugee from time to time on many a long night, finding him to be one of the most gifted conversationalists Allan had ever encountered.

"Your file. Hard data. Most of what they have on

you has been encrypted and scanned into the Chronos master database. I don't have proper clearance to take a peek, and even if I did, they'd soon find out about it. But even records stored on computers have to start somewhere, and when I had a chance to glance through your paper file, I snatched those babies up."

"Will they not be missed?"

"Doubt it. Like I said, most of the idiots in here can't deal with anything unless it comes over a computer screen."

"One day, Allan, one day I shall be joined with them. Dear sweet Emily and my son and daughter."

The large black man nodded. "You mean when you die, old guy?"

Doc snorted. "No, noble Allan. I mean when I find my way back home."

Chapter Seven

"You have me at an advantage," the man who'd introduced himself as Dr. Silas Jamaisvous said in a mild tone of petulance.

"How so?" Ryan asked, the SIG-Sauer P-226 aimed squarely at the heart of the well-dressed speaker. Behind the one-eyed man, the rest of his people had struck similar positions of defense with their own weaponry as they exited the mat-trans chamber. The two sec men Ryan had spied earlier had now lost their nonthreatening stances and held their own autorifles aimed at him, responding in kind to the positions Ryan's group had assumed. "No advantage here. You got blasters. We got blasters."

"All God's children got blasters, my friend. Having a firearm is of no real advantage to either one of us here, since there would be more casualties than survivors," Jamaisvous replied silkily. "What I was referring to was that you have my name, but I do not have yours."

Sometimes the giving of names had been a thorny subject between Ryan and J. B. Dix. The Armorer, being of a more subtle nature would just as soon give out an alias when shoved into an unknown situation with guns aimed at their vitals. Their true names weren't unknown in the Deathlands and both men had left behind plenty of enemies in their travels, at least, the few enemies who had survived the run-in.

Ryan was of a different opinion. As a part of his own personal code a man was only as good as his name, and as such he chose to offer his freely if asked unless doing so would assure him of being chilled on the spot. A long time ago, when he first joined Trader's caravan of war wags, he'd stopped using the last name of Cawdor and rejected the family heritage. Now, he took some quiet pride in being a Cawdor, while remaining true to how his father would have wanted him to live.

Still, Ryan Cawdor might be stubborn, but he wasn't stupid. In this case, his real name wouldn't be a factor in ending or prolonging their current situation.

"Name's Ryan Cawdor," he said to Jamaisvous, gesturing with his head to the rest of the group. "That's my boy, Dean. Lady with the red hair is Krysty Wroth, and next to her in the specs is J. B. Dix. Dr. Mildred Wyeth is on the far left in the denim jacket and beside her is Jak Lauren." Ryan immediately regretted the slip. Usually the knowledge that Mildred was a physician was a closely guarded secret. He hurried. "The skinny gent with the walking stick is known as Doc Tanner."

Taking Krysty's hand and raising it to kiss, Jamaisvous paused after his lips brushed the redhead's warm skin, and recited, "'All that is in you is voluptuous and light—sweet, gentle, caressing and tender. And your moral world owes its enchantment to the sweet influence of your external world.'''

"Is that verse?" Doc asked, his eyes lighting up.

Jamaisvous lowered Krysty's hand and nodded at Tanner. "Indeed."

"How quaint to be greeted in such a fashion, with soothing words instead of bullets. I must confess, as well-read as I am, I do not recognize the poet. Might you enlighten me as to his name?"

"He's a local—was a local. José Gautier Benitez. Died back in 1880. Before my time, but some of his work can be found here in the library. I've tried to immerse myself in the culture and history as best I could. It pays to know your neighbors."

"Doc can't resist a good chunk of verse," Krysty said with a grin.

"So many doctors among you? Your people come equipped with many blessings," Jamaisvous said, and then paused. "Doc Tanner, you say?"

"Dr. Theophilus Algernon Tanner at your service," Doc replied with a slight bow.

"It can't be," Jamaisvous said, his tone now dumbfounded and his face a slack mask of shock.

Doc almost chuckled. "Oh, but I assure you, sir, I am who I am...I think. Truth be told, there are many days I have my doubts as well."

The man in the white lab coat stepped closer, waving back his watchmen, and approached Doc, looking him over from head to toe.

"Christ, Dr. Tanner, what in the hell happened to you?" he finally asked.

"A lifetime of tragedies, I am afraid. Which one are you referring to?" Doc replied, slightly puzzled by the line of questioning.

"I've read of you," Jamaisvous said, pressing on, not hearing Tanner's words. "In the old redoubt computer database records on time trawling. I studied your case from your arrival in prenuclear conflict 1998 until the year 2000, when you were sent ahead as a final part of the experiment. But there was nothing about such severe deterioration on your trawl forward into the future—our present day. And from what I read, I don't think you've been here long enough to have aged so drastically, have you?"

"I have not," Doc replied succinctly. "My current appearance is an unfortunate side effect courtesy of the destructive currents of the time-trawling process. Why it did not occur the first time I was swept away is a mystery to me."

Their newly appointed host exhaled a long sigh. "Well, damnation," he said. "This buggers all of my research."

"Research?" Mildred asked, speaking for the first time since leaving the gateway chamber.

"Yes, Dr.... Wyeth, was it? Research. I've spent the last two years rebuilding and experimenting with the mat-trans chamber behind you." Jamaisvous gestured floridly at the huge room that housed the gateway, a full computer lab with multiple stations and units, a small reception lounge and other odds and ends in the high-ceilinged, yet cluttered area.

"What kind of experiments?" Ryan asked suspiciously, eyeballing the elegant gray-haired man standing next to Doc. Already, Ryan was unhappy with Jamaisvous and his seemingly lackadaisical attitude at having armed strangers pop up in what appeared to be his own private mat-trans unit.

"Why, time-trawling experiments, my friends. Your Doc Tanner and I share something in common regarding our places in this dark future world—neither of us are supposed to be here."

"You were trawled?" Doc asked in disbelief.

"No," Jamaisvous replied quickly. "I was a corpse-sicle. Cryo sleep."

Mildred was about to speak up with a pithy "That makes two of us," but a warning look from J.B. stilled her planned quip. Apparently the Armorer thought that piece of information should remain private, at least for now.

Unfortunately no such exchange of looks occurred with Doc, who, swept up in his excitement over meeting Jamaisvous, blurted out the fact Mildred was also a refugee from the world previous to skydark.

"So, two of my visitors are even more special than I imagined," Jamaisvous said thoughtfully. He snapped his fingers and gave a dismissive gesture to the twin guards. "Garcia! Lopez! You may depart. I have nothing to fear from these men and women."

"But Dr.—" one of the men protested.

Jamaisvous fixed the sec man with a stony look. "Silence! Do as you are told. If you wish to assist, please inform the kitchen we have company for dinner. I'll be along shortly to discuss the meal in greater detail."

"WHERE IS THIS PLACE, anyway?" J.B. asked as Jamaisvous led them upward out of the secured mat-trans chamber and into the antique-appointed fortress interior. "Doesn't look like any redoubt I've ever seen."

"This isn't a redoubt," Jamaisvous replied. "Other than some rudimentary remodeling by myself, the gateway and control you saw in the lowest level are the only hints of any links to Project Cerberus, Operation Chronos or even the Totality Concept. You've arrived in Puerto Rico, Mr. Dix, and this is the famed El Morro Fortress, which has stood watch over the waters here for hundreds of years, and will still be standing after hundreds more and all of us are dust."

"Funny, you don't look Puerto Rican," Mildred noted.

"I'm not. Originally I'm from Ohio by way of Ireland. I take it all of you are from the United States?"

"Has a new name now," Ryan said. "Most call it Deathlands."

"How...charming."

"A man can survive there if he's mean enough and smart enough. Some go out and take up homesteading on their own piece of land, but you'd better be ready to defend it against muties and thieves. If you want safety, there are populated areas scattered up and down the eastern coast, and westward."

"Then civilization can still be found?"

"Didn't say anything about Deathlands being civilized. Plenty of pestholes with nothing more than a place to drink and sleep if you're traveling. Bigger areas with towns and a sort of government breaks down into two basic types of communities—villes and baronies. Villes tend to be a touch more democratic than baronies, which are usually a dictatorship."

"I see. I'm not wholly familiar with how you are using the terms baronies and villes, Mr. Cawdor, but I can make an educated guess."

"Usually a barony is safe enough as long as you stay out of the ruling baron's way," Krysty added. "And if you don't mind being cowed and walking around with your tail between your legs on a daily basis."

"That the situation here?" Ryan asked bluntly. "You the boss?"

"No. I have my small staff here in El Morro. What goes on outside these stone walls is no concern of mine. I do think you'll find life here a tad less restrictive and less threatening than what you appear to be used to."

Jamaisvous gave them all a quick lesson regarding the new land in which they had now taken involuntary residence. Roughly rectangular in shape, Puerto Rico was one hundred miles from east to west, and thirty-five miles from north to south, three times wider than it was tall. Within such a limited space, the island had once possessed it all in terms of a pleasant lifestyle—now, according to Jamaisvous, only the eastern half was habitable.

"El Morro is on Old San Juan—a miniisland, really, located in San Juan harbor. New San Juan—rather, what is left of New San Juan—is on the mainland," their host said.

"What can you tell us about this place?"

"What do you want to know? Old San Juan was a tourist mecca. New San Juan was the most advanced city in Puerto Rico. Together, they created a thriving economy up until the Third World War. Now nothing remains but a scattering of communities, not unlike the villes you described earlier. As far as I can tell, there was severe famine after the war and many of the inhabitants perished, leaving only a few survivors to repopulate."

"So what is the political situation here? Barons? Leaders?" Mildred asked.

Jamaisvous shrugged. "Most of the people here are too poor to think of such aggrandizement. Leaders here are born or made, not bought or elected."

"You said you were in cryo sleep."

"Correct."

"Where are the cryo facilities?" Mildred asked.

"Miles away," the man replied cryptically. "Miles away in the true Puerto Rican redoubt—at least, the only redoubt on this side of the island. I was forced to leave the secure area I awakened in because of problems with the base's nuclear generator."

"What kind of problems?"

"No power. We've reached your rooms."

Jamaisvous had taken them personally to an area in the fortress that had been remodeled at one time or another into a series of guest bedrooms. Each of the tidy sleeping chambers had a small night table made of the finest oak, a double bed with handmade comforter, ample closet space and a dresser smelling of sweet spices.

"I'll leave you to choose your own rooms and sleeping arrangements," their host said smoothly. "I apologize for the lack of bathrooms, but this fortress was not designed for the individual. The bath at the end of this hall has two stalls with bathing facilities and running hot and cold water. There are towels inside on the racks, and additional linens can be found in your rooms in the bottom drawers of the dressers. If you have clothing you'd like laundered, leave it outside your rooms and the maid shall see to it. Supper shall be at dusk. I'll instruct the cooks to prepare a feast, as I haven't entertained here in some time. You're in for a treat—home cooking by a mother-and-daughter team. Fine cuisine."

Jamaisvous stepped back a few paces, bowed deeply at the waist and was gone, leaving the group to make its own choices and go off into the designated rooms.

"Most curious," Doc said, scratching his nape. The expression on his face was one of deep concentration. A few days' growth of beard stubble added to his wan look as he pondered private thoughts.

"What's up, Doc?" Ryan asked.

Mildred bit back a snort of laughter, earning a glare from Ryan. It wasn't the first time she'd snickered when Ryan phrased concern for their elder statesman in a similar manner. "Wish I knew what was so damn funny, me asking Doc a question," the one-eyed man muttered.

"Hmm? What is up, you say?" Doc said, Ryan's query finally weighing in on his mind. "Oh, our benefactor. A most curious man."

"Yeah, he's not exactly what I expected to find when we jumped into this place. Or any place for that matter," Ryan agreed. "Seems to have his shit together. So far he isn't trying to breathe too hard down our necks."

"Yeah, no sec men at all in this part of the fortress," J.B. noted, switching his scattergun from one hand to another. "No cameras, either—unless they're hidden. Has his own hired men, sure, but doesn't seem to be as paranoid as most. And he keeps guards around the gateway control-room doors, but those are the only guns I've seen so far."

Ryan reached out and tapped a finger on the barrel of the M-4000 scattergun J.B. held. "And he didn't bring up the subject of our blasters. Usually, first thing out of any self-styled leader is the demand we turn over the hardware. Makes for a nice change."

"I believe there are probably additional sec men in and outside El Morro," Krysty said. "There's a funny…vibe to this place. I can't put my finger on it yet."

"We can talk about it later. Right now, I could use a bath. Jamaisvous was right—we're all a bit ripe," Mildred said as she started to approach the bathroom. "Krysty, you and I will go first—if it's all right with the rest of you?"

"Sure, Mildred. Go ahead," Ryan replied with a shrug. "We'll keep watch out here. Jamaisvous isn't the only one with a private sec man."

"We'll save some hot water for you…mebbe," Krysty called back with a light chuckle.

"Might just join you," Ryan retorted.

Mildred waggled a warning finger back. "Uh-uh. No, you don't. Wait your turn."

As the women disappeared behind the bathroom door at the end of the hallway, Dean took a moment to sniff at one of his armpits, lifting the arm high and craning his neck over to get a good whiff. "I smell worse than shit in sunshine," the boy groused.

"What else new?" Jak retorted.

Ryan stepped away from the two boys and left them to hold their own debate over who smelled worse. He'd noticed that Doc was still turned slightly to one side from the others, his face far away as he concentrated on his own internal field of inquiry. "Something still on your mind, Doc?" he asked.

Doc didn't turn, but kept his face to the wall as he said, "Ryan, I find I am experiencing a most disconcerting sense of déjà vu."

"Déjà what?"

"Déjà vu. French for a disturbing familiarity."

Ryan cocked an eyebrow. "How so?"

"I have the strangest feeling I have met Dr. Jamaisvous before...which makes his name all the more peculiar," Doc replied as he worked his hands nervously up and down his walking stick.

"Jamaisvous. Sounds like more of your French talk to me," Ryan mused, flexing his fingers in a halfhearted attempt to crack his knuckles.

"Very good, Ryan," Doc said with some delight. "The cognomen is indeed French."

Ryan grinned back. "Hell, Doc, my brain's not as overstuffed as yours, but I'm no dummy either."

"Well, I guess I'm the stupe. Cognomi-what? Translate for us dullards, please," J.B. snorted. The laconic man had grown interested in the conversation. Farther down the hall, Dean and Jak were still continuing to insult each other's personal hygiene.

"Cognomen. Last name," Doc replied briskly. "And that is not a translation, but a definition, John Barrymore. As for the translation, and I'll be the first to admit my mastery of French is a bit rusty, I think the name Jamaisvous means 'a most peculiar sense of time.'"

Chapter Eight

The offer Jamaisvous had made to provide fresh laundry was impossible to resist, and everyone contributed items of apparel to the stack of soiled clothing. In two hours' time the mound of clothing was taken away by a plump woman with long black hair tied in a tight bun, washed in a remote part of the fortress, dried and returned folded.

One of the sec men they'd met in the gateway control room came at dusk to rap lightly at their doors and fetch the group.

"Lopez, right?" Mildred asked as she stepped out of her room with J.B. She felt refreshed from having a bath, and clean clothing to wear for a change.

The big man didn't look amused. "No, ma'am."

"Garcia."

"Luis, actually. I think you have me confused with my cousins."

"You lose again," J.B. said, even as the sec man went on to knock and alert the others of the impending meal. Once all had been accounted for, he led them though a passageway and into an opulent dining room. Centered in the room were a dozen chairs around a long wooden table with an immaculate white tablecloth.

Jamaisvous stood at the head of the table and waited until everyone else was in place and seated before he took his own seat. Ryan sat to his left and Doc to his right.

The Puerto Rican mother and daughter who cooked for Jamaisvous were standing patiently on opposite sides of the table, both apparently serving as hostesses for the meal. He'd introduced them as Elena and Maria, but the pair hadn't spoken in kind, choosing instead to merely nod and keep their focus on the work. Both carried a vibrantly painted orange serving pot on a tray. Upside-down cups on saucers at the upper left of each of the place settings matched the color of the orange pot, so Ryan took the visual clue and turned his cup over, watching the younger Puerto Rican woman pour it full of a steaming brown liquid.

"Mmm! Smell that aroma!" Mildred said, down and across from Ryan, where the mother was filling the woman's cup. "I haven't smelled coffee like this in...well, in years!"

Ryan lifted the smallish mug to his lips, trying to be careful and not burn himself with the hot liquid. He didn't know what Mildred was getting so excited about, since real coffee was hard to come by. Rarely was the real thing found in any remaining quantity except for aged crystals vacuum-sealed in aluminum cans.

Coffee sub was coffee sub, he thought sourly, until he tasted the brew. He took a long pull at the drink before lowering the cup with a wide smile on his face.

"That's triple-fine coffee," Ryan finally said, holding out the cup for a refill.

"I know," Jamaisvous said, appearing to take satisfaction in Ryan's surprise and enjoyment of the beverage. "Puerto Rican coffee is some of the most delicious in the world, but there is very little of it left for harvesting. Even before the unfortunate business of war, it was a local treat only and never exported in any quantity to the mainland. A series of hurricanes in the 1930s destroyed most of the coffee trees, and since it takes seven years for them to mature, the island's farmers were forced to turn to other crops, such as sugarcane. Such storms still rage, and because of that coffee here is a local delicacy."

Jamaisvous went on to explain that coffee was grown mainly along the steep mountainsides in the central section of the island. Obtaining the beans was troublesome and dangerous, but worth the effort.

Baskets of hot corn muffins were placed at either end of the table, along with small shining platters of butter and glistening Guayaba jelly. The main meal was the exotic-sounding Lechon Asado, which everyone was glad to see translated as barbecued pig. The roasted meat had a spicy, pungent flavor that came from an assortment of native seasonings. Jamaisvous pointed out that the dish was roasted over an outdoor fire, not within the walls of an indoor kitchen, and rotated by hand on a regular basis on a pole stuck lengthwise through the animal.

The meat was served with a hot stuffed pepper on the side and a dollop of strong-smelling garlic sauce called ajilimojili that most of the group didn't eat, except for Doc who was glad to partake of both Dean's and Mildred's helpings.

Asopao, a thick rice soup with more of the native herbs, accompanied the meat. Pepper and fresh asparagus tips were mixed into the thick liquids, causing Ryan to reflect that the soup alone was more of a meal than most of them were used to eating.

A pineapple cake with coconut shavings feathering its cream-cheese icing was presented for dessert and even though their stomachs were full, no one could resist taking a slice of the sweet offering. The edges of the dessert plates were lipped slightly, helping to keep the sweet pineapple juice from escaping as forks cut into the delicious confection.

"Keep feeding me like this and I'll never leave," Krysty joked.

"My dear woman, you may stay with me as long as you like," Jamaisvous replied. "All of you. Puerto Rico is my own private paradise on earth, and I'm more than willing to share."

THAT NIGHT, safe and snug in bed, Ryan and Krysty took time out in their private fortress room to make long passionate love, allowing themselves release time and again between the cool sheets. J.B. and Mildred did the same in their own room across the hall, each of them savoring the privacy, since J.B. had never been comfortable with displays of overt emotion or passion in front of others.

The other two rooms in the guest section of El Morro were currently empty. The one belonging to Doc was vacant, since the elder member of the group of survivalists was elsewhere within the majestic fortress. He had chosen to forgo bed and sleep in order to stay behind with a snifter of brandy and continue his discussion with Dr. Jamaisvous.

Dean and Jak agreed to serve as the eyes and ears for the rest of the group. To pass the late-night hours before they were relieved of guard duty, Dean suggested they amuse themselves by playing an old children's game.

He had found the box in a parlor cabinet off the dining room where all had retired after the dessert for drinks. Chuckling over the discovery, Jamaisvous had told Dean to take the game with his blessing, and do with it as he wished.

"What the hell is a 'Cootie' anyway?" Dean remarked, turning the worn cardboard box in his hands to look at the words printed on the back.

"Looks like big bug. Hate bugs," Jak replied with a frown, his red eyes narrowed into dusky rubies as he stared at the photograph on the front.

Dean silently read the instructions that had been conveniently printed on the back of the game box, along with cartoons illustrating proper play. "Seems triple simple to me," he finally declared, opening the lid and taking out a flat numerical spinner.

"See, we spin this thing here, this spinner, and

when it stops it points to a color and a body part. We pick one and start building the Cootie. Whoever gets his Cootie built first is the winner,'' Dean told the watching Jak.

''Stupe game,'' the albino said, rolling his eyes as he held up a yellow segmented insect leg made of soft plastic. ''Making big bug. No need make. Go out find plenty.''

Dean dumped the contents of the brightly colored box onto the surface of the wooden table they had pulled into the hall, right outside the doors leading to the individual bedrooms. Red thoraxes, orange bodies and blue heads joined a scramble of yellow insect legs on the tabletop.

''You think it's possible, Jak?'' he asked after spinning the spinner and selecting a piece of his Cootie.

''What, build bug? Sure.'' Jak took his own turn with the spinner and picked up another plastic leg. ''Got two legs. Need a head.''

''No, not that you dope,'' Dean retorted. ''Do you think it's possible to go back in time?''

''Doc did.''

''No, Doc came forward and then was pushed ahead a second time,'' Dean corrected.

Jak shot him a look, then pondered what the younger boy was saying.

''Hmm,'' the albino mused as he considered the implications of what his friend had brought up. ''Two-way street.''

''That's what I'm wondering. Is it a two-way street

or not?'' Dean said excitedly, pausing in the game. ''And if it is, mebbe we should *all* go back to another time, way back before the nukecaust. Back when everything in the world still worked.''

''Not me,'' Jak replied, tapping one of the yellow insectoid legs against the front of his teeth. ''Like here. Take what we got, not what we might get.''

''Not worth a gamble?'' Dean asked easily.

''Not to me.''

Having become quickly bored with the construction of his cartoon insect, Jak tossed the gathered pieces back in the pile with a snort. ''You win.''

''Aw, come on Jak, there's nothing else to do right now,'' Dean remarked as he absently ran a hand through his black curly hair. ''Dad said for all of us to stick close tonight until we know more about this Jam-ass-voo guy.''

''Ask Doc. He knows. Spending lots of time with him.''

''THIS LIQUOR is...well, words escape me, sir.''

Doc was standing near a stone wall adorned with various black-and-white photographs of the grounds and surrounding area of El Morro, a brandy snifter in one long-fingered hand like it had been designed to be held there.

Seated in a black leather recliner across from Doc, Jamaisvous held a second glass in a nearly identical fashion. ''Then, I shall take that as high compliment, Dr. Tanner.''

''Please do.''

Jamaisvous took a sip of his drink before speaking. ''What do you remember about the time-trawl technology?''

''Bits and pieces. Fits and starts. While parts of my stay with my captors remain in vivid focus, most has blurred due to what I can only describe as damage to my shorter-term memory after they shipped me into this bleak future world.''

''I knew more about how the mat-trans units worked as means of transport from place to place,'' Jamaisvous remarked. ''Other esoteric uses, such as cloning or duplication of living tissue or the fantastic notion of time trawling seemed to be bastardization of the process. The damn things weren't designed for some of the hoops the higher-ups were making the tech boys try and jump through.''

''There were different methods for the trawling,'' Doc revealed. ''That much I do know.''

''How so?''

''We came upon the Chron-Temp portal in Chicago,'' Doc said. ''The original site.''

''Ah, yes. Chicago. They were still attempting to use cryonics as a part of the process then. Were the pods and mat-trans inside the Chicago redoubt still functioning?'' Jamaisvous asked.

''Yes,'' Doc said cryptically. ''And no.''

''Well, I'd wondered. If the Chicago gateway was indeed working, I thought you would have attempted to return to your own time and place without hesitation. From what I remember about your particular case—''

"What do you mean *remember?*" Doc asked sharply, giving Jamaisvous a queer look.

Jamaisvous caught himself, taking back up the thread of conversation as if Doc had never interrupted him and finishing the sentence. "It refers to what I remember from reading about you in the old Chronos data banks, which portray you as quite the single-minded individual."

Doc accepted the breezy explanation and didn't press the matter, since his focus was upon his own convoluted memories. "Single-minded? More like relentless, sir. The Tanner clan has never been known for bending. Stubbornness is a family trait, and by God, I wanted my family back. The bastards would not cooperate with my wishes, so I decided I would be just as unyielding. My captors, well, they did not like that."

"You could have been killed for your dogged pursuit of an impossible goal. Eliminated instead of studied," Jamaisvous mused.

"I did not care. Death would have been one escape, and perhaps the ultimate way to be reunited with my wife and children," Doc replied, and then held up two fingers in a peace sign. "I made two attempts. The first was easily thwarted—they'd been waiting for me to slip. The second one came much closer, since I had my own allies in the corridors of that antiseptic hellhole, but still I failed. As for a third try, well, suffice to say, I was not given the opportunity to make a third attempt."

"Going back to Chicago, what was the status of the redoubt?"

"When I and my friends discovered the lair, the central annex was crawling with spiders. Great albino arachnids," Doc said, waggling the fingers of both his hands like scrawny, jointed legs. "Hundreds of the overstuffed web spinners, with long spiny appendages and eight hooked toes. The chamber was festooned with spun silk as white and powdery as freshly fallen snow. The only colors to be seen were their hideously glowing yellow eyes."

Jamaisvous tilted his head and gave Doc a look. "Giant spiders? Don't be ridiculous. Such mutations aren't logical."

Doc laid a hand across his heart and assumed a solemn look. "Upon my honor, sir, what I say is gospel. After all, logic has no place in Deathlands. Although, I might add in the interest of fairness that the largest of the creatures was only a foot and a half in height, with legs spread three feet in length."

"See? That isn't all that large."

Doc smiled dangerously, showing his fine teeth. "When you have faced hundreds, Silas, they are as big as mountains, and as legion as grains of sand."

Jamaisvous stood, a half smile on his handsome face. "I think you're prone to exaggeration in the interest of a good story, Dr. Tanner, but I'll let it pass. Would you like another drink?"

"No, thank you." Doc also began to stand, but his host waved him back down before crossing over to the bar and refilling his own glass.

"I bow to your firsthand experience, Dr. Tanner. But what happened after the giant spider invasion?"

"After retrieving the young Cawdor child, who had run into the spiders—"

"Yet another good reason to leave the children at home," Jamaisvous said dryly.

"—and sealing off that section," Doc continued, "we went in through an exterior air lock into the Chron-Temp mat-trans chamber, where I was fascinated to see a trio of materialization tubes linked to the standard gateway."

"Tubes?"

"Modules, about the size of hospital beds. A clear plastic cover was over each one, awaiting the arrival of the dolphins."

"Dolphins being code for...?"

"For the trawl subjects."

"Hmm. Chicago was primitive. Lacking in many of the later refinements to come. At that particular point, they were still using cryonics in conjunction with the time-trawling process, a combination that was later abandoned from what I've read. Subjects were phased into their own individual cold canisters made of vanadium and armaglass."

"Oh, bullshit," Mildred interjected from the doorway. She had decided to join the conversation, while J.B. had elected to remain behind in the living-quarters area, relieving Jak of having to join the undefeated Dean in a challenging match of the Cootie game.

Jamaisvous laughed. "Such language, and from an educated lady."

Mildred grinned back. "I never said I was a lady."

"My mistake. Would you like some refreshment?"

"A small one."

"What will you have?"

"Same as you two. Brandy. With a bit of water, please."

"I was frozen after my trawl?" Doc said in disbelief, reaching up with his fingers to stroke the cheeks of his long face. "I have no memory of that, sir."

"How could you?" Jamaisvous replied from the bar. "You were snatched from your time line and taken into the realm of null time via the gateway. For all intents and purposes, you ceased to exist—not here, not there. Nowhere. The problem the engineers of Chronos kept running into was their subjects reappearing during the current time serving as the original source of the trawl. This was totally unlike jumping from one mat-trans unit to another, where your destination was waiting and prepped. When living tissue was trawled, it tended to disintegrate upon rematerialization."

"Thanks," Mildred said as Jamaisvous crossed back to his recliner, handing her the drink before sitting down.

"You're welcome, Dr. Wyeth. Please, be seated."

Mildred took up a position next to Doc on the edge of a small sofa.

"What's the first thing you remember when you arrived in 1998, Dr. Tanner?"

"Shadowy shapes. Masked faces."

"Sounds typical. You would have been disoriented. But you became conscious—fully awake—in a hospital bed."

"If my memory is to be believed, that is correct, yes. However, I find my memory to be seriously lacking in detail and sharpness since I began my travels in time. I used to believe after I was abducted by those madmen in Chronos that I was placed within the confines of a glass coffin, like a refugee from a Grimm's Fairy Tale."

"Cryo pod," Jamaisvous corrected.

Mildred snorted a second time.

Jamaisvous pressed on. "In Chicago, when you were trawled, you arrived through one of the waiting cryo pods—you know, the canisters made of alloy and armaglass. When you appeared inside, you were then immobilized until they could be sure you had arrived whole and intact. Then, over an extended period, your body temperature was brought down and—"

"Please—his entire body would have exploded," Mildred retorted, interrupting the narrative. "The very blood in his veins would've frozen. There would be cellular disruption on a massive and incapacitating level. There is no instant freeze except in bad science fiction. Putting subjects in cryo sleep and then reviving them is a tedious, dangerous process."

Jamaisvous gave Mildred a doubting look. "What makes you an expert, Dr. Wyeth?"

"I was—I am—a pioneer in cryonics, Dr. Jamaisvous." Mildred replied, accenting the word "doctor" as she spoke.

"Really? Got to experience your subject firsthand, did you?"

Mildred frowned. "As did you. We seem to be no worse for wear."

"Right, right," he said dismissively. "Still, as a pioneer in the public sector without military clearances, you know nothing at all of the true nature of cryonics. If you'll pardon the pun, what you and your so-called colleagues were allowed to see was merely the tip of the iceberg."

"And I suppose you're an expert?"

"Not by any means. I can't explain some of what I know of the utilized cryonic techniques. I just know it works. Rather, worked."

Mildred held her tongue, choosing to take another sip of the potent brandy. What Jamaisvous was saying made sense when you factored in some of the advanced technology she'd seen for herself in the redoubts equipped with cryonic sleep chambers. The basics from her past studies were there, but some of the processes were well beyond what she could have accomplished herself using late 1990s technology. The advanced leap of science that had created the matter-transfer gateways also could have been easily involved with cryonics.

"Okay, I give you the possibility. You don't have to be such a jerk about it," Mildred finally said.

"And you don't have to be so damned all-knowing, Dr. Wyeth."

"I am afraid her self-assurance is one of her less endearing qualities," Doc said.

"Well, not to me. I like a woman who speaks her mind."

"How long do you think I was in suspended sleep?" Doc asked, turning back to Jamaisvous.

"A few days, I'd say. Long enough so they could be sure you were intact and whole. The cryo pods served another function, you know. They protected you against any unexpected diseases or exposure. After all, you were in a fragile state, and there were germs and bugs floating around in 1998 you had never dreamed of a hundred and two years ago in the past."

"So, is that how trawling has to be carried out to work, with cryonics involved on the receiving end?"

"No. As far as I know, a year or so after you made the trip into 1998, a modification was discovered that allowed the mat-trans chambers themselves to serve as collector and containment fields for living subjects minus the earlier subzero temperatures needed until the trawled subject was whole and intact. Besides, if cryonic pods were a necessity, than temporal passage into the future would be an impossibility, and you wouldn't be here talking with me."

Mildred yawned in the seconds of silence after Jamaisvous spoke. "I'm sorry," she apologized. "Between my drink and the meal, I'm asleep on my feet, and this sort of technobabble makes my mind ache. I think I'll go back to bed for the night."

Jamaisvous stood and took her hand, kissing it as he had kissed Krysty's earlier. "Good night, Dr. Wyeth."

"Good night, to both of you."

The stocky physician exited, and the den was silent for several moments before Doc spoke. "The gateway you have in this fortress—you are trying to go back, are you not?"

"Of course."

"Even though by your own admission, time trawling was never perfected."

"Until now."

"How so?"

"I am at the final part of the secret. Tell me, Dr. Tanner. Man-to-man. No pressure," Jamaisvous said, his voice becoming faster as he spoke, and the pronunciation of each word more clipped. "Wouldn't you risk it all to go back home to your own time? To pop in seconds before your original disappearance?"

"Not long enough," Doc protested in a murmur. "I could not alter the flow of history's river in a matter of seconds."

"Minutes then. An hour. Long enough to warn yourself—or, better yet, appear at the same time, replacing yourself in the confusion as your other self vanishes into the temporal doorway. Other than a freak storm front that blew up on a dusty Omaha street, no one ever need know you disappeared. You could alter your future. You could save your destiny.''

Doc paced, talking as he walked, his hands shoved deep in the pockets of his frock coat. ''To reclaim the life I should have lived...yes, damn you, yes, yes! Of course, I would!''

Jamaisvous smiled. ''That's what I thought you'd say. I'd do the same, and in fact, I plan to. I have no love of being trapped in a world such as this. No cable television. No pizza delivery. No world wide web. I am luckier than most, but I am also bored out of my mind. Screw fresh coffee, pretty sunsets and sweet-smelling flowers, Dr. Tanner. I want to go home.''

''But what of your disease?'' Doc asked.

Jamaisvous gave Doc a baffled look. ''Disease? What disease?''

''Why were you placed in the cryo suspension plan if not due to illness?''

Jamaisvous gaped at Doc for a long moment, before an explosion of grim laughter erupted from his chest. ''Oh. That. I was placed in the freezer for my brain. Those in the know were aware of the impending holocaust. They also knew they would need men of vision after the bombs fell, and as such, I was put on ice until needed.''

''You agreed to this?''

''Like your own experiences with the Totality Concept, I wasn't given much choice,'' Jamaisvous replied. ''I wasn't conscious to experience the excitement, but from what I can tell, once the war began, it hit with ten times the destructive force expected. The new civilization they expected me and my brain to be a part of was wiped from the map, along with rest of the world."

Doc sat back, his brow furrowed, staring across the candlelit room at his host.

"So why am I needed? What knowledge I held of how time trawling was accomplished has been long lost."

Jamaisvous looked Doc in the eye. "I need a man who's been exposed to trawling before and lived to tell about it, Dr. Tanner. Lesser intellects have no way of comprehending what they are exposed to in the temporal annex between past, present and future. Their puerile brains can't handle it and once the mind goes, the body quickly follows. You have survived two trips. That's two more than anybody else. While I have no explanation for what caused your physical deterioration in the forward trawl other than to say it might have been done purposely—"

"On purpose?" Doc replied, his face pale in the yellow light of the den.

"Yes. That is my theory. You should have arrived here in the future either intact or not at all. Instead, you made it safely, but with more than thirty years stolen. I think an acceleration process was used."

Doc took a deep breath. "Could such a process be reversed?"

"I don't know. To do so would take research that dovetails nicely with my own plans for trawling.

Like yourself, Dr. Tanner, I also want to go back. Unlike yourself, I have never faced a trawl. I need to know more about the process before I can face stepping into that chamber. For I will get only one chance."

"The matter is settled, then." Doc stood. "I will assist you in any manner I can."

"Excellent. I make one request of you."

"And that is?"

"Your companions. Most of them would not approve, I think, of some of my experiments. You may tell them you are assisting me, but I ask you keep the notion of your personally enduring another time trawl to yourself until we are closer to the time of the actual event."

"Of course. There is no need to cause them worry for my well-being."

"Good night, then."

"Good night," Doc replied, and walked out of the den.

Jamaisvous remained sitting, his left index finger idly stroking the rim of his glass over and over in a circle. "The time has come," he whispered softly. "Time enough, at last."

THE MOON ROSE over the walls of El Morro. Far off, in the quiet distance, the unique sound of the coqui could be heard, and for each single cry the little tree frog sent out, a dozen more came singing back in reply from his brothers. For hundreds of years, the native Puerto Rican tree frog had endured, proving that perhaps, things didn't always have to change.

A brief spot of flickering illumination flared into being, only to be extinguished and replaced by a tiny glowing dot of red. J.B. puffed on his cigar, exhaling aromatic tobacco smoke into the night air of the fortress garden.

"Good evening, John Barrymore," a familiar resonant voice said from behind.

"Doc," the Armorer replied in greeting. He wasn't surprised, since he'd heard the older man's footsteps coming up from behind and recognized the sound and pattern of Doc's peculiar gait.

Doc stood silently for a few moments, then turned to his friend. "I wonder, might I avail you of a smoke?"

J.B. blew a plume of the pungent smoke through both nostrils. "You sure? This tobacco has a hell of a kick."

"I am not a lad in short pants, John Barrymore, and I was smoking long before you were born," Doc retorted. "I think I can handle a twist of tobacco."

"Got a point," J.B. replied, taking out the denim pouch of smokes and handing it over to the second figure.

"I'm surprised to find you out here alone at such a late hour," Doc remarked as he rummaged through the pouch and removed one of the sticky black cigarillos.

"Couldn't sleep." J.B. held out his lit cheroot, allowing Doc to use it to ignite his own chosen cigar.

"And I can't light up in the room or Millie starts complaining about secondary smoke."

"I see," Doc replied after exhaling a perfect smoke ring.

"Nice trick," J.B. said, watching the ring elongate and slowly dissipate in the night air. "I guess you have lit up a few cancer sticks in your time."

"Cancer stick?" Doc asked with a frown. "I do not get your meaning."

The Armorer nodded. "That's what Millie calls them. Old predark slang. Said they were supposed to cause lung cancer."

Doc pondered this. "I suppose she would know. Still, I confess I suspect there are many more overt dangers presenting us with cancer-causing radiation on a daily basis than these slender tubes of tobacco."

"Damn straight."

The conversation between the men trailed off, and the sounds of the night seemed to grow louder.

"So, what's your excuse?" J.B. finally asked.

"For smoking?" Doc asked.

The Armorer frowned. Doc could be annoyingly obtuse when he chose. "For coming out here to the top of the fortress so late tonight."

Doc shook his head and his flowing white hair shifted around his skinny shoulders. "My mind, good fellow. I cannot stop thinking long enough to allow Morpheus to bring down his soothing, slumbering touch."

"About trying to go back to the 1800s, you mean."

"I beg your pardon?" Doc said, trying to cover his surprise and doing a lousy job.

"The year 1896, to be exact. This guy with the fancy name, he might have something going with time trawling, otherwise you wouldn't be so worked up."

"John Barrymore, I have to say I'm surprised. You are more of a student of human nature than I ever surmised," Doc stammered. "If such a possibility exists...I have to see it though. Dr. Jamaisvous's work here hints that I might indeed be able to return home someday."

J.B. took off his fedora and adjusted the brim. "Hell, Doc, from what little I know about time trawling, it's a triple-risky proposition with a bastard-poor chance of succeeding. You've cheated the odds twice, which puts you ahead of the reaper double time. Not to mention the second time you crawled into one of those things and got your ass pushed forward you came out on the other side an old man."

"What would you do, John Barrymore?"

"I honestly don't know, Doc. I guess I'm a lucky son of a bitch in that all the people I care about travel with me."

Doc fell silent after that, and stayed with J.B., smoking the cigar down to a stub before leaving the way he came, his thoughts elsewhere.

Maryland, Virginia, 1999

DR. THEOPHILUS TANNER had been moved once more, this time from the caverns of Dulce, New Mexico, to a more civilized facade for a redoubt, with an outer shell of a beautiful white house. With the change in scenery came an ultimatum.

"Have you reexamined our offer, Dr. Tanner?" Welles asked.

Tanner smiled, and his smile was a wonderful thing to behold. "I have."

"What do you say?"

"I say, who am I to challenge the tides of time?"

"We must have your full cooperation in order for the programming to be effective."

"I give it to you, freely."

"Then preparations must be made. And you must understand your place within the machine. Your intelligence makes you worthy. Your future is assured. You will be a great man, a leader in your own time once you are returned with the knowledge we intend to share."

"How will I be readied?"

"Patience. Time is irrelevant. Against my own better judgment, I have been told you must be properly informed."

"Informed?"

"We here at Chronos have temporal windows into the past and into the future. All is not lost. Steps must be taken to influence that the proper chain of events are followed."

"How important is my place?" Tanner asked uneasily.

"You are but one plan," Welles said. "And one

outcome. The right outcome. To assure this of happening, you will be given privileges and taught the future."

So, as a more active part of his eventual acclimation into the Chronos project, Tanner found he was now being treated less as a curiosity in a cage and more as an equal. Many of those involved in the day-to-day operations of the Chronos project were eager to discuss their work with such an avid listener. Knowing that the elegantly dressed man from the past was an essential piece in the overall puzzle of time trawling, they welcomed his insights and deductions. Tanner gave them new eyes, with a decidedly different point of view, since he was a man of the 1800s.

Women, in particular, seemed to flock to his lean form. Whether they found something appealing in his florid gestures and attentive manner was open to interpretation, but he soon found himself always in their company—either in the laboratories or during the meal breaks or even after-hours and socially. Most of the men liked Tanner's company too, seeing a father figure or an older brother in the smiling man's verbal musings.

After correcting a few of the staff members who tried to call him "Theo," and rejecting the more formal "Dr. Tanner," one soul simply dubbed him "Doc." The nickname stuck, and even though his brain burned with wanting to know everything Chronos had to offer in order to devise his own individual escape, Tanner was quietly touched.

In his lifetime, he'd never been a recipient of the signs of affection shown by a fond nickname, and he took quiet reassurance and pride in the familiarity of the abbreviation of his title.

"Not all of those in this future world are black and evil," he mused to himself one night, wishing for a journal to keep his thoughts and impressions in, yet knowing such documentation would never be truly private. "Many of those here seem to be as much prisoners as I, held captive by their insecurities and fears over the highly classified nature of the project they are involved in. I can only hope my studies in philosophy give solace to those who speak to me in hushed tones as they debate the humanity and the morality of what they continue to try to accomplish."

Months passed in this fashion, with the time approaching when Doc would have to allow the hypnotic orders and suggestions to be implanted in his brain, orders he knew in his heart he would never be able to accept, thereby tipping his hand that he had no intention of aiding these madmen in their schemes to alter the fabric of time and space.

Before that day arrived, he knew he would have to escape.

Dr. Theophilus Algernon Tanner made two attempts to flee his keepers.

The first came after a year and a half of his participation in the various machinations of Project Chronos. By this time, Doc was a familiar staple among the staff. His natural charm had won over many of them to his side, on a private one-to-one basis. None of the scientists or engineers felt secure enough in their positions to publicly take Doc's side in his continuing debate to be allowed to return home a free man, but he knew he had many allies.

And there were so many other projects in various stages of completion within the redoubt.

One of these involved genetics. Doc was prevented from seeing much of the work in this sector, but as was his wont, he listened and he learned.

Among the scientists on this project was an individual who seemed impossibly old and seemed to be suspended in a perpetual case of what Doc used to call "the shakes." The man, whose name was Pennyworth, spoke with a thick English accent that the years he'd spent among his fellows, all of whom appeared to be American or Japanese, hadn't blunted.

His day over, Pennyworth would fold his white lab coat, look back at the sealed sec door of his laboratory and announce to his fellows, "And that, gentlemen, concludes the entertainment for today."

Doc agreed. He'd seen enough, and was no longer entertained in the slightest.

"WHY ME?" he asked after being captured outside the redoubt's gateway mat-trans chamber. Doc hadn't even made it into the control room before his attempt to leave was foiled. He had been betrayed by one of his fellow scientists, but by who Doc could not be sure. "The truth, this time, if you please."

Welles placed both of his hands on his paunch and gave Doc a pitying look. "You weren't the first choice. We tried trawling a noted judge from the United States Supreme Court, but after the judge was picked up in the temporal annex, he didn't survive the retrieval process. How can I put this? Judge Crater arrived here in 1997, yes, but he arrived...incomplete. We might have saved his life, but he wouldn't acquiesce."

"Which explains his disappearance—a mystery never solved."

"Oh, Operation Chronos has been responsible for a deluge of urban legends and unexplained cases, Dr. Tanner. There are entire books written on the subject of strange disappearances and miraculous reappearances. Some, like our good judge, have been famous. Others, less so. Take, for instance, the case of Dr. Geraldo Vidal. On June 3, 1968, Vidal and his wife were traveling in Argentina late one night when they drove right into what they later described as a cloud of swirling mists. Sound familiar?"

"I imagine this was the same sort of mist or fog I encountered during my own time trawl," Doc said.

"Correct. Upon entering the mists, the Vidals were rendered unconscious. When they awoke the very next morning, they discovered their car was in Mexico. The time trawl failed, but at the same time, succeeded! We didn't bring them into the future, but we did manage a successful mat-trans jump on two living subjects thirty years in the past. Can you comprehend the implications of such a weapon?"

"Yes, I am afraid I can," Doc replied.

"In an earlier attempt, we trawled a limousine off

the Fujishrio Bypass in Japan with driver and passenger, a woman of ill repute in transit from a whorehouse to a wealthy client. Our aim was to bring back living matter, not automobiles, but in this case what appeared in the mat-trans chamber here was an amalgam of both parties. Suffice to say, neither man nor woman survived."

Welles got up from his desk and walked over to where Doc was seated, bending to whisper in his ear. "Do you want to survive?"

"Yes."

"I don't think so. You have damaged your credibility with such a foolish escape attempt, and you are now under arrest. All of your B12 access privileges to Chronos are revoked. You are not to be anywhere without a guard."

"When am I to begin your treatments for reverse trawl?"

"Soon, Dr. Tanner, soon. After all, the millennium is fast approaching."

AS WAS HIS ROUTINE in Chicago, then Dulce, and now Virginia, Allan Harvey paused in front of Doc's holding quarters to talk. His security team had been transferred each time with Tanner and Welles, all of them traveling across the country together. He'd seen less and less of Doc once the doctor had been allowed access to Chronos, but now, after the escape attempt, Tanner had been returned to the holding area.

The room was spare, but complete with bed, desk,

television set and other amenities. As was his habit, Doc had the television on with the sound off, allowing him to read without intruding noises and yet able to look up from time to time to see what was unfolding on the screen. If it looked interesting, he merely hit the mute button and brought back the sound.

"Good evening, Doc," Allan said. Tanner was sitting up in his bunk, his back propped up against the wall with a pillow. He was holding a scuffed hardcover book with the unlikely title of *A Brief History of Time.*

"Salutations, my friend."

"What you reading?"

"The theories of a man named Hawking. I have studied this book half a dozen times since my arrival. He seems to have unknowingly hit upon some of the techniques being carried out within Operation Chronos, and yet while agreeing some of the time, he goes off in entirely different directions. According to Hawking, much of what is being done here is impossible as the world now understands science."

"Yeah, I guess. You hear all kinds of rumors, Doc. My favorite has the U.S. government in an alliance with some alien cartel that gave us all this technology."

Tanner snorted. "Poppycock."

"I know. It does sound like a crock, doesn't it?" the burly security man agreed. "Glad to see you're back in your old habits. After that escape attempt, I guess you're settling in, Doc, from what I've been hearing."

"Aye, noble Allan, that I am."

The security man shrugged. "Looks can be deceiving, though, can't they? I mean, you know and I know that you're not exactly doing what the bosses think you're doing, are you?"

"No, I am not." Doc flashed his teeth. "Nothing is ever what it seems."

"They might have killed you instead of just limiting your access in the redoubt, you know," Allan said in a matter-of-fact tone.

"I was willing to take the risk. If I succeeded, to hell with them. If I failed, well, I am beyond caring whether I live or die. I have outlived all I knew, all my friends, my—" and his voice caught "—my loved ones. My family. No, they did not kill me. I remain too valuable. They yearn for my agreement."

"Agreement?" Allan looked puzzled.

Doc put down the book and stared at the flickering television set. "I am but a cog in a greater plan, Allan. Their wishes are my own. They wish to send me back home to my proper time and place."

"So, what's stopping them? Or you? I mean, that's what you want, right?"

"Yes...and no."

"So who's the hold up?"

Doc sighed. "I am."

"You?"

"Me. And my hesitation comes from what they call an 'alternate event horizon.' See, if I had not been taken away from Omaha in 1896, I would have gone on to become a very important man. I am not bragging about this, merely stating a fact. My studies and oratory would have influenced generations."

Allan whistled. "No shit?"

"None. Now, *how* this was to have occurred, I do not know, but I have been assured that eventually I would have had access to the president's ear, and as such, would have, *could* have, influenced national policy in times of great crisis. The two world wars I have read about? Those and other pivotal events would have been substantially altered by my presence."

"Damn. For better or for worse?"

"Who can say for sure? That's why they call it an alternate event horizon. The flow of time—the time line would have been different."

"So what? Go back anyway. What will be, will be."

"Que sera sera, Allan?"

The sec man showed off his own shining white teeth. "Damn straight. And fuck Doris Day."

"I would risk doing as they wish, my friend, but with the knowledge I now possess, who is to say how I might change things? My own guess is that if I go back with their mental programming, the facts of the future I already know consciously or subconsciously would assure them of occurring...at least, within my sphere of influence. However, I would not be in full control of my actions. They will not tell me how or why, only that my cooperation must be absolute for the planned mental programming to work. To regain my wife and children, I must become a pawn and follow a combination of predetermined maneuvers on the chessboard. To take back what I have lost, I must give them my soul."

"Can you do that?"

"No, Allan, I cannot."

"Then you're going to need some help." Allan opened the door to Doc's cell, stepping inside.

"Now, if I were to turn my back on you, like this, I might be accidentally opening myself up to another one of your escape attempts, mightn't I?"

"Yes," Doc said, feeling his heart sing in response to Allan's ploy. He got to his feet. "You just might, were I the type to betray your trust."

"And there wouldn't be a damned thing I could do if you bashed me over the head with that bookend next to the TV, would there?"

Doc reached over and picked up the object, hefting the heavy ceramic bookend in both hands.

"Not if you were taken by surprise, no."

"Two things before lights out, Doc."

"Yes?"

"Take my tunic and pull up the hood like I was wearing it before and you might make it past the security cameras in this sector. Once you're past the cell block, they won't be looking for you immediately, and you can move a bit more freely."

"Very well. What is the other thing you wished to relate to me?"

"When you raise that bookend up and clobber my noggin, try not to kill me."

DRESSED IN THE SECURITY bodysuit with the hood pulled up over his head, Doc hoped Allan was right in assuming he would escape detection from the security video cameras scanning the hallways of the redoubt. He had quickly memorized by rote the numbers to push for entry into the control room of the Chronos mat-trans device, and was hoping against hope the chron-jump transport was still using the same command codes.

As he already knew from his previous freer days, a skeleton crew would be on duty inside the control room. Looking inside through an observation portal, he spied three figures—two men and a woman. Doc hovered outside the access door for a moment, his fingers poised to tap in the entry code, and then he decided to wait. He nimbly stepped into the nearby men's room and went into a stall and sat. He knew the shift break would come soon, and if he were quick, he could go inside with the advantage of having only a single technician watching over the dormant equipment. Time-trawling tests were rarely done after daylight, and those on watch inside were only there to run computer simulations, more or less.

Doc checked his wristwatch, also liberated from Allan. He'd made note of the patterns of the curious lair he was kept within and found all of those who shared his world in the redoubts to be almost painfully predictable in a military sort of way. If, at a designated time Tab A were to be inserted within Slot B, nothing short of World War Three could prevent such an order from being carried through.

Reciting bits of poetry and famous monologues from the theater in his mind to pass the time, Doc was rewarded when his ten-minute wait passed quickly.

He stepped out of the washroom and peeked back through the small window into the mat-trans control room. Only a single figure now remained, the other two having retired for coffee and conversation in the commissary two levels up. They'd be gone for fifteen minutes.

Fifteen minutes. An eternity if one knew how to use the time well.

Doc looked up at the warning sign posted above the doorway. In red and black letters on a laminated yellow backing, the sign read: Entry is Absolutely Forbidden To All But B12 Cleared Personnel Or Higher. The word *Forbidden* was underlined for added emphasis.

"I'd say I've regained my former rank and clearance," he said softly, counting on the masters of the redoubt to not have changed the locking codes for the heavy vanadium steel door. Taking a deep breath and mentally crossing his fingers, Doc punched in the trio of digits for the entry code, tapping first the number three, followed by five and then two. He was rewarded by the door sliding upward silently into a ceiling slot, allowing his entrance. Turning, he reversed the code and the door slid down and locked into a floor groove, sealing the control room from the rest of the complex.

The man on duty turned from a flickering computer screen. He was slight of build and very short, coming in at a height of five feet. He wore wire-rimmed glasses that accented his tanned skin and Asian features. Doc had hoped he wouldn't encounter anyone he knew, but as their eyes met, he knew his luck had finally run its course.

"Good evening, Dr. Tanner," Chan said. "Can I help you?"

Chapter Nine

Dawn arrived with the fabulous multicolored beauty of the Caribbean sky.

Before beginning the day, Ryan decided to pay Dr. Silas Jamaisvous a quick visit. In the doctor's bedroom, he discovered his host was doing a most curious thing, and since it was an action Ryan had never associated with the male member of the species, it made the sight even more unsettling. Once he identified it, the feminine undertones made him wonder about their host.

Jamaisvous was carefully, studiously, meticulously filing his fingernails with a small brown nail file, vigorously rubbing it back and forth in a sawing motion, pausing every thirty seconds or so to look at the back of his hand to make sure the manicure was proceeding as planned.

The doctor was nattily dressed in a similar manner as the day before, now wearing a black-and-gray patterned blazer with a new burgundy dress shirt and narrow black necktie with matching black slacks. The long white lab coat was draped over the back of a nearby chair.

"Good morning, Ryan Cawdor."

"Morning. Thought I might take my boy and look around the island some today."

"What a delightful idea! I only wish I could spare the time to come along. Your good Dr. Tanner will be assisting me today with my continuing attempts to use the matter-transfer unit for something besides a glorified ferryboat."

"What's the situation outside the fortress walls?"

"Well, the western side of Puerto Rico suffered terrific losses and from what I understand is nigh uninhabitable, unless one enjoys squalor and disease."

"Rad sickness, I'll bet. Must've been a nuke," Ryan guessed. He'd noticed upon their arrival in El Morro that the tiny rad counter on his long coat hadn't indicated dangerous levels of radiation, but that didn't mean other parts of Puerto Rico hadn't suffered from the same radioactive fire that had plagued the rest of the planet.

Pausing to blow on the nails of his left hand, Jamaisvous responded in the negative. "No, Ryan, no nukes. At least, no major direct hits. The island's trials have been generated thanks to the queen of havoc herself, Mother Nature. Hurricane season used to run here all summer and fall. Storms would develop out in the Atlantic, then wind their way northwestward, sometimes striking Puerto Rico, but as a rule, the island was spared. After the nukecaust, the storms seemed to increase in ferocity and regularity, and Puerto Rico was no longer so lucky. I have suffered through two powerful storms myself, but none as deadly as the one that hit the western side."

"So, any dangers I should know about outside?"

"In Old San Juan? Not hardly."

"Fair enough. Thanks for the advice."

Exiting the expansive grounds of El Morro by way of the short stone bridge stretching across the moat around the fortress, Dean, Krysty and Ryan went out after his talk with Jamaisvous to look at the sights. In reality, Ryan needed to assess their surroundings, be prepared and familiar enough to move through the area without hesitation, if need be. Besides granting his hearty approval, their host had also suggested they leave as early as possible to avoid the heat of the afternoon.

Outside El Morro, the first thing they encountered was the ruin of the Santo Domingo Convent as they stepped out onto Cristo Street. Even in its dilapidated condition, Old San Juan was magnificent, rich in the coin of history. The night before, Jamaisvous had commented that this part of Puerto Rico was essentially his own private lair. The old part of the city had originally been separated from the mainland by three bridges, and in addition, the buildings of the inlet were walled off, surrounded by high imposing towers thanks to the old fort nearby known as Castillo de San Cristobal.

Before leaving El Morro, Dean had taken a printed leaflet from a wire rack in the foyer of the fortress, next to what was once a combination information desk and souvenir stand. The pamphlet had obviously been designed for the edification of visitors, and the boy had delighted in reading from the tri-folded sheet of glossy paper as the three of them walked along the narrow sidewalk.

"See that chapel, Dad?" Dean asked, pointing to a little building at the end of Cristo Street.

Ryan took in the decrepit church, noting the cross jutting from the roof was the only part of the construct still completely intact. "Sure," he replied.

"They built it because a slowie retard was racing his horse and couldn't stop before hitting the wall," Dean said confidently. "The retard's mom and dad wanted to help prevent more racing accidents from happening to other stupes."

"Keep it up, son, and you'll be giving Doc a run for his windpipe," Ryan replied. "You're telling me a lot more than I want or need to know."

"Well, I appreciate it," Krysty said, giving Dean a quick hug as they walked. "Somebody has to play tour guide."

"Place feels like the walls are closing in. Lots of places for an ambush," Ryan noted.

"Says here the streets and sidewalks are so narrow that ped...pedestrians must often walk single file," Dean read, his voice stumbling over the unfamiliar word. "What's a pedestrian, Dad?"

"Beats me," the tall man replied. "Means 'people,' I guess. You'll have to ask Doc when we get back."

Krysty's attention was on the street beneath their feet. The roadway was made up of a series of rectangular bricks of a dark blue substance. "Feels kind of strange here, walking down paths thousands of years old," the redhead said. "Not a bad feeling, just...strange."

"Old ghosts?" Ryan asked.

Krysty nodded and gave him a dazzling smile. "Mebbe so, lover."

"'Some of the streets in Old San Juan are still paved with the original blue-glazed blocks brought over on old Spanish sailing ships,'" Dean read aloud.

"Need to get your nose out of that pamphlet and look at what's around you, Dean," Ryan suggested, plucking the booklet from the boy's hands and shoving it into the back pocket of his trousers. "You're missing half the sights by reading about them."

The morning air wafting through the streets of Old San Juan was pleasant, and Krysty was glad for the opportunity to lose the extra layers of clothing she and everyone else had grown accustomed to wearing at all times. It was much easier to wear a jacket than to tote it. Not having it on your person could also mean forgetting the item of clothing and leaving it behind if trouble started.

However, here in Old San Juan, things appeared to be much more relaxed.

A few of the locals gazed at the three, but didn't approach or speak. One man nodded in passing but kept his eyes lowered. Once, on Luna Street—identified as such by a rusted old street sign—Dean spotted a deeply tanned boy who looked to be his own age and he walked over to speak. However, the child responded to his greetings in Spanish, and Dean returned to Ryan and Krysty wearing a frown of disappointment.

The houses along the streets were a crowded sprawl of color and design. Some were in good repair, others obviously abandoned. The narrow streets were the dividers between multiple grilled balconies, brass-studded doors housed in ornate doorways and an explosion of colorful flora. His own curiosity working against him, Ryan returned the tour book to Dean and asked the boy to go ahead and tell them what they were looking at. Meanwhile, he scanned doorways and walk-through buildings fronting on two streets and noted dead-ends.

Krysty felt as though she had been on the receiving end of an unexpected chron-jump. According to Dean's informational booklet, Old San Juan dated back to the year 1521, and the architecture that remained intact along the streets and alleyways supported the claim. A mix of Spanish colonial mansions mingled with colorful plazas and shops.

"Blue," Krysty said, speaking aloud.

"What?"

"First time since I was a little girl back in Harmony I can remember the sky being the right color. My Uncle Tyas, he said the world above us was supposed to be blue, and he always made a point of showing me the right hue in picture books or bits of old vids. I've seen the sky colored blue before, but it was always dark, like a storm was brewing. More often than not in Deathlands, sky was orange, red, pink. You got used to it, but I always wanted to see that color of blue Tyas told me about. Nice to see he was right, as usual."

"'Natives say that the sky in Puerto Rico is bluer than any other place on earth, and the white clouds are whiter,'" Dean chimed in, reading a predark line of advertising copy.

"Doesn't surprise me," Ryan said easily, stooping to pick a smallish bright red flower that had grown up in a bare patch of dirt near the curb.

"You should give it to the lady, *señor,*" a voice said. "It matches the crimson of her hair."

They looked up to see a heavyset man in a straw hat looking down at them from a second-story window.

"Yeah, I was going to do that," Ryan said warily, handing the flower to Krysty.

"Thank you." Krysty was slightly annoyed at having her private time with Ryan and Dean interrupted by the native's appearance. She'd been charmed by rogues before, and knew the drill. Still, her mutie ability to read a person was giving her an all-clear signal regarding the man looking down, as opposed to the conflicting impressions that radiated like flaming tendrils from the always smiling Silas Jamaisvous.

"That flower is the Maltese cross, named because the petals of its flowers have the shape of the cross. You can see them if you look closely," the man noted.

"Hot pipe! He's right, Dad! Check it out!" Dean said excitedly, pointing at the flower.

"Thanks for the tip," Ryan said, turning to go. But the man wasn't to be put off so easily.

"My name is Soto," he called out. "Might I ask who you are?"

Ryan turned back and made quick introductions. "Ryan Cawdor. Krysty Wroth. My boy, Dean. We're staying at El Morro."

Soto made a show of appearing impressed, whistling softly before speaking. "That explains much. We don't see newcomers around here very often...at least, not human newcomers."

Ryan and Krysty both wondered what the man meant by such an odd statement, but didn't inquire further.

"We get around a lot. We tend not to stay in one locale for very long."

Soto nodded sagely. "Ah. That explains your weapons."

Ryan had already dropped a hand to rest lightly on the butt of the SIG-Sauer. "Man has to be armed and ready to defend himself."

Soto nodded enthusiastically. "Oh, I agree. It's just in Old San Juan, we rarely have need of such means of self-defense, at least, we had no need until recently."

The one-eyed man frowned. "That's twice you've dropped some kind of hint. If something's on your mind, say it."

Soto waved a hand, batting at the air in a submissive motion. "Please, don't get upset. I have no wish to cause trouble for you or your family. Why don't I come down where we can speak more privately?"

"You alone?"

"Yes."

"Okay, we'll wait."

Soto leaned out through the window and pointed with his left hand to the side of the building. "If you open the gate and go around the side, you'll see a garden. I'll be coming down the back stairs."

The garden along the wall was overflowing with flowering plants and ornamental bushes—hibiscus, gardenia, bougainvillea, jasmine, oleander, golden trumpet, cup of gold, and the queen-of-the-night, so called because its pale fragrant blossoms open only after dark. Flaming red poinsettias sixteen feet tall were growing wild at the edge where the ground met the concrete of the partition.

"Gaia, but this land is beautiful," Krysty said, sighing.

"Thank you," Soto replied as he stepped gingerly down the steps. He wore a white shirt, sandals on wide, flat feet, and near-white blue jeans. A pair of binoculars dangled from his neck. There was no visible blaster on his hip, although a large knife hung from his belt in a leather sheath. The straw hat was perched at an angle on his head.

"You wanted to talk?" Ryan asked, as blunt as always.

"I did, Mr. Cawdor. There is a darkness here in Old San Juan an outsider such as yourself might be able to help eliminate. A man with blasters and experience."

"Experience?" Krysty repeated.

Soto clarified. "In dangerous affairs."

"Guess you could say that," Ryan said. "Just so you know, I'm not a mercie or sec man. I don't kill for profit."

"That is good since I have no currency to pay you with. What I can offer is food and drink and a story."

Ryan glanced at his wristchron. He'd reset the timepiece for local time that morning before leaving El Morro. It was high noon. "Reckon we can spare a moment to hear you out and break your bread."

"Good! Now, come, come. A café is not far from here."

THE CAFÉ WAS SMALL and intimate, open at the front to allow natural lighting, yet still sheltered enough to provide shade from the blistering heat. When Ryan had spoken of "breaking bread," he hadn't realized how accurate his statement would prove to be, since lunch was indeed hunks of freshly baked bread with sweet-tasting sides of butter for flavoring. A bowl of fruit was placed next to the platter of bread, and all were given water to drink.

They had been joined by another man whom Soto had introduced as Jorge, and the two made an interesting contrast. Where Soto was plump and compact, Jorge was tall and muscular. Where Soto's clothing was heavily worn and drenched in sweat, Jorge was bare-chested and wore a pair of clean nylon swimming trunks.

The taller man didn't share in his friend's efforts to be friendly, and he gazed across the table with open distrust. When first introduced, there had been multiple exchanges of Spanish, some heated, before Soto had turned with his usual smile and asked them to sit.

"There a problem?"

"No," Jorge replied. "Not yet."

"Your food, it's good?" Soto interjected.

"Yeah," Ryan said, chewing on a piece of the blackened bread. "Good."

"Probably not as fine as the fare you've been dining on in El Morro," Jorge said with a sneer.

"No, it's not," Ryan answered. "But bread is bread."

"You said something about a story?" Krysty asked in an attempt to clear the air.

"I did," Soto said, wiping crumbs from his chin. "There is a creature who appeared here in Puerto Rico many years ago before the final war, the conflict that destroyed the world. First found with blood-stained teeth crouched at the side of a goat, the creature was quickly dubbed El Chupacabras—the goatsucker—since the poor animal the demon had killed was completely drained of blood."

"You don't say," Ryan replied, breaking off another hunk of the bread.

"The name of goatsucker soon proved to be misleading, since other carcasses began piling up in this region of the island. Sheep, cattle, horses, rabbits, cats, dogs, chickens, and many other recently killed animals were discovered daily for weeks afterward, and all of them shared the same symptoms of attack. Each dead animal had small wounds, punctures through which all of the blood had been sucked out."

"Wow!" Dean interjected. "Sounds like a horror vid I once saw."

"So, your goatsucker was some kind of predator. That was dozens of years ago. What's it got to do with the here and now?"

"El Chupacabras was no ordinary predator, Señor Cawdor. Here, I have a drawing."

Soto stood and took a leather pouch from one of his pockets. Unfastening the pouch, he removed a folded sheet of paper and handed it to Ryan. The one-eyed man unfolded the sheet, revealing a detailed drawing of a frightening-looking beast standing on a pair of muscular hind legs. Covered in coarse black hair, the *chupacabras* had a series of sharp spines running up its back. Clawed "hands" were at the ends of stubby arms, and under the arms were bat wings.

In the drawing the creature faced outward, showing an oval-shaped head with a long jaw and pointed chin. Huge eyes stretching across the upper half of its forehead rested above two tiny nasal slits. A mouth of jagged fangs was hissing a silent warning.

"Damn, looks like some kind of mutie," Ryan said in a soft tone, speaking more to Krysty and Dean than the two Puerto Ricans at the table.

"No such animal has ever existed in nature, my friend," Soto said.

"So, what's the problem?" Dean asked. "If this thing was running around more than a hundred years ago, how can Dad help you out?"

"Got a triple-bad feeling El Chupacabras is back, Dean," Ryan told his son, before turning to Soto and Jorge.

"That's why you're telling me all this, right?"

"Yes," Jorge said. "El Chupacabras is back, only he is no longer content to kill our animals. Now, he kills our women, our men and our children."

"You called it a 'mutie.' I know of mutants. Do you think El Chupacabras was created by man, Señor Cawdor?" Soto asked.

Ryan nodded, sipping at the mug of cool water. "I do."

"Why? You have now seen a picture of the beast. Do you not agree it looks as though it is the spawn of hell?"

Ryan scratched the stubble on his chin while pondering an answer. "First, all I've seen is a drawing. And yeah, it's butt-ugly, but I think we can leave the red-faced bastard with the pitchfork and pointed ears out of the game, Soto. I've seen this kind of shit before. Screamwings. Stickies. Dwellers. Swampies. All kinds of muties, some of them humanoid and others throwbacks to a world before man ever came crawling out of the muck. Back in Deathlands, we brought hell down on ourselves. From what I've learned in recent years, we're the ones responsible for most of the horrors that now walk, crawl and slither on the surface of this mudball."

Soto looked at Ryan with a thoughtful expression. "The world has always been a most dangerous place, Señor."

"Mebbe," Ryan agreed, wiping the sweat from under his chin. "Wish Mildred was here, she'd probably be doing a better job of explaining about mutations."

"Is there more than one?" Krysty asked.

"Oh yes," Jorge answered, and then shrugged. "Ten? Twenty? One hundred? I have no way of knowing for sure how many. I would say the number is low due to the rarity of earlier sightings here, but now it must be growing, since the attacks have increased. Little is left in the way of livestock, so they have gone the extra step of killing men for the needed blood. Seventeen of us are dead so far. A little girl was attacked and drained just a few days ago."

"I would hope the number of *El Chupacabras* is low. A few of us here have seen them, but I must wonder at the truth of what witnesses have said," Soto mused.

"You think they're lying?" Ryan asked.

"No, they have indeed seen something, but stories conflict. The truths do not match. One young boy said the two *chupacabras* he saw were floating in the air in total silence. The spines along their backs were vibrating at incredible speeds, and all of the colors of the rainbow were generated in an aura around their bodies, which in turn caused him to blank and fall unconscious.''

''Triple crazy,'' Dean commented.

''So why haven't your men gone and killed the things? Don't you have a group of sec men to enforce the peace?''

''There is no government or police force here. People are trying to survive the best way they know how, and we do so together. All is shared,'' Soto said.

''But there are few willing to fight what many think to be a creature from hell, Señor Cawdor. I and Soto are the only two who will take up weapons,'' Jorge said. ''But we have little experience in such affairs.''

''And you think I do?''

''Yes.''

''And all I have to base my decision on to help out is a yarn about a blood-sucking demon and a pencil drawing of an overgrown bat. Not much to go on.''

''Lover,'' Krysty interjected, ''can I talk to you alone?''

Ryan stood and Krysty followed. ''We'll be right back,'' he said.

Dean sat alone at the table with the two Puerto Rican men. ''You guys ever hear of a game called Cootie?'' he asked.

Outside the café, in the blinding hot sun, Krysty took Ryan's hand and squeezed it, pulling him along to a patch of shade beside the brick exterior.

"Sounds wild, doesn't it?" she said.

"Not really. Compared to the shit we're used to wading into back in Deathlands, a vampire goat demon is tame," Ryan replied. "They could be wrong, you know. Old folktales dreamed up to explain a rash of deaths."

"Yeah, but there's something in the telling. I don't think these guys are lying. Whatever this *chupacabras* is, it has them scared," she said.

"Guess Puerto Rico isn't such an island paradise after all."

"Guess not. You going to help them?"

"Mebbe. I want to get J.B.'s and Mildred's input on this. Doc's and Jak's too."

"I say we should try and do what we can, within reason," Krysty said.

"Why? Nothing in it for us. Could be an easy way of getting chilled, chasing around an angry bloodsucker."

"He mentioned children, Ryan," Krysty said firmly. "I won't have dead children on my conscience."

Chapter Ten

By the time Ryan, Krysty and Dean returned to the fortress, night had fallen. Retiring to their quarters after yet another spectacular meal courtesy of Jamaisvous, Ryan explained to the others about the encounter with Soto and Jorge. All agreed to return to the streets of Old San Juan the next day, even Doc, who had been told earlier by Jamaisvous that his assistance in the mat-trans chamber wouldn't be needed for the next twenty-four hours.

They had arrived to find Soto and Jorge at the site of their first meeting in the two-story building with the beautiful back garden, where the story of El Chupacabras was told again. Now, even more questions were being asked, not only about murderous mutants that struck in the night, but also regarding Dr. Silas Jamaisvous.

"When Jamaisvous showed up, how did he end up staying in the fortress?"

"Us locals, we had no interest in staying there. A cold and drafty fort made of stone held little or no appeal. Only after the doctor arrived and figured out how to reactivate the electricity did El Morro live again. It is said he has unlimited power at his fingertips. One would wish him to share his bounty, but he keeps all electrical energy within his own walls."

"It's a wonder he hasn't been chilled."

"A few hold grudges. This is why he employs guards. One or the other of them is always at his side. Some men and women who have grown close to the doctor have entered the fortress and never been seen in San Juan again."

"Almost like he's some kind of slave owner or overseer. Surprised you put up with it."

"Puerto Rico has a history of being...overseen, Señor Ryan."

"Going back to these *chupacabras.* Why the need for blood?" Mildred mused.

"Mebbe they're some kind of offshoot of the Cornelius family," Ryan suggested, referring to a bizarre sect of scientifically created "vampires" the group had encountered in the Bayou country south of Lafayette. "They supposedly needed the specific DNA in human blood to survive, at least, that's what they told us. I never did quite get a good understanding of what drove their engines."

"The concept of ingesting DNA through human blood to survive is ridiculous," Mildred said. "And I agree with you, Ryan, there was more going on with those poor bastards than met the eye. If I'd had more time and inclination, I might have figured out what drove them after human blood so relentlessly. I don't think it was just biological. I think they got some sick thrill out of playing vampire."

"While I scoff at the notion, one can find an historical precedent within a supernatural context,'' Doc said in a tone of authority, his voice strong even as he wiped at his overheated brow with his kerchief.

Mildred rolled her eyes. ''This I got to hear.''

Doc frowned, hefting his swordstick and pointing the tip at the dubious Mildred. ''You should cease and desist with the eye-popping and lip-smacking. Such overblown exaggerated movements, Dr. Wyeth, make *you* look foolish, not I. Right now, you put me in the mind of a poor pickaninny forced to perform in the confines of an old minstrel show. I half expect you to break into an arm-swinging tap dance in hopes of being thrown a penny.''

J.B. snickered before reassuming his usual poker face. ''That tears it! I like you better when you're a moron,'' Mildred said tiredly. ''I'm amazed to hear myself saying this, but you're less annoying when you don't have a brain in your head!''

''Come on, now, what's got into you, Millie?'' J.B. said, reaching out a hand to lightly brush the back of Mildred's plaited hair. ''Ease up.''

The physician was having no soothing from her man, and she spun on one heel to make an exit away from the men and into the house. ''Supposedly people are dying while we talk about evil spirits and freaks in vampire capes. I don't have to stand around listening to this garbage. If I want to hear this crap, I can pull out an endless supply of moldy old Stephen King novels.''

''Go ahead, Doc,'' Ryan said, sitting on one of the deep windowsills in the outer wall of the home.

The older man stuck a hand in one of the pockets of his coat and held the left lapel with his other, assuming a more formal stance before picking up the threads of his tale. "Blood, Ryan Cawdor, is the crimson elixir of the gods and their followers. The mortal blood of man has always been a liquid offering of significant value and importance to those who watch us from above...or below."

"The gods have abandoned us, Doc Tanner," Jorge whispered. "That is one answer."

"I don't believe that, and neither should you," Krysty said.

Jorge drummed his fingers on the arm of his chair. "Six months ago, a man riding a bicycle came upon a single *chupacabras* at the side of a road. Fearing for his life, he pulled a blaster—a 6-shot revolver—and fired at the monster. Six shots were unleashed, and the monster was not harmed."

"Mebbe he missed," Ryan suggested.

Jorge gave him an annoyed look, then refigured his handsome face into a wan smile. "At a distance of less than twenty feet, I can assure you I did not miss, Señor Cawdor."

"Okay, fair enough. What I don't understand is why you haven't done anything about these muties sooner?" J.B. asked.

"As I said before to Señor Cawdor, there had been no reason. Our livestock was being attacked, but the occasional lost chicken or goat was an acceptable loss. Grupo, he stayed up night after night, his weapon held between his legs as he hid under a pile of straw and watched intently in his coop for the creature who had been killing his poultry.''

''What happened?''

''One night, Grupo found his murderer,'' Soto continued, ''and fell prey to the beast himself. His son found him the next morning, soon after sunrise, when he ventured out to collect the morning eggs. Like the other animals, his father had two puncture wounds on his neck. All of the blood had been drained from his body.''

''Grupo was the first. Many now think the *chupacabras* had been content with the blood of animals, until tasting the life fluid of man,'' Jorge added.

''Uh-huh.'' Ryan grunted.

''You do not believe me?''

''Didn't say that. Seen enough in my time not to discount what anybody tells me, till I check the situation out for myself. You want to tell me mutie fruit bats or blood-sucking earthworms or even talking palm trees are running around Puerto Rico and tearing up the neighborhood, fine. I'll take your word for it, but still want to see some proof.''

''As do I,'' Mildred added, having rejoined the gathering.

''Proof,'' the muscular man snorted, working his cheeks and coming up with a glob of saliva to spit it disgustedly. ''You want proof, visit the cemetery. Ask for your proof from the recently departed dead.''

''Yes,'' Mildred said, stepping forward with a frown. ''Let's do that.''

NO MATTER HOW MUCH death she had been forced to witness in the dark future world she'd been awakened from cryo sleep to find herself thrust into, Dr. Mildred Wyeth had never been able to numb herself to the heartbreaking sight of a dead child.

She found the chosen site where the little girl had been placed in repose to be one of infinite sadness, since in life, in another time, this very same sanctuary would have been a place of learning and security for a child. Now, alone as only the dead can be, the girl rested under a threadbare sheet on a long wooden table, inert and eternally still. The upcoming funeral and burial services were planned for the next day.

Unlike many children, Mildred had never feared or dreaded going to school. The locker-lined hallways of academia served as order against the chaos of her life, and gave off light against the darkness of ignorance and fear. Born too late to experience the insult of segregation, she'd always thought of school as her second home, and after her father's brutal murder by Klansmen—an act in itself an aberrant throwback of a hate crime that she'd never been able to fully erase from her mind—Mildred had come to rely on the educational system more and more as her primary residence as she grew older.

"That Mildred...always got her nose in a book," one of her two aunts was always saying, even after she'd graduated from high school and entered into college, finding a new home and leaving behind the old shell. What would those very same two aunts now have to say regarding her current life-style?

Mildred sighed. These days, she was getting entirely too much in the way of exercise, and she couldn't remember the last time she'd sat and read a good novel from cover to cover.

Besides, there were no more schools, except for the few private affairs such as the Brody School where Ryan had sent Dean. Mildred turned away from the dead girl and walked over to the boarded-up windows along the side of the classroom. She peered out across the overgrown schoolyard at the remains of the playground. She imagined the skeletal jungle gym out back hadn't been touched by innocent hands in many years.

Reaching down, she took the hand of the dead girl and was stunned to discover it was still flexible. Rigor mortis hadn't begun to set in, even though the flesh was cold.

"How long did you say she has been dead?" she asked Soto.

The short Puerto Rican managed to twist his face into an even more morose expression. "Since three nights ago."

Mildred frowned as she flexed the fingers of the child's hand with ease. "The body...there's no stiffness."

"I know. That is how we can always tell a true victim of the *chupacabras.* You might wait a handful of days, and still little Rosa would not stiffen, her body still limp even in death."

Mildred frowned. "The blood," she said softly.

"Que?"

"The absence of rigor mortis must be related to the blood loss. Some sort of secretion given off by the *chupacabras* during its...feeding." Mildred suddenly felt completely helpless. "I could try and do an analysis, but without the proper instruments and laboratory equipment, my hands are tied. Dammit."

"Now do you believe?"

"Let's just say I'm leaning closer to your side."

"I'll accept that as a yes."

"Why here? Why a school as a storage spot for a corpse?"

"This is a safe place. Many live here."

"No, what I meant was why keep her body in a school and not in a church?" the woman demanded. She was by no means an expert, but she'd always understood most Puerto Ricans to be both deeply religious and firmly Catholic. She knew many of the social customs and mores had disappeared after the arrival of skydark, but from what she'd observed of this community, the men and women still held the concept of God close to their bosoms.

Soto took off his battered straw hat and sheepishly ran his fingers through his lank black hair. "The child...she is unholy," he said in a halting voice.

"What?"

"The *chupacabras*'s bite has left her unclean. Any mourning will have to take place outside the church."

Mildred felt her posture tighten as she struggled to

contain any outburst. "You believe that crap? Evil or not, the *chupacabras* is definitely of this earth."

"What I believe does not matter. The community believes, her own mother believes, and their wishes override my own."

Mildred continued her examination of the body. There were twin puncture marks at the front of Rosa's fragile neck, on line with the jugular vein. The tiny wounds were perfect, and almost seemed to have been cauterized. There was no evidence of the usual tearing or mauling that the fangs of a normal predator would have left behind in the child's flesh.

"Enough. I need some air," the physician finally said, walking out of the classroom, out of the school, and onto the playground.

"You have examined the body." Jorge looked down at Mildred who sat and swayed in an old metal child's swing.

"I have."

"And...?"

"And I have to say there are oddities here I can't explain," Mildred admitted.

"Such as the *chupacabras*'s bite and the condition of the body."

"That's right."

"My ancestors, they also battled El Chupacabras," Jorge said easily. "Distant relatives have told me the stories of those who came before, who shared my name and blood."

"Yet, these bastards didn't start giving you hell now until a few years ago."

"That is true, yes."

"Have you ever wondered what triggered their reappearance?"

"There have been some terrible storms to sweep the island. Perhaps a door—a passageway into our world—was blown open, allowing them access to Puerto Rico once more."

"And you want Ryan to lead an expedition to close this 'door.'"

"Close it? I hope with his help to nail it shut and melt the hinges," Jorge replied.

"All we have is your word on what has been happening here."

"My word is my word. Soto and me, we do not lie. Question others here in Old San Juan. They will tell you."

"Oh, I have. I talked with the one person I could get to speak to me. She wouldn't even say the word *chupacabras* for fear of bringing one swooping down on her head, but she had a high opinion of you. Not so much of Soto. She thinks he is slightly mad."

"Aren't we all, *señorita*? Aren't we all?"

THE GROUP OF SEVEN FRIENDS gathered that night in the back garden of El Morro, standing and sitting among the lush flowers and bushes. The sky above San Juan Bay was as clear as any the companions had ever seen before and the stars looked down on them impassively, watching, waiting, their starlight having traveled for millions of miles to this last point, burning in time for an eternity over their heads.

"There's no getting past what's been said and what's been shown to us. There are some kind of mutie killers around here. Jamaisvous isn't worried. He's hiding up here in his own little world, safe in a fortress. The native Puerto Ricans—the ones still alive in the city and the villes around here—they aren't so lucky," Ryan said.

Krysty picked up the discussion. "Soto said the *chupacabras* started giving them problems about six months after Silas Jamaisvous appeared out of nowhere. They went to the new arrival to ask for help, since Jamaisvous had previously offered food and supplies to any men wanting to work in exchange for assistance."

"Assistance?" Mildred asked. "I must've missed that part."

Ryan gave the woman a look of grim amusement. "He needed strong backs to do some heavy lifting. Needed wags for transport. Ended up using some gas-powered trucks and—"

The sound of leisurely footsteps alerted them, and they turned their heads to see Jamaisvous stepping down the small maze of steps and into the garden. He was alone, although Ryan had spied movement farther up the walk, indicating that one of the sec men who always seemed to dog the doctor's heels was close at hand if needed. "Good evening, all."

"Thanks for the fine meal," J.B. said. "Really appreciated it."

"You are more than welcome, Mr. Dix," Jamaisvous replied, sipping from one of the orange mugs of coffee. "Still, I couldn't help but overhear you talking as I approached."

"Eavesdropping, Silas?" Ryan asked easily.

"If you are curious about my past, Ryan Cawdor, why don't you just ask?" the elegantly dressed man replied. "I have tried to be as open and honest with you as I know how."

"Then consider this a request."

"Very well, then. What would you like to know?"

"Funny thing, Silas," Ryan said in a dry voice that indicated he didn't find a single thing amusing about what he was going to say. "I've been here in Old San Juan for three days now, and I can't seem to find any of the lucky bastards who got to help you cart that mat trans out of the wilderness and into this stone shell of a fortress."

"I didn't know you were looking for any of the 'lucky bastards,' Mr. Cawdor."

"I wasn't, really. Just making conversation with the locals. One of them said the boys who gave you a hand vanished once you made this overblown tomb your home."

"Vanished? My, that is amusing. My legend continues to grow within the walls of Old San Juan. Evil white man comes to the village. If you think for a moment, I'm sure you'd become aware that most of the men who assisted me now live here within El Morro's walls, serving as my gardeners or security force. And I did not 'cart a mat trans.' I merely absconded with a few key components and used them in the modification of the gateway hidden here in the fortress.''

''Two gateways?'' Dean asked, wrinkling his nose. ''Weren't they pretty close together?''

''Not so unusual, my boy. The other one was used primarily for advanced experiments in time trawling—a prototype facility. The gateway located here in El Morro was for nothing more than quick transportation. Obviously, despite its formidable exterior and historical reputation, El Morro is no hidden redoubt or modern military installation.''

''Seems like a stupe move, and you don't strike me as a stupe,'' Ryan noted. ''Why not just stay in the redoubt?''

''If fate had been more kind, I would have. However, once I had come out of cryo sleep, I discovered the true reason my hibernation had been interrupted, and it had nothing to do with a faulty timer. The nuclear generator at the lowest level was beginning to malfunction, causing power fluctuations to spike and burn out all through the facility.''

Ryan caught Mildred's eye. The woman gave an almost imperceptible shrug. The story did appear to be truthful, at least on the surface.

''Since my reaction to this bleak world after nuclear exchange was the same as your own Dr. Tanner's, I decided after research to make the attempt to go back in time before the conflict. Since Puerto Rico seemed to be a chosen spot for advanced trawling attempts—or rather, it would have been had war not broken out when it did—why not take advantage? To do so, I needed to utilize a matter-transfer device for my experiments. However, I needed a steady source of power I could rely on without interruption. I did attempt a few transports while housed in the redoubt and all of them ended badly from a lack of necessary energy."

"You look okay to me."

Jamaisvous grinned. "I was not fool enough to climb inside the gateway myself. I used objects. Sent them out and brought them back. The drain of power required to activate the mat-trans unit was too much for the weakened nuclear generator, so I had to stop. Within a month's time, I realized another solution would be needed. Knowing of the second gateway, I decided to avail myself of it."

"But, how?" Ryan pressed. "How did you know?"

"Know what?"

"About the second mat-trans unit? How did you know it was in El Morro? Why even suspect Puerto Rico to have more than one? Like Dean said, two in close proximity is unusual."

Jamaisvous frowned, as if annoyed by the question. Finally he said, "When my own cryogenic chamber malfunctioned and I was brought out of cryo sleep, I was afraid, perplexed. The redoubt I found myself in was like nothing I had ever seen before, especially once I realized some of my own theories regarding matter transfer were in fact in use. I had no concept of shadowy government groups beyond what I'd read in fiction or saw on television. The late nineties were a hotbed of stories for conspiracy buffs."

"So how do you know so much?" Mildred asked.

"Luckily, Dr. Wyeth, when I awoke, my mind was intact. Unlike yourself, there was no one waiting to assist in my adjustment. Still, I was and am, an intelligent man. I read, and in my research of the redoubt, I discovered many secrets within that cavernous hole. The curious case of Dr. Theophilus Algernon Tanner, for one. Secret codes, for another, which allowed me to travel from one sealed sector to another. And also, I discovered the existence of a second mat-trans unit—one close at hand, since I also read about my current home."

"You've been in other redoubts?" Krysty asked.

"Briefly, yes. I didn't linger."

"Well, I've been in more redoubts than I can count on my fingers and toes, and none had a book of operating instructions lying on the floor," Ryan said. "Seems standard operating procedure called for carting out all sensitive data, and if it couldn't be taken out manually, it was destroyed on the premises."

Jamaisvous sighed. "Not here, Ryan. Not in the Puerto Rican redoubt. Here, files remained, and a most fascinating compact disc listing gateways and their locations, at least, all of the ones in the former United States and its close, personal allies."

Ryan dwelled on the implications of what Jamaisvous was saying. Such a guide book could prove invaluable, allowing quick transport across the globe.

"Now, if you have any other concerns, please relate them."

"You know anything about these goatsuckers that have been killing off livestock down in Old San Juan?"

Jamaisvous gave Ryan a look of amused disbelief. "You must be kidding me. The *chupacabras* myth? Legend, Ryan. The Puerto Ricans have been bothered by these blood-sucking monsters for years. Goats. Sheep. Pigs. Any and all small animals that end up dead under mysterious circumstances get blamed on the bad *chupacabras*."

"More than some goats these days. They've started going for people."

"People?"

"It's true," Mildred said. "I've seen one of the bodies myself. Little girl."

"I am sorry to hear of any loss of life, but what can I hope to do?"

"Something's out there killing people," Ryan said. "Since there seems to be a lack of experienced sec men in Old San Juan, or even men who know which is the proper business end of a blaster, I agreed to look into this matter at least. However, my signing on didn't mean the rest of you have to follow suit. This isn't anything to do with us—at least, not at this point."

"I go where you go, Dad," Dean said.

"Me too. I'm already climbing the walls of this

gussied-up mausoleum. You know I hate standing still,'' J.B. added.

''Me, too, lover,'' Krysty added.

''I go. Something do,'' Jak said. ''Get bored here.''

Doc had been looking hesitant, but apparently came to a decision. ''Ryan, I...I fear I must decline. I am needed to assist Dr. Jamaisvous in some delicate procedures.''

''No need to apologize, Doc. You've got your own road to follow.''

''I also have a request,'' their host said. ''I wish Dr. Wyeth to remain behind as well. According to Dr. Tanner, she also has a practical working theory of the mat-trans gateways. Plus, an experienced third hand could prove useful in reaching our eventual goal.''

''How about it, Mildred?'' Ryan asked. ''You want to hang back?''

The woman thought about it for a moment before replying. ''I suppose. If it'll help Doc.''

''Your presence will be invaluable,'' Jamaisvous said.

''Okay, looks like it's a trio,'' she said.

''Tell you what, Silas. Since you're taking two of my people, how about loaning me some of your sec crew in exchange?'' Ryan asked.

Although he didn't look pleased at the notion, Jamaisvous nodded curtly. ''I can spare an extra set of hands, but only one. If this creature is indeed developing a taste for human blood, we shall need to be vigilant. El Morro is quite large—in this case, a minus rather than a plus. Luis will accompany you.''

''Good.'' Ryan looked over the group of friends. ''And I am sure the others in Old San Juan will see it as a neighborly gesture.''

''When are you leaving?''

''Tomorrow, midday.''

''I shall inform him of his new assignment. Our stores here are limited when it comes to weaponry, but please take along extra ammunition and any other survival supplies you think you might need. Where are you starting the hunt?''

''Don't know yet. Soto said he'd show us the way to where he thinks a nest of *chupacabras* might be hiding.''

''Then, I will bid all of you a good-night. Dr. Tanner, if you want, we can discuss my plans for you in greater detail in the morning.''

''I am looking forward to it. I shall see you at breakfast.''

Jamaisvous strolled out the way he came.

''Still don't trust that bastard. Be on guard, Mildred. Especially for Doc.''

''Of course, Ryan.''

''All right. Dean, you'll stay with Doc and Mildred—''

''The hell I will!'' Dean exclaimed.

Ryan's face fell into a stoic frown and he gave his only son a cold glare.

''What did you say to me, boy?'' Ryan said in his quietest tone of voice.

Dean knew that tone. Feeling the contents of his stomach turn to stone, the boy stood his ground and repeated himself, only without voicing the annoyance or anger in the reply.

"I said, 'the hell I will.'"

"That's what I thought I heard. What makes you think you have a choice in the matter?" Ryan asked.

Dean continued to stand his ground. "I'm tired of getting left behind. I can protect myself."

"Yes, you showed keen judgment back in Freedom," Ryan retorted. Dean didn't look pleased at being reminded of how he'd ended up as a bargaining chip for the flamboyant Beck Morgan, who'd been serving as the mall's baron in charge. Morgan had snatched the opportunity of Dean's being incarcerated to force Ryan and the others to serve as sec men, supplementing his own weak task force.

"Not his fault. Was mine," Jak said simply. "Dean backed play. Caught us both. Baron let me go work while kept him. Knew you'd feel stronger about kin."

"I would have done the same for either of you," Ryan replied.

"Yeah, but baron didn't know."

"True. All right, then. Mildred, looks like you and Doc are on your own here with Silas. Dean's coming along. And Doc, there's more here than meets the eye... Don't know much about that man. He wants your help, but mebbe what he wants is to make some use of you. Use that could leave you worse off."

"Thank you, my friend," Doc answered, and

lifted a hand in farewell as they moved off. His mind kept repeating Ryan's words like a mantra, "Make some use of you...worse off," a mantra that sent his thoughts tunneling back through time....

Maryland, Virginia Redoubt, 1999

CHAN HAD SEEMED unsurprised when he glanced up and greeted Doc, until he had a delayed reaction with a shocked double take.

"Greetings and salutations, Chan, my boy," Doc replied easily, stepping closer to the seated man. "I see they still keep you on the night shift."

His approach sent Chan skittering to his feet. The small man nearly lost his footing as the wheeled chair he'd been sitting in rolled away from the desk. Striving to regain his composure, he gasped out, "Wh-what are you doing here?"

Doc made a waving "bye-bye" motion with his right hand. "Leaving, I hope."

Chan frowned, taking in what Doc was wearing. "Aw, shit, Doc. Where did you get the sec gear?"

"I liberated it, just as I plan to liberate myself."

"Not again. You can't be serious."

"I am deadly serious," Doc replied flatly, all humor and warmth erased from his voice as he stepped closer to the technician's workstation. "Now, I am hoping you will just pretend I am not here while I borrow your keyboard to access this computer and make a few entries and corrections into Operation Chronos's temporal guidance array."

"You want to make a chron-jump, Doc? That takes time."

"Time? Do not speak to me of time, you twit!" Doc said with a sneer, suddenly losing all patience. "What I have no 'time' for is useless debate!"

"I can't let you do this," Chan replied as he scooted over to the panic button mounted on the far wall of the control room. Such buttons were mounted in flip-top Plexiglas boxes and scattered throughout the redoubt in case of emergency. "There's no telling what you might screw up. Besides, you haven't been prepared."

"None of us have been prepared," Doc replied. "I sure as hell was not prepared when I was sucked up into your little science project."

Doc had hoped Chan wouldn't push it to the limit, but knew now he had no choice but to pull the Glock pistol from where he'd hidden it behind his back in the waistband of his trousers under the white sec-man cloak. He shakily raised the weapon and pointed it. While he was familiar with handguns, the more destructive and powerful guns of this future age left him a bit breathless, especially since this was the first time he'd actually threatened a fellow human being with such a weapon.

"Please, Chan. I beg of you. Let me be. This is my risk and my risk alone."

"I can't, Doc. You know I can't," the man replied. "Just like I know you can't use that gun. You're not a killer, and the sound of the shot will bring everybody running."

"Logic, Chan?" Doc asked.

"And emotion," Chan replied. "An unbeatable combination."

"This gun could be silenced," Doc pointed out, seeing Chan's face fall for a millisecond as the possibility ran through the man's mind.

"Why?"

"Why indeed?"

"Put it down, Doc. This attempt, it's suicide."

"Well, I had to try," Doc replied mildly, letting his shoulders slump and assuming the air of a beaten man before coiling every muscle and springing forward, plowing bodily into Chan and crushing him against the wall before grabbing the technician's clothing and pulling him in a sprawl to the lab floor. Having abandoned using the gun, Doc managed to maneuver himself on top of the younger man and he pressed his advantage as best he could, covering his struggling adversary's nose and mouth with one hand while trying to maintain his balance with the other.

"Ow—damnation, boy!" Doc bellowed as Chan bit down on the fleshy inside of his unprotected hand. Doc pulled away the injured limb, slinging drops of blood from the bite. His mouth and nose free, Chan sucked in a needed gasp of air before lunging up and confronting Doc once more. Bending upright as best he could at the waist with Doc's weight on top of him, Chan looked him in the face.

"You tried to kill me!" the Asian accused.

"No, I did not!" Doc protested. "I just tried to render you unconscious. If I wanted you dead, you would be shot, you idiot! Get it through your mind, son! I am a desperate man!''

Chan lowered himself back on his elbows, sighed, and then sprang up a second time, managing to lean forward even farther and whack his foe bluntly in the nose with his forehead. He was rewarded with a cracking noise as Doc cried out in pain a second time. Taken by surprise at Chan's ferocity, Doc slid sideways, staggered by the head butt.

Chan wasn't in much better physical shape than Doc, but he was more of a natural brawler. The advantage Doc held over the technician was his desperation. He knew if he didn't succeed in this second attempt to go back home, undoubtedly it would be his last time unaccompanied into a mat-trans chamber.

Doc swung a punch with his right fist and caught Chan full in the jaw, causing both of them to cry out in agony from the pain of the blow.

''Shit, Doc!'' the smaller man hissed, a trickle of blood pouring from his mouth where the older man's desperate blow had loosened two of his teeth.

''I do believe I have broken one of my fingers,'' Doc replied mildly, flexing his hand even as he prepared to swing another punch with his left.

The second blow caught Chan in the upper part of the face, above the nose and around the forehead. He fell and landed flat on his back on the floor. Finally, to Doc's relief, the man was unconscious. Doc's hands were singing a duet of pain as he sat at the computer, activating the operating software that was linked with the time-trawl hardware. The only sounds in the room beyond his own two-fingered typing were the usual ambient noise of the computers and a raspy breathing from Chan.

Then, an alarm Klaxon went off, screamingly loud and disruptive. A metallic voice said, "Warning! Intruder alert within the matter-transfer control room."

Doc knew the pair of scientists couldn't have returned from their break so soon, and Allan's unconscious body was hopefully still slumbering in his bed, the covers pulled high...so what had tipped them off? Doc looked up, craning his long neck and pointing his chin skyward, and saw the sec camera staring down at him, a small red activation light winking on and off.

At some point during his fight with Chan, the overhead video camera had seen the struggle.

Doc supposed he should be glad for his keepers and their lack of subtlety. If they hadn't hit the alarm, he wouldn't have heard them coming in time to try to make a stand.

He picked up the chair he'd been sitting in and ran over to the control keypad for the vanadium steel security door to the room, swinging up the solid metal legs in a sideways arc and smashing the plastic casing. The liquid crystal display went blank, and there was a smattering of white sparks from the inside wiring of the number keys.

Having retrieved the Glock, Doc fired a series of bullets into the door's mechanism as well. The pistol had a slight kick, but he had braced himself instinctively before pulling the trigger. The gunshots were horrendously loud in the confined area of the control room, but when combined with the shrieking of the alarm, they seemed inconsequential.

Rolling the chair to the computer, he sat back down and began to type even faster, hoping in his haste he wouldn't make a mistake. Recalling the commands from his scholar's trained memory, which had observed, organized and stored away during previous stints watching and learning in the mat-trans rooms, he was able to bring up the proper entry screen for the time-trawl settings on the computer monitor.

Sweating now from the exertion and nerves and the double layer of clothing he wore, his brow glistening with perspiration, Doc typed in the destination date as that November day of 1896, along with the exact moment the "eye of God" appeared in the sky before his daughter. While Doc might not have been certain of the precise second, all of the essential information regarding his trawl was already stored in the computer's data banks, and as such he was able to time his planned reentry as best he could to the very instant he was first sucked away. In essence, he was attempting to superimpose himself upon the scene.

The date in place, Doc closed down the time-trawl data banks, retaining the translation code the computer had offered that he would need to program by hand for his destination when he entered the gateway site itself. The code was more complex than the ones he'd seen for using the gateways to travel from one location to another. He imagined that extending the process to include the opening up of a temporal doorway accounted for the extra series of numerals.

The intercom speakers crackled into life a second time, struggling valiantly to be overheard against the whooping of the alarm. "Tanner, this is Welles. Halt what you are doing immediately and open the control-room door or there will be terminal repercussions. If we have to blast our way inside, we might damage the gateway controls, and if that happens, you won't ever be able to go back."

Doc ignored the voice. "Lies," he murmured to himself. "All lies."

He raced into the anteroom between the armaglass gateway and the control room, stripping off the security uniform. He held the pistol he'd taken from Allan out from his body for a second, pondering whether to take it along or not, and finally thrust it down into the front of his trousers and belt, hoping the weapon's safety would stay in place and he wouldn't be blowing off the Tanner family jewels.

Pausing before the gateway keypad, Doc tapped in the needed code, bringing it up from where he'd stored it in his short-term memory and taking grim confidence in knowing he'd remembered the sequence perfectly. The small display on the control pad of the gateway blinked twice after he thumbed the enter key and began counting down. Doc looked away, knowing time was short, and lifted the rubber and metal handle of the heavy armaglass gate to the six-sided chamber.

The door swung open easily and he stepped inside, pulling it closed behind him.

The curtain of mists fell down like water through a drain, swirling, twirling, growing thicker and whiter, obliterating all sight and sound. There was a queer sensation of being pressed upon with a giant hand, and his ears popped as if he'd made the transition from a higher to a lower altitude. Doc tried to speak, but couldn't. The last thing he remembered before falling into unconsciousness was how the metal plates on the floor of the chamber felt hot against his cheek, while the other side of his face was as cold as freshly fallen snow.

DOC AWAKENED to find he was inside another chamber. The code had proved wrong. He hadn't gone back in time, but instead had been shuttled down the line to another one of the multitude of gateways that dotted the United States as part of the project.

"Fuck!" he screamed, and Doc's current state of mind could be easily guessed by the usage of the vulgarity. The curse was one of the few he rarely, if ever, used, but none other seemed to sum up his situation as perfectly. "Fuck! Fuck! Fuck!"

Then he realized the color of the walls were exactly the same shade as the ones he'd just departed. Yet, he'd been told no two gateways were alike and all had different colors of armaglass. Rather than number them, one of the design engineers had hit upon using colors as a security measure. If someone transported into a chamber and didn't know the location from the color, the jump would be quickly recognized as unauthorized.

Doc realized he hadn't even left. He was still on the floor where he'd started from, and the stolen pistol was cutting into his stomach something fierce.

The door of the hexagonal chamber swung open and there stood a squad of the security men, a frowning Allan among them.

"Dr. Tanner, consider yourself under arrest," one of the men announced.

A hundred retorts went through Tanner's mind, ranging from "On what grounds?" to "I would rather be under arrest than under attack." He used none of these.

"Fuck," Doc said again, raising his hands.

Then, Welles pushed his way through. "You're finished, Tanner."

"Nonsense. I barely got started before ending up back here in your charming company."

"We rerouted your signal," Welles revealed. "Chan was able to stagger up and do a bounce back on the chronal-nav guidance computer. You went one way, hit a wall, came screeching back. Do not pass go. Do not collect two hundred dollars."

"So, my computation and calculations were correct."

"Yes. Still, you couldn't wait, could you? We trust you and this is the result. I ought to have you shot where you stand."

"You would not dare. I am too important to your little project."

Welles stroked his double chin. "For now, Tanner. For now."

Chapter Eleven

"Why here?" Mildred asked. She was taking in the tropical breeze from the open balcony and enjoying the feel of the air on her bare shoulders and neck. She was dressed in a midnight-blue summer dress with white collar and trim, a scavenged piece of attire Jamaisvous had obtained for her from one of the boutiques still intact in Old San Juan. She had refused the gift at first, but then decided she was being silly, and why not spend a day feeling feminine?

She was surprised to find Jamaisvous alone. Doc was nowhere in sight.

"Why here?" Mildred asked a second time, turning to face Jamaisvous.

"Why not?"

"Rude to answer a question with a question."

"Then I will attempt a compliment. You look most beautiful, Dr. Wyeth."

Even though Mildred knew she was being hosed, she returned his smile. Her own lover rarely tossed out such commonplace courtesies and compliments. Manners, like so many other social niceties, had gone the way of the nukecaust. While the woman knew she never would have been confused for Emily Post, by the very nature of her former positions as researcher, physician and Olympic champion she knew her way around a cocktail party or formal dinner.

Then, there were occasions she missed getting dressed up for a night of entertainment as opposed to trekking through a world that was not only consistently crude and inelegant but also held an inexhaustible stock of nasty surprises for them.

Dressing up and dining out. Too bad the man sitting across from her wasn't J. B. Not that the Armorer would have been enjoying himself. For all of his talents, he wasn't a man for casual finery or amusement. To a woman who had once lived in the late span of the twentieth century, the Armorer could seem almost supernaturally cool and dispassionate.

Still, Mildred mused, while J.B. was predictable, he was usually predictable in all the right ways.

Jamaisvous, on the other hand, was still an unknown commodity. Charming, handsome, silver-tongued, and like herself, intelligent, he seemed to be more the type a woman like herself should be attracted to.

So, why didn't Mildred trust him?

"I said, would you like some more wine?" Jamaisvous asked, snapping Mildred out of her reverie. He held up the bottle from the silver ice bucket and presented it to her.

Mildred held out her empty glass. "Pour."

Jamaisvous did so with a flourish of the wrist.

"I always thought you government types preferred a cold, sterile environment," Mildred remarked, stretching like a lazy cat in the island heat. The balcony offered up a spectacular view of the ocean, and the warm sea breeze blowing across her body was most comforting.

Jamaisvous leaned on his arm and watched her as he spoke. "Really, Dr. Wyeth, I was hoping for some time away from talking shop. That was one reason why I left Dr. Tanner to his own devices for brunch."

"Sorry, the subject just came to mind."

"What you really mean is why did 'they' choose Puerto Rico as a site for Operation Chronos's trawling experiments?"

Mildred turned back to face him. "Yes," she replied directly.

Jamaisvous paused, the wind whipping through and tousling his graying hair, then idly checked the backs of his hands, holding them out, extended from the front of his body. "Would you believe the group wanted to work on their tans?" he asked, deadpan.

Mildred couldn't help herself. She had to chuckle. "No."

"I didn't think so."

The phrasing, the joking—Jamaisvous's speech patterns were unlike any of those she'd heard since coming back to life in Deathlands, and after some thought, she'd understood why. Of course they weren't unfamiliar to her since he was also a freezie. His speech, the teasing sarcasm, the timbre of his voice, the predark slang he used—it was all very comforting.

While making her uneasy as hell.

"You have a most fascinating voice," she said, forthright and boldly.

Jamaisvous looked up from his omelette with a quizzical expression. "Is there something wrong with the way I speak?"

"Exactly the opposite. I like listening to you talk."

"Thanks."

"Don't mention it...and you never answered my question."

"Of course I did. The possibility of their working on their tans. I asked if you would believe such a statement."

"No, Silas. I wouldn't," Mildred said.

"I thought not. The project is long dead. Why concern yourself with trivial matters now?"

"Nothing involving the Totality Concept ever dies. At least, that's been my experience," Mildred said, a tinge of unease in her voice.

"In this instance, you are incorrect. What does it matter why they chose to set up here?"

"It matters to me."

"They had their reasons. Just as you do."

"What are you talking about?"

"Like you and Dr. Tanner, two members of the merry marching Cawdor band that seem totally out of place. The intense redhead, the skinny one with the glasses, the bloodless albino teen—even the Cawdor boy. They're of a kind with Ryan, those four. Not much of what you or I think of as being civilized among them. Stand all of you against a wall and ask even the youngest child to pick the two who weren't quite the same and the success rate would be most high."

"No, they're not civilized, *if* by that you mean *urbane*. And yes, any child could pick out Doc and me—because he's an oldie and I'm the only black," Mildred retorted hotly.

"Oh, please, that's not what I meant at all. Don't twist my words to bring up your unwarranted ire," Jamaisvous replied, holding up a hand to still Mildred's burst of anger. "You and Doc Tanner are the only two members of the group with something on the ball beyond innate cunning and alpha-male dominance. I think your former places in time have something to do with that. We don't belong here, Dr. Wyeth. We're all lost."

"Not me. And watch what you say about the skinny one with glasses."

"He means something to you, this Dix?"

"He does."

"Could have fooled me. Where's the affection, Dr. Wyeth? The secret smiles, the holding of hands... from my observation, limited as it might be, he treats you as one of his fellows."

"And what's wrong with that?"

"Well, for one thing, if you were my companion, I'd treat you with the attention and care a woman such as yourself deserves. Like I'm doing now. Good food. Nice clothes. Intelligent conversation."

"Look, Silas," Mildred began, "fine wines and

new clothes aren't the only things a woman is seeking in a mate."

"I know, but aren't they a nice bonus?"

Their eyes met for a second, and then each turned attention to the meal. No words were spoken for a series of lengthy moments, until Doc Tanner stumbled up and announced himself.

"I say, I had wondered where the two of you had gotten off to," he remarked. "Are those scrambled eggs I smell?"

Mildred bit back a giggle. "Why don't you join us, Doc?"

"A splendid suggestion." Doc slid back one of the two unoccupied chairs and began to serve himself from the covered tray of eggs and potatoes.

"Well, you wanted us to stay and assist you—we're doing so. Now it's time for you to come clean and explain why to me. Are you serious about trying to trawl yourself home?"

"I am. And my dear Dr. Wyeth, Puerto Rico has long been a site of the most infinite possibilities. What I find amusing is that even in this far-flung age, decades upon decades after the final nuclear conflagration, this tiny island remains as unstable as it was in the 1990s."

Mildred's brow furrowed. "Unstable in what way?"

"Electromagnetically, of course," Jamaisvous said. "And Puerto Rico is on the edge of one of the great mysteries of life, the Bermuda Triangle."

"Of course!" Doc agreed in between bites of a piece of toast smeared with jam.

"An electromagnetic field covers the world like a blanket," Jamaisvous continued. "When combined with gravitational forces, we have the status for our little network of matter-transfer gateways. When the mat-trans units are focused on the grids of ley lines currently crossing the globe, we tap into the very molten power of Mother Earth herself for transport, and our earth parent is a most powerful entity indeed."

Although she didn't attest to it, Mildred knew Jamaisvous was correct. She'd seen the power of Gaia harnessed before in the form of Krysty Wroth, power that made the woman seem to glow with an inner energy—an energy that gave her terrific speed and strength. Krysty once described the sensation to Mildred as sinking down into a thick whirlpool of heated molten goo, all-encompassing, all-comforting. While your own movements were unencumbered by the substance, the world around you seemed to fall into bizarre slow motion. What to her seemed to be nothing more than a casually launched counterattack against a foe appeared to others as a blur of destructive power and force.

Mildred had seen Krysty rip off a man's arms as easily as she might break a twig. Back in Kings Bay, Georgia, at the naval base of Admiral Poseidon, while under the influence of the Gaia force, one well-placed kick had sent a man's head flying up, tearing away from his shoulders and spinal column like a punted football.

"Such forces aren't easily controlled," Mildred remarked.

"I don't understand why you weren't brought here, Dr. Tanner," Jamaisvous mused. "In my reading, this site appears to have been a nexus point for advanced chron-jumping. Instead of devoting such a large part of their time and funding to waging war, their undivided attention and Herculean efforts should have been focused on time trawling."

"Too late now," Mildred said and took a bite of toast.

"Actually it isn't. Such is the joy of having access to time travel. If it works, one can always go back to put a fix in, right?"

Doc and Mildred exchanged concerned looks.

"Pass the salt," Doc said.

Chapter Twelve

According to the legends, the lair of *El chupacabras* was supposed to be farther up the island, somewhere within the dank boundaries of the El Yunque Rain Forest.

"How far out to El Yunque Mountain?" Krysty asked, shielding her eyes and straining to see farther ahead on the road.

"From San Juan? Thirty miles or so. The road is still good in most places with the right transportation, and travel by day is relatively safe from attack," Jorge noted.

"Attack by whom?" J.B. asked.

Jorge looked at him as if he were dim-witted. "The *chupacabras,* of course. No sane man can be found out in the open once the sun goes down."

"Thirty miles is a long way to walk," Ryan stated. "Take at least two days' travel time on foot."

"Makes my feet hurt just to think about it," Dean added.

"Well, I'm sure as hell not walking all the way out to El Yunque," Luis muttered, obviously not happy to have been taken from the El Morro fortress and assigned to Ryan's group. The sec man was standing in a patch of shade beneath the overhang of an old two-car garage next to the ruin of a house.

"You said the road is still good with the right transportation. You got a wag?" Ryan asked the two Puerto Ricans.

"Better than that, I have two wags," Soto said with a flourish, and the portly man was proved correct when Jorge stepped past Luis and rolled up the garage doors to reveal two well-used, but operational Jeeps. Unlike some of the armored tanklike vehicles Ryan and the others had used for transportation before, these were stripped down little runabouts, both convertibles with roll-up canvas tops in case of inclement weather.

Soto rode with Ryan, Krysty and Dean, and J.B., Jak and Luis joined Jorge. Some dull red jugs of crude gasoline provided full tanks of fuel. For a sixty-mile trip, not much gas would be needed. Progress out of Old San Juan and into the newer part of the city was slow, but soon became easier once they turned onto the open highway going northward.

The heat was heavy, drenching the group in sweat, and a long two hours passed, with stops to move debris from the roadway.

"We're making good time," Soto said, turning to speak to Ryan and Krysty once the odometer revealed they had gone past the twenty-five-mile mark.

No sooner were the words out of his mouth than the steering wheel of the Jeep twisted out of his hands. One of the front tires of the lead transport burst in an explosion, bringing the agile little vehicle to a sliding stop, angled across the road. Luis had been driving the second wag and was able to hit the brakes, stopping quickly enough to avoid a collision.

"What've we got?" J.B. grunted, stepping up to the first Jeep.

"Flat," Soto said, getting up from his knees where he'd been looking at the tire.

"Is there a spare?" Ryan asked.

"No. No spares for either vehicle."

"How about a jack?" Dean asked.

"That we have," Jorge replied. "In the second Jeep, bolted underneath the back axle."

"Then we need to go ahead and take a tire off the wag with the bum leg so we have a backup for the working Jeep," Ryan said, pointing at the back of the first vehicle. "Guess we're going to have to ride double the rest of the way. How long to swap tires, J.B.?"

"Since we're just taking one off and not having to put on new ones, Jak and I can probably have us a spare in ten minutes."

"Do it."

THE SUN WAS PAST the height of noon in the sky, but the temperature was still as hot as could be expected in the Caribbean. Unfortunately, soon after the spare tire had been obtained, a misty rain had begun to fall. The lone Jeep buzzed along on the two lanes of elderly paved blacktop, overcrowded and uncovered to the elements.

Still, even with the rain, a few hours of daylight remained when Ryan tapped Jorge on the shoulder.

"Que?"

"We camp here," Ryan said, using a finger to point at a clearing to the left of the cracked black highway. A frame of a former roadside attraction was at the back of the pull-off area, but whatever message or offering it promised had long vanished to the elements. El Yunque Mountain loomed ahead of the Jeep in the distance. Leaning forward to the driver's side, Ryan added, "Stop the Jeep up there under those trees, J.B., next to where the guardrail ends."

"Right," the Armorer replied as he downshifted and hit the brakes of the sturdy little vehicle, slowing to turn off the pavement and onto the grass. Everyone stepped out of the wag, stretching and circulating blood back through their bodies. All were cramped from the close conditions.

As Ryan did a deep knee bend and was rewarded with the sharp crack of both knees popping, Jorge squatted next to him. Ryan knew from the expression on the muscular Puerto Rican's face the man hadn't cared much for camping so soon. "We should continue while the sun is still up. Night is the *chupacabras*'s friend, Ryan Cawdor."

Not used to having his orders questioned, Ryan felt his temper start to flare, until he got a good look at Jorge's face, open and innocent. The statement hadn't been a challenge, merely a fact. "If so, Jorge, that's the best time to go hunting for them, right?"

The Puerto Rican looked puzzled. "Yes, I suppose, but I'm not sure I like your logic."

"I do," Jak said stepping next to Ryan. "Take battle to them, they make first move."

"If that's the way they want to play it. Either way, we've been traveling all day. We need to get some rest, let our bodies cool off. We've still got a few hours before dark. It's best to grab some sleep and downtime before going into the rain forest any farther."

Jorge slapped at a flying insect that resembled a mosquito. "If you say so. You are the one with experience in such affairs, not I."

"That's right, Jorge. Now get some shut-eye."

THE LIGHT WAS DIM. It was time to move out and into the forest proper.

Ryan had chosen to ignore his own advice, keeping watch over the small party. After an hour or so of trying to sleep while swatting at the swarms of mosquitoes and other winged insects in the heated air, J.B. had done likewise, getting quietly to his feet and joining his comrade.

Neither of them had spoken as the Armorer took up position across from Ryan, enabling each man to watch the other's back as they guarded their resting friends.

After consulting his wristchron, Ryan had walked softly among the others, shaking them gently awake. All had come to alertness slowly, except for Jak, whose warrior senses were ready to go the instant Ryan tapped his shoulder.

Luis had stood, moving more slowly than the others but not noticeably so. When erect, he bent to pick up his weapon and promptly fell forward on his knees, dropping his retrieved long blaster as both hands went frantically to his throat.

Noticing his plight from the corner of her vision, Krysty was at his side first, kneeling as she tried to determine what was wrong. Her strong hands grasped him by the shoulders, trying to stop the frantic spasm creeping through the Puerto Rican's tanned body. A coating of sweat had spread across his skin as if he'd walked through a fine mist.

"Luis? What is it? What's wrong?" the redhead asked, her eyes narrow.

By that time, Soto and the others had joined Krysty and Luis, surrounding the kneeling pair. Soto made a series of clipped inquiries in English, then Spanish. Luis didn't respond to either language. The big man looked at them, panic in his eyes, and tried to speak, but all that came forth was a thick grunting sound from deep within his barrel chest.

"Can't breathe," Luis wheezed, the two words an effort. He tried a third. "Hurts."

"He some kind of epileptic?" Ryan asked suspiciously. "Going to throw a fit?"

"We need to get him down if he is," Krysty said. "I saw Mildred deal with an epileptic once and that's what she said to do."

Then came a shrill shriek, an inhuman sound that

poured forth like water from a pitcher, poured forth in a sonic fury from Luis's entire being. The skin on his face was taut and cherry red as he shrieked again and again. He pulled free of Krysty's hands and fell on his side, the unearthly wailing still coming from his mouth until the sound was cut short and replaced by a bubbling of crimson. Dark, nearly black blood splattered on his shirt and face as he thrashed in the dirt.

"What do we do?" Jorge asked.

"Nothing we can do," Ryan replied.

Dean stood next to his father, watching, an expression of sheer horror on his young face. He'd seen death before, but usually it came from an outside source, not from inside a man's own body.

Luis bent his dying physique, his neck muscles taut as bands of stretched steel. His upper torso arched into a backward U-shape, the spine beneath contorted into a direction never intended by nature. The man's arms twisted and shook, his entire body writhing in a mass of agony before he flopped over on his back. His legs kicked a few times, feet bent out like the graceful arc of a dancer, then his heels drummed a last tempo of pain as he finally died.

At that second, Krysty spotted new movement, like the fin of a shark breaking the surface of the ocean under the front of his sweat-soaked shirt. "There, lover," she shouted, pointing it out to Ryan.

Ryan drew his panga and stepped close, reaching down and slitting open the tight cotton T-shirt. The cloth, damp with sweat and blood, tore easily as he pulled the blade of the panga up and across the fabric, revealing Luis's bare torso.

There were wiggling movements under the dead man's skin, as if something was trying to frantically break out—an angled something, like a broken bone trying to rip free of the skin.

Only there were no bones in the immediate area of the disturbance.

"What the hell is that?" J.B. demanded in a tight voice, his knuckles white as he clutched his well-maintained Uzi, ready to send a barrage of 9 mm bullets into the mystery inside the corpse on the ground before him.

"Don't know offhand," Ryan replied, stepping back and watching the queer undulating movements at a safe distance.

"There's something inside him," Soto murmured, speaking the obvious.

As if in reply, a single oversized mandible two inches long poked through the flesh of Luis's stomach, a shiny black eyetooth all wet and glistening in the dim light as day continued to fade into night.

"Bug," Jak said, a hint of distant disgust in his flat voice. The albino had seen all kinds of insects during his youth in the fetid swamps of Louisiana, all kinds of squirming, crawling, creeping insects, and most of them large and nasty—biting bugs, sucking bugs, flying bugs—the kind where it took far more than a single well-placed stomp to end their scurrying across a kitchen floor.

There was very little blood as the size of the

wound increased in diameter. The cut was jagged, but straightforward, like the release of a zipper as it widened. Some clear stomach fluid and digestive juices spurted up at one point but quickly trickled down to nothingness.

Both cruel black mandibles were free now, along with the insect's small head. Overblown fangs, sickle-shaped like inverted question marks extended from the front of the bug in an almost comical display of exaggeration. Above the quivering mandibles on the shiny black head was a mass of compound eyes. Festooned about the eyes were four horned antennae, quivering in the naked air.

Approximately five inches long and streamlined, the creature continued to eat its way free, poking out the rest of the shiny black carapace and six legs, and coming to a stop on the lifeless form of Luis. Each member of the group had the uncomfortable sensation of being studied, the watchers being watched in return by the insect.

"I know this insect," Soto breathed, his voice a mix of disgust and awe. "They are very rare and unusual. They eat more than your flesh, see, for since they burrow inward, they also have the access—and the hunger—to devour your soul. But no one I know has died from the beetle's kiss in many years."

"Saw one like it once," Ryan replied, as he exchanged a knowing look with Krysty.

In his mind's eye, Ryan summoned up memories of being forced to helplessly watch as Cort Strasser and his underling Kelber prepared to use a similar black beetle as an instrument of torture on a bound and helpless Krysty Wroth, and it wasn't until Ryan agreed to tell Strasser what he wanted to know that the insect had been removed from her bare buttock. Now he saw Krysty shudder, her eyes hypnotically fixed on the gleaming horror.

Deciding there was nothing left worth eating inside Luis, the beetle scurried off the dead man's stomach and into the forest grass with surprising mobility and speed.

Before a single word could be spoken, Jak had responded to the grotesque insect's movement by selecting and throwing one of his lethal leaf-bladed knives. The albino was a lightning-fast blur of motion as he aimed and hurled the knife downward, effectively sending the blade home into the beetle's glistening black shell and through the insect's softer underside.

Red blood spurted out as if from an overripe piece of fruit, and the insect's twin mandibles clawed at the air like miniature ebony hands, reaching up and wiggling for the sky before becoming as still as the lifeless body of its victim.

"Hate bugs," Jak said flatly as he stepped forward to retrieve the knife. He raised and lowered a boot heel and twisted his foot to crush the remains of the insect into the grassy soil of the forest floor. "Hate 'em."

Maryland, Virginia,
December 28, 2000

DOC TANNER DIDN'T BOTHER to look up when the smooth metal alloy and Plexiglas door of his one-room holding facility slid sideways into the far wall. His attentions were on the thick hardcover book he was holding, one of more than two dozen family biographies he'd read recently about the famed Kennedy dynasty.

A tragic fall of three, beginning with the president and ruler of Camelot, the one-and-only lusty Jack; then his second-in-command with his own eyes on the prize, the compassionate Bobby; and finally ending with the lesser of the trinity, poor, sad Teddy, who'd fallen prey to circumstance and timing and seen the dynasty crumble to dust on the cold banks of the Chappaquiddick.

The floor of the small quarters was covered with stacks of books and magazines. Overhead a color television set was on, but Doc had the sound turned down, finding himself quickly bored with the images. A fantastic invention, he had to admit, but as for the choice and quality of what was being broadcast, a lot was left to be desired.

Aware of another's presence in the crowded room, and also aware that whoever it was didn't intend on leaving, Doc decided to speak.

"More questions?" he barked, still not gracing his visitor with a glance. "Perhaps I shall be allowed to clamber half naked upon your wondrous treadmill and run myself ragged for the amusement of your note-taking associates. Better still, perhaps we shall test my psychic abilities. Tell me, what do you see in your mind? A circle? A square? A picture of a cross? Your own rancid smiling face?"

"No, none of that."

Doc lifted a bony arm. "Or do you require yet another pint or three of my bodily fluids?"

"Why take a pint when we have drained the entire store?" Welles replied silkily.

The tone of Welles's voice sliced through Doc's concentration and he looked up from his volume on the trio of Kennedy brothers. The fat man's three chins were jiggling as Welles struggled to contain his laughter.

"What, pray tell, does *that* mean?"

"Tanner, you are, without a doubt, the biggest, most puckered asshole I've ever had the fortune to encounter. Stubborn, arrogant, prideful, and for all the wrong reasons. You get on my nerves like no one else, not even my first wife nor my sainted mother, damn her immortal soul may she rot in peace."

"Am I to take comfort in your compliments?" Doc retorted.

"I had the option of having you terminated, you know. A simple order. My decision. No one cares, really, about you anymore. You are no longer special. And while I know it makes me sound like the villain in a third-rate television melodrama, I have the extreme honor of telling you your usefulness to Operation Chronos and the Totality Concept has ceased."

Doc drew himself up on the bed and set his jaw firmly. "So. The day has come. I have never feared death.''

''So you say. So you've said. Got some video interviews with you saying just that very phrase, same ramrod posture, same twitch in your jaw. I spent a sleepless night debating my next move, imagining the joy I'd take from watching your death throes—from a purely scientific view, of course. Then, I decided death was too good for you, Tanner. Much...too...good.''

Doc decided he didn't like the slant this conversation was taking.

''Make your boasts or do as you will, Welles. Or get out.'' Doc turned his attention away and opened his book to the page he'd been reading before. The words of the paragraph were meaningless now, and he read the same sentence over and over without retaining any of the content. His eyes were on the page, but his ears and his mind were on Welles.

The administrator hadn't paid any heed to his patient's request to leave. He was just getting wound up as he continued to speak, his tone even and modulated. The only hint of his rising excitement was a darkening of his facial coloration.

''You weren't a team player, oh, no, not the mighty Dr. Tanner, owner of two doctoral degrees. No, most men would bow to their betters, acknowledge their masters and beg for whatever crumbs of glory they might be content to pass along. No, not you, bleating about your sainted wife and bratty children. We gave you an out, would have allowed you to return and you spit in our faces, all smug in your limited command of backward faith and knowledge of right and wrong,'' Welles said.

''You made your proposition for your masters, Welles,'' Doc said softly, turning in the cot and placing his feet on the cell floor, and then resting his hands on his knees. ''As their faithful lapdog, I know you were disappointed when I refused your most...generous offer. A man of character would have known then I was not to be blackmailed or bought, and as such, should have been returned to my proper place in time. For time, you see, has checks and balances, and by plucking me away from my particular slot, you have upset the apple cart. My wife has endured a life without a husband, and my children have endured a life without a father.''

''Your children,'' Welles said with a snicker. ''Life without Daddy.''

Doc gave his keeper a scathing look of contempt. ''That is correct.''

Welles continued to chuckle. ''Your children are dead, you pathetic fool.''

Tanner wasn't biting. ''Dead now, of course, unless they were incredibly long-lived, and while the Tanners are a hearty bunch, I harbor no illusions of a hundred-and-ten-year-old Jolyon being wheeled through the door to say hello to his father.''

''No, no, not dead now—dead *then,*'' Welles said, his voice starting to rise in tone and volume. ''They died within seconds after you were trawled! While you were in flux, held within the temporal containment field, random fluctuations of wild energy escaped, Tanner, escaped crackling and gibbering and killing. Any living tissue it came in contact with resulted in violent cellular disruption.''

''You, sir, are a liar,'' Doc said, all pomposity gone from his voice as he struggled to maintain his composure.

''And you, sir, are a trusting, mewling fool. We didn't lie to you. We told you your children were long dead and the Tanner bloodline had stopped with their demises. All true. What we neglected to inform you of were some of the details.''

Then, Doc was on him, his hands around Welles's portly throat. In his brain, which was colored now with a killing haze of red, Doc saw his oppressor's head pop off his neck like a cork from a bottle of champagne and a geyser of blood spurt into the air.

Such a scene remained imaginary, however, locked inside Doc's mind, for one second after his lunge for Welles, his cell door slid back a second time and a knot of grim-faced security men came rushing into the room, peeling the whip-lean man off his much heavier foe.

''You lie! You are playing mind games, punishing me for my noncompliance! I will not have it! Send me back!'' Doc screamed, spittle flying in a spray from his lips.

''Too late,'' Welles gasped as he tried to raise himself from where he'd sprawled across a mound of books and papers. ''Too late!''

"I—I accept your damnable agreement. Return me to my family!"

"Too late for deals, too late. We no longer need you, Tanner. You have outlived your usefulness by, oh, say a hundred years!" And then Welles unleashed an almost feminine cackle of laughter.

"I could help you! I could be of assistance," Doc wailed as he was carried out into the hallway.

Welles made a show out of considering this. "Perhaps. That was our intention, but now we're not so sure it would be the correct action to take. Such an act might create a paradox, or it might not. Right now, my good man, I don't care. So, buck up and allow me to give you my Christmas present."

Welles had chosen four of the burliest men he could find to accompany him to Doc Tanner's holding cell. His estimate was still off by two, since it ended up taking six of the security men to effectively pry their charge out of the room and into the waiting elevator, where Doc screamed, bit, stomped and yelled.

Welles had debated the advice of sedating Tanner, but finally decided it would serve his purposes to have his test subject awake for the process.

As for what his purposes might be...? Welles wasn't sure of that, either. He did know he wanted Tanner to suffer, and a chron-temp jump into the future seemed to be the perfect way of assuring the man's agony.

Welles took the entire Doc Tanner affair quite personally. He'd been on the committee to select Tanner, drawn up the plan to trawl him forward, push him back, overseen the man's acclimation into Operation Chronos, and now, after the ungrateful bastard had rejected their offer, and on top of rejection had tried repeatedly to escape, Herman Welles was going to take immense pleasure in showing the skinny shit the door.

In other words, he had no desire to see his most famous failure make his last journey unconscious.

And then, they were out of the elevator, and moving at a fast jog down the corridor, Doc caterwauling the entire way. After entering the triple numerals into the entry keypad, Welles led the way into the massive chron-jump chamber control room itself, and past the consoles, past the monitors, past the banks of flashing lights, past the eyes of the watchers, all of them dressed in white lab coats. A few personnel turned away, distaste on their bespectacled faces, but most watched the scene unplay before their eyes with a mix of concern and horror.

Except for a figure lurking at the edges of the outer control room that Doc didn't immediately recognize—a lean man, tall, yet solid and imposing, and with the same easy assurance and carriage as had been Doc's in better days. Long silver hair was combed back from his forehead, giving his narrow face a severe look. His eyes were unreadable, hidden by the shadows and by a pair of imposing silver eyebrows.

The man appeared to be glacier cool as he stood apart from the others, alike in form only through the long white lab coat he wore. A raspberry-purple necktie was tied at his neck in a proper Windsor knot.

All of them save this new figure knew Doc personally. Some had engaged him in debate, seeking the viewpoint of a living anachronism in their midst, and none took pleasure in seeing him screaming at the top of his lungs while being brutally manhandled.

The only person enjoying the spectacle was Welles. In a display that would later bring him reprimands, the fat man was enjoying himself far too much. Even while serving as point man of the hour, he was eagerly awaiting the chance later to review his performance on the security tape being made on the redoubt's elaborate security system.

The group was now within the anteroom that separated the mat-trans chamber from the central control area. The room was small, only ten feet by twenty, keeping the guards pressed close to the wiggling Doc. Welles stayed at the back, wishing he was taller in order to truly oversee the scene as it unfolded.

The unadorned white bodysuit that had been assigned as his regular attire after the second escape attempt was ripped from Doc's struggling form, leaving him naked as a newborn. The fingernails of one of the security guards raked his arm, drawing blood as the suit was torn away. Doc felt his genitals shrivel up, trying to stay as close to his body as possible. Being nude just made the fate he was to suffer even more humiliating.

There was no gentleness taken with the prisoner.

After the removal of his suit, he was lifted high by the six security men and thrown bodily into the matter-transfer room, where he came crashing down painfully on his left shoulder. Doc landed on one of the steel floor disks, but also felt the jab of some object poking into his body.

As he rolled over to his side, he found beneath his aching form two round spheroids, test objects used in previous jump experiments. Doc reached across the disk and picked up the perfectly metal balls from the tiled floor.

"Didn't want to send you off without what you came in with," Welles called out from the open armaglass chamber door, then threw in a double armload of clothing—a black frock coat, a pair of tan britches, two thigh-high black boots and other pieces of the apparel Doc had been wearing when trawled two years earlier. Apparently the clothing had been kept in storage after being studied by researchers of the project.

The bundle hit the floor and scattered lifelessly next to the aching Doc, and he spied a button on the sleeve of the shirt he remembered Emily had sewed on a lifetime ago.

"No," he whispered, even as the air began to thicken and his brain began to shut down. Struggling to his feet, the skinny man staggered to the chamber door like a drunken mantis and used the metal sphere he held in his right hand to begin pounding on the unbreakable surface of the armaglass. Again and again, he raised his arm and brought it smashing down.

"Wasting his strength on such a futile show," the silver-haired man with the raspberry-purple necktie calmly observed from control, watching Doc on a wall monitor, the picture beamed from an interior security camera hidden inside the armaglass chamber. "He should sit down and compose himself or he'll never survive the trawl."

"I don't think Dr. Welles wants him to survive, Mr. Burr," Chan said from a nearby station, his own prior conflict with Doc now put aside as he, too, stood back and watched what was about to occur. Burr shot Chan a withering glare, and the technician fell silent, choosing to no longer peer at the live video monitor. Instead, he sat and focused on the readings coming in on his computer screen.

The tragedy of the biography he'd been reading scant moments ago still fresh in his mind, Doc cursed them from within the armaglass prison. "By the three Kennedys, a plague upon your houses, you white-coated malcontents!" he bellowed, swinging the metal balls with all of his fading strength even as the mists fell upon him, swirling into his brain.

"Jackbooted thugs! Blind thoughtless cretins! Gibbering jackanapes! Rapists of family members and small children!" recited the agonized voice from behind the armaglass, even as the lights within raced up to an unbearable brightness.

As Chan had before, the other people in the gateway control room without safety goggles were forced to turn their heads and look away from the video monitors. Many of them had already done so when Doc's fate became inescapable and apparent.

An unworldly humming like a thousand alien hives raced through the chamber, the anteroom and into the control area of the mat-trans gateway. Just when the sound became almost unbearable, Dr. Theophilus Algernon Tanner was gone in a puff of smoke, vanished in the fog. He was a missing person once more, taken away a second time as if he had never existed.

Welles strode to the armaglass chamber through the security of the adjoining anteroom and wrenched open the heavy gateway door. Inside, there was nothing left except the nostril-tickling stench of burnt ozone. The heat from the mat-trans unit filtered out and wafted across his body, sending fresh trickles of sweat running down from his armpits.

"He's away, Director Welles," a technician informed him over the intercom system, her eyes scanning the readouts on the oversized computer console on her observation station. "We're showing a ninety-eight-percent probability of a successful matter transfer via temporal annex, but have no way of tracking or knowing the exact destination."

"Do you think he made it, sir?" Chan asked, his reedy voice coming over the intercom.

"I don't care whether he arrives in one piece or not," Welles replied, wiping the tail of his jacket over his perspiring face as he stepped down from the elevated gateway chamber and into the anteroom. His skin color had taken on an unhealthy purple hue, and his small eyes were crinkled and leering, a crazed look topped by a manic toothy smile.

"So, what was the point, sir?"

"Peace of mind. And I'll tell you this much. I hope Tanner made it. Hell, yes, I hope he made it, the arrogant son of a bitch, and wherever he is, I hope he's choking on whatever future hell he's trapped in now."

Chapter Thirteen

Always the master of understatement, Jak delivered the most precise and telling description of what the group of friends were now facing in the darkness of the rain forest.

"Caves."

The albino always used a minimum of words, even fewer than the usually closemouthed J. B. Dix. Sometimes, such abbreviated ways of speaking made conversation with Jak a frustratingly one-sided experience. Other times, the tautness of his verbal expression summed up a situation so perfectly that the florid Doc and his love of language could never conceive of competing.

This was one of those occasions.

"Yep," J.B. added. "And lots of them."

Ryan didn't bother to restate the obvious. The impressive face of the rock wall was a honeycomb of cavern entrances, dark womblike mouths opened wide and indicating the presence of random holes of varying sizes. J.B. dug in one of the many pockets lining his leather jacket and took out a small flashlight he'd "liberated" from Jamaisvous's supply room back in El Morro.

Thumbing the switch, he used the beam to illuminate the wall and the caverns, darting across the dark openings, spotlighting in a flickering white circle the varied entryways. J.B. moved the light over the holes one by one for the group's visual perusal.

"Plenty to choose from," Krysty said. "Take your pick."

"Too many," Dean added disgustedly.

Soto coughed, and cleared his throat. "I am afraid all of El Yunque is reported to be honeycombed with such caverns. Some are easily seen like these, others less so. This area is a good place to start, since there are existing tunnels already in place that were used by the local Indians for hiding dating all the way back to the time of Christopher Columbus."

"Who?" Jak asked.

"A white man. He came to Puerto Rico like most others—to claim land in the name of his Spanish masters," Jorge explained.

"Typical white male power fantasy," Krysty added. Ryan shot her a look and she shrugged. "That's what Mildred always says."

Once they had arrived within the section of Puerto Rico considered to be the rain forest, Jorge had taken time out to explain a bit about the area to the outlanders. The forest was named for the 3,496-foot-high mountain looming above and in front of them, El Yunque. The forest itself was a rough 28,000-acre stretch of jungles, hills, streams and waterfalls. Two hundred species of trees were to be found inside this dank, overgrown area, and El Yunque was almost always wet from the thunderstorms that sprung up two or three times a day to violently drench all within.

Such abundant rainfall, when combined with the rich soil, was responsible for giving the area lush and exotic greenery.

"Most of the tunnels only go down and back for about twenty feet before they dead-end," Jorge continued, as he hitched up his gun belt. "A few of the passages intertwine and connect with others. Those are the ones where it is suspected *El chupacabras* make their lair. The legends state they breed here, where there are few people and no interference."

"Make sense," Jak said. "Stay where nobody comes."

"So the question is, why have they been heading out to San Juan?" Ryan mused, still not fully sure of the how or why of the queer-looking muties and their hunting habits. "You'd think there would be enough wild game here. It's a bastard long trip to the city."

"*El chupacabras* are hunters," Jorge noted. "They have probably expanded their area to find new prey. Besides, a distance of thirty miles is nothing to these creatures. They move quickly, and some of them possess the ability to fly, although only for short distances."

"Sure wish you two had some idea of what we're going to find," J.B. said sourly to the Puerto Ricans. "This could be a wasted trip."

"No, Señor Dix. All the evidence we have collected from the old tales, along with what we researched for ourselves, points to this site as the *chupacabras*'s lair.''

''Well, then, we'd better get looking,'' Ryan said, stepping forward and rubbing the back of his neck. Another one of the sudden rainfalls that had soaked them all was starting to pick up in intensity, and he wanted to go ahead inside and get out of the rain. ''Guess we'll start at the far left and work our way down.''

''Do you want to split up?'' Soto asked, his worried expression revealing his own doubts of such a tactic.

''No,'' Ryan said, his eye following the path revealed by J.B.'s flash. ''We're in no hurry. Stick together—there's safety in numbers. We check out the caves one by one.''

The band of travelers fell into a defensive stance before entering the first of the many black openings. A routine was quickly established. Ryan took the point. Soto, Jorge, Krysty, Dean, Jak and J.B made up the rest of the search party. Go in one cave, follow it back, check on any side tunnels, turn and exit.

Soon, an hour passed. Then another. The similarity of the rocky clefts' interiors began to press on their minds, making each of the caverns interchangeable. When the second hour passed, Ryan's wristchron gave off a soft beep, and he called for a break so they could clear their heads.

The one-eyed man stepped over and sat on an outcropping next to Krysty. ''Hey,'' he said to her, running a hand down the back of her soaked red hair.

"Hey yourself."

"How you feeling?"

"As good as you."

"That lousy, huh?"

"'Fraid so. At least the rain stopped for a little while."

"You picking up anything out of the ordinary? Any echoes of the earth power in those caves?"

Krysty got a focused look in her vibrant green eyes, as if she were peering down a hallway in another place far, far away. "Nothing in particular," she finally answered. "But there is something old and dark and ancient about this place. Like these caves are older than man, and will still be here long after we've taken the last train West. Know what I mean?"

"Right. Place gives you the creeps."

The redhead smiled. "And Doc's supposed to be the one with the vocabulary."

Twenty minutes later, the pattern began anew. Soto suggested going back a few caves, since the last ones checked might have had a hastier scrutiny than earlier ones when they started. His own weariness now beaten back, Ryan agreed. If the others felt as refreshed as he now did after a quick break from stumbling around in the darkened caverns, something might very well have been missed through fatigue.

It was inside one of the caves being searched for a second time that Ryan spotted something he hadn't during the first go-round. "Wait a minute," Ryan said. "J.B., get that flash back over here on the wall. To the right."

J.B. did as his comrade asked, raising the illuminating beam and playing it across the back stone wall, seeking out whatever had alerted Ryan. He patiently moved the beam and revealed a familiar-looking steel doorway framed in dull silver vanadium steel. On the right side of the frame was a keypad display.

The doorway imbedded in the rock wall was open, the vanadium-alloy door itself recessed into the narrow ceiling slot of the reinforced support frame. The familiar and standard entry code numerals were still glowing patiently on the tiny screen, unwiped by the last person who had exited from what was clearly another redoubt.

"Black dust," J.B. breathed, his amazement echoed by the use of the arcane epithet he used only in times of complete and utter surprise.

"Gaia's heart," Krysty added, equally surprised.

"Dad, is that what I think it is?" Dean breathed, his eyes squinting at the door.

Ryan nodded. "Answers one question that's been bothering me about the timing of Jamaisvous's appearance in San Juan with the return of *El chupacabras*. The goatsucker must've come out of the redoubt."

"JAMAISVOUS KNEW? He knew!" Krysty breathed, her crimson hair tightening about her face and neck in an unconscious mirroring of her inner turmoil. "This explains everything."

"I know," Ryan replied, placing a hand on her shoulder. "And we left Doc and Mildred back at the fortress alone with him."

"Millie's a big girl," J.B. said, his face a tense mask. "She can take care of herself."

"It's not Mildred I'm worried about. She's been leery of Jamaisvous since the beginning. My concern is for Doc. He'd do anything to get back..." and Ryan trailed off, not wanting to raise questions or suspicions in their Puerto Rican companions about Doc's origins. "To his own place. Where he's originally from. He has a wife, kids."

"Sure," Soto said. "I understand."

Jorge took up the conversation. "This...'redoubt' I believe you called it. You honestly think *El chupacabras* live inside?"

"Yeah. Like I said before, I believe the bastards were cobbled together by some mad doctor working on some sick project," Ryan replied. "At the very least, they must have lived in here. Don't know if any are left or not."

"Only one way to find out."

When the keyed-in code admitted them, Ryan stepped past the doorway. The layout inside was functional and to the point: stripped barracks, with skeletal bed frames and empty footlockers; a closed-out kitchen, the cabinets barren of foodstuff, utensils, anything not nailed down. Long-lived autocircuits clicked into life, causing the overhead strip light panels to flare as the group made its way down the main level to the single elevator car at the end of the hallway. The heavy steel entry door to a stairwell left of the elevator was crumpled as if hit by a massive battering ram. The door had been hurled across the hall, and lay ripped from its mounting hinges.

"Somebody wanted out in a powerful hurry," J.B. said, running a hand along the twisted metal. The front of the ruined door that had been on the inside of the stairs was covered in jagged scratches, some light and quick like the tracks of a domestic tabby, others deep and long like the aftermath of an enraged Bengal tiger.

"Or something. See if you can fetch us a ride, Dean," Ryan said, jerking a thumb toward the elevator.

"Right, Dad," Dean responded, stepping past J.B. and the stairwell door to the front of the elevator. He pushed the call button, but the plastic activation disk mounted in the steel plate to the right of the elevator doors remained dim. He tried it a second and third time, pressing with all of his might, and still received no satisfaction.

"Elevator's out," he announced. "Must be busted."

"Not like elevators," Jak said. "Make me nervous."

Memories of previous elevator escapades went through Ryan's mind, including one precarious escape from a stalled car that had hung between floors, suspended over nothingness. They'd been able to exit via the ceiling hatch, but then were faced with a lengthy climb up an emergency shaft ladder, after which the only exit to the top floor was guarded by snipers.

"I can't say I care much for elevators, either, Jak. Jamaisvous said there were power problems here with the nuke gen," Ryan replied. "May be why the elevator isn't working. No choice in the matter—I guess we walk. I'll take the point."

Then a weight fell on Ryan's shoulders. He felt long crooked fingers try to grab on to his face, snaking claws toward his nostrils, his mouth, even a small hooked claw that tried to insinuate itself into the empty socket behind the tooled leather of his eye patch. Hot breath blasted on his neck like an open flame, and visions of vampires skittered through his brain.

Ryan didn't frighten easily, but the cold sweat of fear involuntarily popped out on his brow. Dropping his blaster, he reached up with both hands to snatch the animal who'd fallen on top of him. His gloved fingers found purchase on a series of quill-like appendages sticking out of his attacker, and he used them to lift and hurl the beast to the floor. Two of the razor-sharp quills cut through the leather of his gloves and into his fingers and palms, but Ryan ignored the bite of pain to rid himself of the animal.

Landing upright, the creature flapped a pair of wiry arms and skittered across the floor, half running and half hopping with a seeming clumsy agility. And speed. A pair of powerful hind legs assisted in the quick, rapid motions the creature was making as it scurried away.

Like many of the other mutations Ryan had glimpsed or come face-to-face with in the Deathlands, this one possessed a pair of glowing red eyes, and a softly hissing mouth filled with sharply pointed teeth. Pupils of a pale yellow-green were slitted dots within the centers of the red.

The drawing Soto had shown him back in the café hadn't begun to illustrate just how ugly and frightening *El chupacabras* truly was. The beast's head was oval, with a strong lower jaw. Small holes served as a nose, and, like stickies, the mutie had no ears. Two small arms ended in three-fingered clawed hands. The powerful hind legs also had three claws, and Ryan took note of the bat wings under the creature's arms, much wider and sturdier-looking than in the illustration.

"El Chupacabras!" Soto gasped, his round face flushed with excitement.

Jak's Colt boomed twice, both slugs catching the creature high in the chest, and while the force from the shots drove the *chupacabras* back for a second or two, it still kept coming, silently, eerily, with eyes of glowing crimson lit by the darkest of inner fires.

Dean chose to unleash his own firepower, drawing his Browning Hi-Power and cocking and firing the blaster in a single fluid motion. The round was useless for any kind of long-range shooting, but at a mere twenty feet from the target, the payload the

Browning delivered on impact was utterly devastating.

When the bullet hit the freakish mutie, it struck with pile-driver force. The *chupacabras*'s head was obliterated in a cloud of wet grue and bone, leaving behind a stump of a neck that spouted pinkish blood, even as the body continued to be propelled forward by sheer momentum.

"Thing runs 'round like chicken with head cut off," Jak noted.

"Got news for you, Jak. This sure as hell ain't no chicken," J.B. retorted as he kicked out with a booted foot and halted the now-headless creature's charge.

"I didn't expect them to be so tiny," Krysty said as she eyed the dead mutie.

"What's the deal, Soto?" Ryan asked. "That little thing couldn't have been over two feet tall. You mean to tell me the entire island's been hiding in fear of *that?*"

"No, you misunderstand, Ryan Cawdor. This *chupacabras* is a mere child, a baby."

"Oh."

"You're bleeding, lover," Krysty said, running her hand along one of Ryan's stubbled cheeks and wiping away a red smear. "Claw must've got you on the way down."

Ryan pulled off one of his tight-fitting black gloves, revealing additional superficial cuts on the top and heel of his left hand.

''Spines got me, too,'' he said. ''Who's carrying the first aid and playing medic this trip?''

''Me,'' Jak said, reaching back into the pack slung over one shoulder. The albino removed a tightly wound bundle of cotton gauze and a roll of white adhesive tape.

''These goatsuckers—any poisons or toxins in the spines?'' Ryan asked, wincing as Jak sprayed a stream of hissing antiseptic from a small med can onto his exposed hand.

''Hope not,'' Soto replied, kneeling at the corpse, using the muzzle of his long blaster to poke at the creature's exposed underbelly.

''You're a lot of help,'' Krysty snorted to the smaller Hispanic man.

''I answer true, girl. I don't think the spines are poison, but I don't know for sure. I never tried to find out, if you know what I mean.''

''You test subject, Ryan,'' Jak said, grinning, showing off sharp-looking teeth. ''How you feel?''

''Felt better,'' Ryan replied as the gauze was wrapped around his hand. ''Felt a lot worse. Don't feel sick or poisoned.''

''Looks like Jak has the makings of a decent field medic,'' J.B. noted, glancing at the albino's handiwork on Ryan's injuries. ''If Millie doesn't watch out, she'll be out of a job.''

''Tough for you,'' Jak replied. ''Not share your bed.''

Dean snorted and laughed, but didn't turn. He remained alert, his Browning Hi-Power cocked and ready to shoot if more firepower was needed.

Ryan held a hunk of the remaining gauze to his bleeding face. Jak had offered to attach a pad with some of the white adhesive tape, but Ryan told him no. The bleeding was already starting to ease.

"All right. Let's go on down," Ryan said.

Deathlands, 2095

DOC TANNER CAME to his senses in the middle of what he believed to be the worst fog he'd ever encountered in his life. And how long was that life? Thirty years or a hundred years? An unruly mass of days and decades and he neither cared to nor could he keep count. He was flat on his stomach in the dirt, now in a world whose floor had been jerked out from beneath his feet.

Somehow, he'd managed to gather up his clothing and dress himself, but having lost track of time long ago, he had no real concept how long he'd been stumbling down the treacherous mountain path. Chunks of his conscious mind, along with his immediate short-term memory, were missing, as if sliced away by a butcher's blade and discarded in some charnel pit.

Even worse, there were a few times he knew for certain, or at least, as certain as he could be in his addled state, that he'd blacked out while trying to stagger along his chosen path in the damp mist.

The last memory he could pull up from his brain

was that of Emily. In the memory, the hour was early, perhaps seven in the morning. He'd dined on poached eggs, crisp bacon and day-old bread recovered from the previous night's meal that had been toasted to disguise its origins. He and Emily were standing at the front door of his home, and she was nagging at him in a pleasant tone to not be late, as they were expecting her parents for supper.

Emily was still in her nightclothes, covered by a filmy pink robe for modesty's sake. However, for some reason, the robe wasn't tied around her middle—her more than ample middle. The belt wasn't long enough, he supposed, since her frame was normally so petite. In fact, blessed Emily was getting quite the gut on her, but Doc was so happy he didn't care.

She gave him a kiss on the cheek and he stepped through the front door of the apartment. And everything appeared normal, except he didn't recall Emily being so overweight.

"By the Three Kennedys!" he said aloud. "Emily was pregnant!"

Pregnant with their first child? Their second? Doc had no clue.

The apartment...they hadn't lived there in how many years? Before Rachel was born, yes! That much he was sure of, and when her young face appeared in his mind's eye, Doc felt an almost inconsolable, unbearable tidal wave of wrenching pain and loss inundate his entire being.

All around him, the fog was growing heavier, but

Doc didn't notice in the slightest, since he was weighted down by an even heavier fog from within. Night and day and another night passed as he stumbled along, sleeping when he was tired, hungry beyond imagining, but he never seemed to black out for very long.

He was found facedown on the broken tarmac of an old highway, his skull coming close to being crushed under the wheel of a small armored transport. The occupants believed the long-haired elder to be a drunk from the nearby town of Mocsin, but none of them could identify the face. The direction he'd apparently been traveling also gave them pause. Behind Doc was nothing but the mysterious Black Hills, a mystery which those above them in the chain of command had expressed an interest in.

Doc was kept alive. There were men who would want to talk to him.

He awakened in a toilet, his long legs bent and hanging over the side of a bathtub. After struggling to gain his footing, Doc looked in the cracked mirror hanging crookedly over the filthy washbasin. He squinted once, twice and closed his pale blue eyes to refocus before taking another peek.

"What carnival jest is this?" he wondered aloud to himself, for what was looking mutely back at him wasn't *his* face, no, couldn't be his face, since he knew damn well the visage he was seeing was that of his own sainted father.

"No more," he said in a quavering voice, watching his chapped lips move in the mirror's reflection.

"Gods of the universe, I can take no more of this. How many more pounds of flesh can I give before nothing is left but barren white bone? Accursed speculum, why do you show me such a terrible sight?"

What stared back at him from the mirror was his transformed image, skull-like and hollow-eyed, topped off by the silver-gray hair he knew was his own, matted with dirt and sweat.

The hair remained healthy, but the rest of him appeared to have aged more than thirty years. He appeared to be a man of sixty-plus years.

At least thirty years, three decades of time, had been foisted upon his personage, and he remembered none of it.

Doc smashed his forehead into the reflection while starting to incoherently wail at a fever pitch. A wordless jumble of sounds bubbled out, interrupted only when he had to stop and suck another breath of air into his chest. He banged his head again and again, feeling the mirrored glass crack under the assault and cut his forehead. Blood began to run down his bushy silver eyebrows and the left side of his long nose.

Doc looked at the man in the mirror and cackled insanely, until his stomach began to violently cramp, driving him to a crouch. Feeling as though he were about to become violently, messily sick, Doc dropped his trousers and sat on the filthy toilet seat, thankful even in his current state of near-insanity that he hadn't soiled himself.

The metal door to the small bath chamber swung open partway, blocked from fully opening by Doc's bony knees. Doc remained hunched over the porcelain toilet, his pants around his ankles and his bare, bony knees sticking pointedly up. His stomach was gurgling, still expunging itself of the vile water he'd drank from a ditch many hours before.

The bearded sec man threw in a dingy towel many washings removed from its original color of orange, and spit out a series of orders to the captured man.

"Use the tub behind the plastic curtain. Water works. Hope you like cold. When you're clean enough, you moldy old fruit, the baron wants to talk to you."

"Baron?" Doc whispered. Such a form of address was medieval to his ears and reeked of the past, not the future land to which Welles had so arrogantly claimed he was sending him. In a quick second, Doc's mind lost the patina of confusion he had feared to be permanent and began clicking on all eight cylinders again.

Doc wondered whether he could have been shunted back in time instead of pushed forward. The prospect was grimly appealing, until he considered the appearance and manufacture of the bathroom in which he was now sitting. While it didn't look any more modern than the small bath he'd been allowed to use during his stays in Dulce and Chicago, it was certainly in much poorer condition.

Leaning out from his seat, Doc pulled back the dank, slimy shower curtain and looked at the condition of the bathtub. The interior was nearly black. A vapid green millipede as long as his forearm crawled back and forth, all one thousand of the ghastly insect's legs trying vainly to find purchase on the walls of the enamel to crawl out to safety.

Although repulsed by the sight, Doc felt a certain kinship with the many-legged insect. He, too, was trapped, and scrambling for a way out, but the walls surrounding him were as smooth as pure spun glass, and in his present condition, just as insurmountable.

CHOOSING TO WASH his face and upper body in the sink, Doc had removed the layer of road dust he'd picked up on the trail and was actually feeling half-way human again. A bar of soap would have added to the ease of bathing, but none had been offered and he didn't dare ask. The same gray-bearded man had come to fetch him, making many unfunny comments about the way Doc had "smelled up the shitter" to the amusement of the other fellow who served as his backup.

Together, the three had left the bath and entered a long hallway. Once upon a time, Doc noticed, the far side of the hall had been made of nothing but inviting panes of glass, offering a view of the world outside. Now, the glass appeared to have been mostly broken out, and huge slabs of plywood and scavenged metal nailed in place to contain the walkway. One piece of metal used was cut in the shape of a colossal red circle, and a white star rested in the center. The letter "T" was in the middle of the star. The color red and the star itself made Doc wonder for a brief moment if he'd ended up inside the borders of Asia, or one of the Soviet states, but no Russian was spoken and the design of the hall furnishings ended this line of thought, as well as seeing the sign's mate farther along, and this time the word "Texaco" could be easily read.

"Texas," Doc mused. "Funny. I have been through Houston, and it does not feel hot enough for Texas."

The comment earned him two things: a snarled "Shut your mouth," from the bearded man appointed to be his keeper and a whack to the back of the head from the butt of the rifle held by the second guard. While the blow wasn't hard enough to send Doc crashing into unconsciousness, or even send him sprawling to his knees, it was ample and unexpected enough to shake his brain loose from the coherent mooring he'd reestablished and start him careening from topic to topic once more inside his damaged mind.

After the long walk down the side hall, Doc and his captors entered through a large double door into a great room, a high-ceilinged monstrosity. The room was empty, barren of any decoration or furniture. Industrial carpet of olive green had been lain upon the floor, muffling the sounds of footsteps. A second carpet, this one of royal red, stretched across the expanse like a lazy tongue that led to a mouth of equally red draperies, slightly parted. Soft, flickering light was escaping from the gap left in the massive curtains, which helped cover the worn condition of the carpets underfoot, royal red and olive green, equally ratty and dirty.

A figure behind the curtains beckoned. For a moment, Doc's addled mind proposed the possibility he was but an actor, waiting to go on and deliver his latest performance. Trying to remember his lines, he stopped walking for a second, and struck a pose, one hand on a hip and the other one extended, palm up, just so.

Doc cleared his throat.

"You got a problem?" his keeper asked.

"'All the world's a stage, and all the men and women merely players. They have their exits and their entrances; and one man in his time plays many parts, his acts being seven ages,'" Doc boomed.

The new figure stepped out from behind the curtains and took in the sight of Doc and the waiting guards. He smiled and it was phony and insincere, a cold-hearted smile belonging to a cold-hearted man. It was a smile with no joy, a cruel twisting of the lips, like a pasted-on appliqué. A dead smile.

"Greetings, friend. And who might you be?" Doc said brightly. "I hope I have not missed my cue."

"My name is Strasser. Cort Strasser," the man said, silky smooth. "And you haven't missed a damned thing, old man. In fact, you're just in time for the festivities."

"Fancy that!" Doc said.

"Fancy that," Strasser echoed.

Making an "after you" motion and holding out a hand to the gap in the curtains, Strasser stepped aside, the smile across his lower face frozen in place as he waited for Doc to move. As the older gent passed, squinting to see as he entered the dimly lit room beyond the curtains, Strasser cuffed him across the back of the head, causing Doc to stumble forward. He managed to break his fall with his hands, but still landed painfully on his knees, which seemed to have developed all-new aches and pains after his latest mat-trans chron jump.

"I'll have none of that crazy babbling, old man, stuff about entrances and exits. Keep it up and the only exit you'll be taking is the slow train West, get me? I've already heard enough of your wailing and crying. If you try and embarrass me in front of the baron, I'll chill you on the spot, one slug right to the head, okay?" Strasser grated from behind.

"Take heart that I meant no embarrassment. The words, sir, the words I spoke came from the Bard. And William Shakespeare, for all of his faults, was far from crazy."

"Do I look like I give a good long happy shit?" Strasser demanded, his face visibly angry even in the subdued lighting of the wide room.

"I must confess, no, you do not," Doc answered truthfully.

"So you aren't a total half-wit."

Doc didn't reply as he carefully looked around the room in which he knelt. The lighting was as bad as what passed for illumination outside in the great hall, but at the same time the room still seemed bright because of an abundance of mirrors—on the walls, mounted in freestanding racks, on the ceiling above. And in the mirrors were the reflections of lighted candles. Candelabra were placed on a series of small tables that Doc would have recognized as being old even during his boyhood, so this baron had to have an affection for antiques. The scent of incense hung in the air, thick and heavy, almost covering other, more undesirable smells of body odor and decay.

The floor beneath his knees was covered in rugs of all sizes, shapes and colors. They were strewed upon the floor in haphazard fashion, overlapping in a scattering of patterns. Doc had the impression that a series of new rugs were brought in on a daily basis and slapped down wherever, covering the older soiled ones.

He turned and addressed his reflection in one of the long mirrors. He didn't have to look far to see himself, since the mirrors were indeed mounted all around him. "Last scene of all, that ends this strange eventful history, is second childishness, and mere oblivion. Sans teeth, sans eyes, sans taste, sans everything," Doc said, finishing his earlier scene.

"So, you're the one," a voice from on high said. "The one I've been hearing about. What secrets you got to tell me, old man, before we chill your sorry ass?"

Chapter Fourteen

"At least this maze of stairs is lit," Dean said, memories of the quickly fought but intense battle back at the hospital in Carolina still fresh in his mind. The stairs were made from the same sturdy vanadium steel as the walls, with dark rubber strips on the top of each step for added safety and traction. All in the group had noted the dizzying array of scratches and claw marks left behind in the rubber.

"The old one, she told me I would have to stride bravely into the bowels of hell to face my quarry. I know now she was correct," Jorge said firmly. "I visited a seer. She predicted victory for us all, my friends."

"If you've been down to hell once, you been there a dozen times," Ryan replied cryptically. A journey into one of the redoubts was nothing new or exciting, and the only difference offered up by this one was the possible presence of the murderous mutated *chupacabras.*

As if conjured by his thoughts, a hissing noise like the leaky pipes of some magnificent steam boiler came from a source near the rear of the group.

"Company," Ryan said softly as he whirled and quickly spotted the lurking presence of a single *chu-*

pacabras at the wide bend where the stairs turned to wind their way up another level. The large unreadable eyes of the creature peered down at them impassively, as if the goatsucker were waiting for them to make the first move.

Unlike the one that had landed on Ryan, this *chupacabras* was at least two feet taller, and much more muscular. Dean decided to himself that he'd prefer to stick with the younger muties, if given a choice in the matter.

"Wonder what he wants?" Dean asked.

"Hungry. Mebbe," Jak replied. "We snack."

"We're on his turf. Must've come in behind us somehow," Krysty said. "Or perhaps he's angry that we chilled his little buddy."

"He can stick around and be curious all he wants as long as—" Ryan didn't get to finish his sentence as the hissing creature decided to attack, swooping down in a half-gliding, half-falling motion and landing close to the waiting group. The spines on the monster's back undulated, and the unearthly rainbow wash of colors Soto and Jorge had previously mentioned radiated outward in jagged beams of light.

"Trying to hypnotize us," Soto cried.

"Too late," Ryan replied, and fired a single burst from his pistol. Despite the baffle silencer, the noise of the shot was distinctly audible in the confines of the stairwell. The 9 mm bullet launched from the powerful blaster hit the squatty creature in the throat and careened up through its neck. The high-velocity impact lifted the four-foot-tall mutie off his feet and hindquarters, raising him until his powerful legs came crashing down, kicking and flailing for balance.

Since Ryan had fired up at an angle, the bullet exited out the back of the horror's head, taking a fist-sized chunk of misshapen bone with it.

Threads of blood and brain tissue sprayed out in a fine mix of red and gray. The head of the *chupa-cabras* then lolled back and forth in a half circle on its thick neck before coming to rest awkwardly on a scrawny shoulder, then the entire corpse tumbled down to a resting place on a level floor landing of the stairwell.

Ryan had watched impassively as the sack of dead guts flipped past his combat boots.

"Wonder how the bastard thing got behind us?" he mused. "I've had more than enough surprises come slinking up from the rear."

"Perhaps he followed us from outside the cave door," Jorge said. "Back from another part of the forest of El Yunque."

"Knew we should of locked the damn door behind us," J.B. noted.

"Well, I don't know how it snuck up on us, lover, but I can tell you something else," Krysty said in a worried tone as she rested a hand on one of Ryan's broad shoulders. "The way my head's been ringing since we set foot in this redoubt, the one you just chilled isn't traveling alone. This place is as cold spiritually as they come. Went through a graveyard after dark on a dare once back in Harmony when I was a little girl. Picked a night with no moon. Halfway in the boneyard the whole world seemed to go quiet. This place gives off the same kind of feeling."

"In other words, we should get out of this redoubt," Soto said.

"Ready," Jak said succinctly. "Go back lock door."

"Scared?" Dean challenged.

"Hell, no!" Jak retorted as he turned his ruby eyes on Dean. "You?"

Dean cocked his head over at Ryan. "Not with Dad here."

"Appreciate the confidence, but there's nothing wrong with a little caution, Dean," Ryan replied. "A man who isn't a bit scared of the unknown might find his nerves are too dead to be much good to him or his allies. Besides, we can't leave. Not yet. Not until we've found the nest and made sure there aren't going to be any more of these things."

"This one must've been coming down the stairs for a reason. I don't think he was intentionally following us, otherwise why attack now instead of waiting for a better opportunity? We were just in the way. His home must be down farther in the redoubt," Krysty pointed out.

"Okay, we find this home. And then...?" Jorge asked, a sheen of perspiration plainly visible on his neatly trimmed mustache.

"And then, once J.B.'s dismantled any of the remaining safety sec systems in this redoubt so we don't get foamed or blasted by fire-retardant gas, we blast this entire redoubt...with whatever sick kind of genetics lab they have precisely at ground zero."

"Señor Cawdor, what I said earlier back in the camp? I take it back. I am beginning to like the way your mind works," Jorge beamed.

"NOISE," Jak said, tapping Ryan on the shoulder. "Hear it?"

Ryan held his breath and listened hard, but heard nothing more than the heartbeat in his inner ears. He looked down at his friend and shook his head. His hearing was good, but Jak's was even better.

"I don't hear anything," Dean said.

"Well, I do," Krysty replied, confirming the albino's detections. Like Jak, the woman possessed uncanny abilities of sight and sound, and drew upon them now. "Can't identify what the sound is, though."

Jak didn't say anything else, choosing instead to kneel on the metal floor of the redoubt, placing his hands flat on the ground, turning his head sideways, his fine white hair extending outward from the crown of his skull as he leaned his ear against the cool alloy for a closer listen.

There were no other sounds but the rhythmic in and out of their own individual breathing patterns. Far off, around a corner, Ryan could just catch the mechanical whir of the redoubt's vent system as it cycled air through the complex. Jak stayed in place, prone on the ground and listening hard, his eyes shut. All eyes were on him, as he strained to listen.

"What is it?" Ryan finally asked in a whisper.

Jak opened an eye and peered up at Ryan. "Vibrations," the albino said. "Hard tell. Floor solid, metal on rock."

"You don't really hear them, you just feel them," J.B. added, shifting the M-4000 scattergun from the crook of his left arm to his right.

"Uh-huh," Jak agreed, standing.

"Must be something big, or lots of somethings big to cause enough of a vibration to be felt on flooring as solid as this," Jorge said.

"Could be the *chupacabras* nest, Dad," Dean added.

"Still not picking up any vibes, lover. Earlier on, I could. Now, there's nothing. Almost like I'm being jammed by the little bastards."

"Jammed?" Ryan replied. The term didn't seem to fit in with life functions.

The redhead shot him a look, her fiery hair undulating about her face and shoulders. "Best word I could come up with for how I'm feeling."

"The *chupacabras* have long been rumored to possess the power to cloud the minds of men and women, Krysty Wroth," Soto said. "Make them feel weak, powerless, sick enough to vomit. Entire groups of people have been driven to nausea when faced with a single *chupacabras*. Your special gifts might indeed be compromised in combating the goatsuckers."

"Which way you think the vibrations were coming from, Jak?"

The teen pondered Krysty's question for a few seconds, then pointed at the left fork of the twin corridors. "Down there."

Soto stepped over and looked at a laminated wall map. "That passage leads to an area called Research and Development. Entry Absolutely Forbidden To All but B12 Cleared Personnel."

"Good thing we've got a B12 clearance isn't it?" J.B. said.

THE DESIGN OF THE LAB was reminiscent of others they'd previously seen in military redoubts. Entryways provided by polished air locks of silver chromium rings irised open and closed at the touch of a keypad, each hexagonal-shaped chamber leading into a massive central control area. That, in turn, looked either out and across an interior room or down on med-sterile arenas where the actual grunt work was performed, and in the case of genetic manipulation and the creation of mutants, where the products of said experiments were housed and caged.

The lab area below was dim. All of the fluorescent strip lights that usually illuminated redoubts had either burned out or had been broken and removed. No movement could be seen among the darker shapes of the tables, cages and other pieces of larger gear on the lab floor.

One of the cages was close to the ob window, and allowed the group to see that it was made of clear armaglass on three sides and solid steel on top and bottom. A fourth wall was a mix of vanadium bars and a sliding armaglass portal. From his viewpoint, Ryan noted most of the other cells also appeared empty.

The closest of the confinement cages showed damage—claw marks.

Massive panes of thick and clear armaglass kept the overlords separate from their charges. A series of interior vid cameras were mounted high along the ceiling. Black-and-white vid monitors that took the images seen by the cameras and played them back in the ob booth were mounted in a wire rack next to the armaglass. At the moment, most of the monitor screens were dark. The two still functioning replayed views of what they could already see on the main lab floor below.

Down at the other end of the ob window, Soto gave a startled shriek.

Hell eyes gazed back at him through the glass.

Then, unexpectedly, more eyes appeared as a mass of the *chupacabras* hovered inside, silent, like a swarm of angry insects.

"How many you count?" J.B. asked.

"Eight. Nine. A dozen. Shit," Dean replied.

"Wonder how they're getting in and out? That section below looks sealed," Ryan noted.

The voiced question was answered when a wall-mounted vent covering clattered to the floor, followed by a beating sound of wings and a hissing noise almost painful to the eardrum.

"They're in the redoubt's air ventilation system," Ryan said in disbelief.

"Bastards must be contortionists," J.B. replied, setting the sights of the M-4000 scattergun and preparing to fire. He blinked once, twice, and focused. One thing about using the scattergun—precise aim was the last thing a man needed to worry about.

The scout for the *chupacabras* delegation came bounding over, a fleshy ping-pong ball with bat wings and glowing eyes. J.B. didn't hesitate as he gently caressed the trigger. A double load of fléchettes burst from the wide bore of the blaster, spinning for their intended target.

The squat beast exploded like a burst party balloon, spraying blood and entrails in all directions. A pungent stench of sulfur wafted into J.B.'s nostrils and he struggled to hold back a sneeze, but failed mightily.

"That's one," J.B. muttered, sniffing lustily.

A trio of the hell-beasts bounded out this time, keeping their distance from one another as they came at the party of humans. Krysty rolled across the ob floor toward the cover of a fallen table, hoping for a clear shot. She was moving on instinct in a desperate series of maneuvers, keeping low as one of the creatures zeroed in, hissing in triumph. Her bare arms and hands hit broken glass where beakers and other glass paraphernalia had fallen and shattered after the table had been overturned.

"Dammit!" she cursed as a half-dozen cuts and punctures oozed fresh blood from her skin. The injuries weren't life threatening, but they blazed hotly with pain. She lifted her left hand to her mouth and using her teeth, gingerly pulled one of the larger slivers of glass from her throbbing palm.

The scent of blood sent the pursuing *chupacabras* into a spastic dance of joy. The ugly beast waved its arms, waggled its wings and shook its pear-shaped abdomen, all the while cocking its head and sniffing the air. A hop, two more and it was on the spot where Krysty had just left a few drops of crimson fluid behind as she rolled away through the jagged hunks of glass.

A long, pink tongue lolled out of the beast's mouth and stretched out and down to lap at the fresh blood. While the creature was distracted, Krysty scrambled onto her stomach and crawled on her bleeding hands and knees behind the sanctuary of the fallen lab table.

Across the room, Jak pulled the Colt and fast-sighted, pulling back the hammer of the blaster in a one-two motion so quickly that the twin shots fired sounded like one. The first round missed by less than an inch the creature approaching Krysty. The second landed on target, hitting the mutie high in the general area of the shoulder and driving the beast backward and to the ground.

The *chupacabras* unleashed a wail of pain, and Jak was beset by one of the creature's brothers. Jak went for lower ground too, taking a dive like an Olympic swimmer and rolling nimbly with the agility of a born athlete as he came up into a crouched position with Colt in hand next to Krysty. Even in the taut danger of the moment, Krysty couldn't help but notice the lithe albino wasn't even breathing hard.

The youth fired two more bullets, and both rammed home, blowing a fist-sized hole in the *chupacabras's* midsection. The mutie flipped backward from the force of the gunshots, screeching in agony for a few long seconds before dying.

"Need practice. Not good with gun as knives," Jak said casually to the woman at his side.

"Good enough," Krysty answered with a smile.

"I think we have found the nest, Ryan Cawdor," Soto called out, his face flushed red with adrenaline and fear.

"You think?" Ryan replied, biting back a more sarcastic remark. "We've been lucky so far, but I think we need to back off. J.B., we got enough in the way of those grens you boosted from Jamaisvous to close this place down?"

"Yeah," the smaller man replied, patting a pocket of his jacket.

"Everybody head for the stairs!" Ryan bellowed. "J.B. and I will lay down covering fire. We're going to blast and seal them in!"

Ryan didn't have to give the order twice. There was a scramble as Krysty, Jak, Dean, Soto and Jorge hit the silver ring of the air lock. J.B. had the Uzi set on 3-round bursts, periodically fanning the duct where the creatures had entered the deck of the lab.

"Everybody's out."

"Okay," the Armorer replied, taking out one of the four unusual, small, yet deadly high-ex grens he'd taken from El Morro. "I'm setting the timer for twenty seconds."

"See you outside," Ryan replied, and exited the room.

J.B. flicked a small timer switch and gave an underhanded toss, landing the gren inside the open vent of the circulation system, and then he was gone, out of the room, through the air lock and into the outside hallway, running with the others even as the walls shook and the loud sound of the gren explosion echoed through the lower section of the redoubt.

The group kept moving, Ryan now in the lead, as they made their way back to the emergency stairwell.

"Missed a few!" J.B. bellowed, and fired off a stream of lead behind him, taking down one of the pursuing *chupacabras* that had waddled out of the haze the high-ex gren had created.

The stairs reverberated the terrific clatter as the group climbed higher and higher, continuing their way to the top.

And below, more of the fearsome *chupacabras* gathered, ten or more by the Armorer's quick count. Apparently there had been more of them elsewhere in the redoubt, or more likely, in the air circulation system. They were joining forces, as if a silent, psychic message had gone out to all of them to garner their strength to take on the threat.

"I'm going to drop another gren in ten seconds," J.B. warned.

"In the stairwell?" Jorge asked. "You'll kill us all!"

"Keep moving," Ryan replied. "J.B. knows what he's doing."

The Armorer threw a second gren behind him, counting down loudly as he ran, relying on the decreasing numbers to speed his comrades. He'd set the timer for ten seconds, but as always with old ordnance, trusting the fuses to perform accurately was like plotting the path of a lightning strike. You always heard the thunder after the bolt had fallen.

Ten seconds later, and the stairs underfoot seemed to try to grab their own ankles in an attempt to lift themselves from their moorings, hurling all those on them into the air. Each member of the group had known to keep at least one hand on the railing, and some had placed both for an extra-secure grip near the end of J.B.'s shouted countdown, but such precautions were still not enough to keep them on their feet once the gren went off in a massive exhalation of fire and concussive force.

"Help!" Soto cried as he pitched over the rail, his legs dangling into the rising cloud of smoke and debris. Managing to grab the bottom rail, he hung on for dear life until Ryan and Dean could reach over to rescue him from plummeting downward.

"Help, somebody!" he screamed again as they tugged. "It's got me, one of them's got me!"

Krysty was there, thumbing back the action on her .38-caliber Smith & Wesson blaster and firing three bullets, one-two-three in rapid succession as she pulled the trigger, taking aim not so much at the horror that had attached itself to the squirming Puerto Rican hanging over the banister, but instead taking greater pains not to shoot the man who needed the assistance.

The *chupacabras* was nearly completely hidden in the smoky haze of the damaged stairwell.

"It's biting me!" Soto screamed. "Blast it! Blast the fucker!"

Krysty fired another volley of shots, and this time one of the bullets found a home in a vital organ of the creature. The clawed hands went slack as it fell from the helpless and kicking Soto.

At the back of the stairs, J.B. reached into a pocket and took out a third gren, his fingers flying as he set it for yet another ten-second fuse.

"I'm sending down another package," he yelled as he pulled the ring and opened his hand, releasing the gren on its deadly path.

"J.B. Wait—" Ryan called, a fraction of a second too late.

"What?" the Armorer asked tersely, before continuing the countdown. "Nine—"

"We've got company."

Above them glowed three pairs of eyes.

"Dark night," the Armorer said, disgusted.

"Going to get darker," Jorge replied.

Chapter Fifteen

Mildred had awakened in her quarters before dawn, much earlier than she would have liked, but she was a person usually unable to fall back asleep once she was roused from slumber. Without getting up from the bed and keeping busy, she knew she'd end up missing J.B.'s presence at her side and staring at the ceiling even as fatigue continued to rest upon her weary bones.

What had awakened her? The room was surprisingly cool, the stone construction within the fortress not holding any of the previous day's heat.

Her bladder twinged as if in answer.

"Too much wine," she said aloud, and then giggled. "Drink too much and you have to prime the pump."

As she padded barefoot down the stone hallway toward the washroom of this section of the fortress, she strode past Doc's room.

The door to the old man's quarters was hanging open. Curious, Mildred looked inside, and immediately realized from the taut bedspread and perfectly centered pillow the bed hadn't yet been slept in, nor had someone lain on top for a quick nap.

Unlike herself, Mildred knew from the many times

they'd shared a campsite together that Doc was a man who could sleep through anything.

So where was he now? Worried, she took a moment to retrieve her clothing, shrugging into the blue dress Jamaisvous had given her the previous morning, since it was close at hand. She also picked up her blaster, holding it at her side as she started looking. Her search led her to the control room of the oddly configured mat-trans unit that Silas Jamaisvous had modified in the bowels of the mighty fortress.

Her eyes went first to Doc, who was standing next to the mat-trans chamber, the door of the booth open and the handle gripped in one hand as if he were saying a silent prayer before entering. Doc wore a guilty hangdog look, like a naughty pet caught in the midst of shredding a favorite sock or shoe. He twisted his swordstick in his other hand.

Mildred then directed her intense gaze at Jamaisvous, who was sitting at a control center with his back to her. Various comps, vid screens and readouts were actively chattering and blinking away in front of him.

"What in God's name do you think you're doing?" Mildred demanded loudly.

He turned and gave his unexpected guest a quick smile. "What am I doing, Dr. Wyeth? What I've been doing for two long years now. I am conducting an experiment. You were not expected nor invited for this final phase, but you are more than welcome to watch."

Mildred took one step forward, and a sec man in

green pants and black T-shirt stepped into view from his hidden vantage point next to a tall comp data bank.

"Garcia?"

"Lopez."

"Sorry, I get you two confused."

"That's okay, Dr. Wyeth. I have trouble telling your people apart, too."

Mildred started to stride forward once more, and the sec man lowered his weapon in reply.

"Uh-uh. You may watch, but don't think of interfering," Jamaisvous said easily.

"What are you going to do, Doc?" Mildred asked.

Jamaisvous spoke instead. "Dr. Tanner is going to add the final piece to the puzzle of chron-jumping. I've given him a series of medical injections to counter some of the temporal side effects, and now we're going to try to trawl him forward and back in time. If this works, everybody wins."

"And if it doesn't, Doc ends up dead. Or worse."

"I do not think my life could get much worse, Dr. Wyeth," Doc replied sadly. "This is my decision."

"Uh-uh," Mildred replied. "You need to think this out."

"He has made his decision," Jamaisvous snarled, spinning toward the woman. "Imagine waking up, Mildred, and discovering you had no human companionship to welcome you into the future. I wish I had been a freezie instead of a trawl. I had to shoot myself forward just to survive the coming war, only unlike Dr. Tanner, I used another mat-trans chamber as a destination point. Chamber-to-chamber time trawls are a hell of a lot safer in case anything goes wrong."

"You lied."

Jamaisvous continued to speak, paying no attention to Mildred's accusations. "I made it there alive, but I was the only one, and when I checked the rest of the redoubt, I discovered all of my fellow sleepers were mutants, ugly little demons waiting, sleeping and dreaming their dark thoughts."

"The *chupacabras*...?" Mildred asked with dawning realization.

"Yes. I sent some of them back, you know. Back in time, right from the source of the first redoubt in El Yunque," Jamaisvous said with a smirk. "I was only able to do this six times before the power fluctuations from the failing nuke generator started to create massive problems."

"What kinds of problems?" Mildred asked, her mind racing as she tried to think of a way out of the situation in which she now found herself and Doc trapped.

"Most of them were computer related. It takes an infinite number of calculations to accomplish even a simple same-time mat-trans jump. When you add the complication of a temporal destination, even more juice is needed. The *chupacabras,* as the locals dubbed them, would not have been my first choice as test subjects, but since I was there and they were the only other living creatures at my disposal, I made do."

"You made do by sending violent, murderous creatures into the past?" Doc asked in tones of disbelief.

Jamaisvous shrugged. "Frankly I was curious to see if such moronic boobs would survive a reverse time-trawl intact. The information stream I beamed into the quantum interface and bounced back for a picture never did function correctly—then again, the masters of Chronos never perfected the chronal window for temporal peeping, either."

The whitecoat turned back to Doc. "As I recall, that was another reason for their delight in you, Dr. Tanner. They'd somehow managed to keep the window open into your particular time and locale, actually getting some video footage of you and your wife doddering around the wooden sidewalks of Omaha."

"I know," Doc replied quietly. "I have seen the tape."

"The goatsuckers... You said you sent them back?" Mildred prodded, wanting to keep him talking, wanting to extend the situation before Doc crawled into the waiting gateway.

"Right! And from published reports of the time, I was even more successful than I could have dreamed. Amusingly enough, the media of the 1990s deemed the genetically created *chupacabras* a living creature designed for war, as having extraterrestrial origins."

"You're right," Mildred said. "Soto and Jorge, from Old San Juan, had researched those accounts, too."

Jamaisvous gestured with both hands, adding a visual commentary as he talked in the clipped manner he assumed when spewing information. "Imagine! Savor the irony! Packs of EBEs—extraterrestrial biological entities—flying over the islands of the Caribbean! Bug-eyed Martians wanting a beach vacation! All of them, racing around the Puerto Rican countryside in their flying saucers, taking time out to suck the blood from goats and cows in some arcane ceremony. Utterly hilarious."

"None of them were ever captured or found?"

"Of course they were! The United States government, the 'aboveboard' contingent, knew something strange was going on after they took away a pair of the beasts from the island to the mainland for observation and autopsy, but their response was predictable. Taint the evidence and ridicule the believers, while destroying or distorting any real proof."

Mildred realized where this was leading. "They could tell the *chupacabras* were genetically engineered creations, couldn't they?"

"Of course! And here's the kicker. They took what they could learn from the two animals and used what they thought were alien strands of DNA to make their own living, breathing *chupacabras!* Next thing you know, we have a paradox. Take into account the eternal question of the chicken or the egg? Doesn't matter any longer, for you no longer needed the egg in the first place! Which came first—the future or the past? Damned if I can say for sure, but it certainly makes for top-notch entertainment."

"I'm not a geneticist, but this sounds far-fetched even to me."

"Not when invoking chimeric DNA, Dr. Wyeth."

"What?"

"'A fearful creature, great and swift of foot and strong, whose breath was flame unquenchable,'" Doc said from his position at the opening of the gateway, pulling up specs from the depths of his incredible memory.

"Sounds like he needs a bottle of mouthwash," Mildred retorted. She'd heard Doc's lengthy dissertations on these topics before, and the end result was always one of two things: either Doc's yammering drove her to distraction or bored her to tears. Now, she welcomed it, knowing as long as she kept the discussion going, the odds were greater of holding these two off until Ryan returned, hoping the one-eyed man would never allow Doc to take such a risk without knowing more about the boundaries.

"The Chimera was a mythical fire-breathing monster, with the great head of a lion, the body of a goat and the tail of a hissing, striking serpent," Doc continued. "Held to be unconquerable, with the ability to spit bolts of fire...until Bellerophon rode winged Pegasus up and over the beast, shooting her with arrows from a safe distance with no risk to himself."

"You know, I used to enjoy mythology until I met you," Mildred said wearily.

Jamaisvous laughed in delight. "She's right! Count on you, Dr. Tanner, to ruin all the fun. But, he's correct in his words, Dr. Wyeth. The term 'chimeric' does indeed come from mythological origins and, in this instance, refers to certain combinations of DNA. Take genetic material from one animal, and place it in another. Shake well, and see what surprise combo you've come up with this time."

"Playing God," the woman said with a frown.

"I agree. I also postulate that if man has reached the heights of such creation and manipulation of life, then man has become godlike."

"I don't agree," Mildred said. "I've always believed there are limits, and lines that should not be crossed."

"This from an expert in the field of cryonics? What about the eternal body and soul debate? The morality of freezing the dead for eventual reanimation? Dr. Frankenstein would have heartily approved of your field, Mildred."

"There's a big difference between trying to preserve existing life and creating anew, Silas," Mildred pointed out.

"Perhaps, but it doesn't matter here. Like yourself, Dr. Wyeth, genetics aren't my specialty, but I'm a fast learner and have spent quite a few nights going through the existing videotapes of the many processes that led to the creation of the mutants known as *chupacabras*. Here a protoplast, there a hybrid and boom—a single cell containing the chromosomes of both parent cells. I believe vectors were also used, a vector being an unsuspecting DNA molecule into which foreign DNA can be easily inserted."

"There goes the neighborhood."

"Yes. Once you've added the new element to the old, you then have an entirely different creation that is fully accepted and taken up by the confused host cell."

"All you're describing to me is pantropic science," Mildred said. "I've seen it and experienced the horror of it firsthand. Why the government didn't think a nuclear conflagration was sufficient punishment for the world is beyond me, but the artificial creations generated by the distortions of nature make me sick to even call myself a member of the human race."

Jamaisvous laid a hand over his heart. "Spoken like a true patriot, my dear. Still, Dr. Tanner and I have an appointment to keep, right?"

"Yes," Doc replied.

Then, Mildred surprised them all. She raised her pistol and fired a quick shot into the heart of one of the comps on the table next to Jamaisvous, followed by a bold lunge for Doc, which was doomed to failure by the equally quick reaction time of Garcia, who pulled a small black-and-silver handheld device from his belt and shoved the suddenly sparking gadget against Mildred's body.

The last thing Mildred saw before being plunged into unconsciousness was the electric-blue strike of a compressed lightning blast.

"YOU COULDN'T BACK OFF, could you? I'm sorry, Dr. Wyeth. Sorry for both of us."

The leader of the El Morro Fortress glared down

at his guest, all pretense of polite host long lost. The tazer Garcia had used to subdue Mildred emitted faint crackling sounds as Jamaisvous, who'd taken control of the woman's target pistol, idly caressed the hammer of the firing mechanism. "I suppose I should kill you to insure my plans of succeeding, but I'm a fair man, so what I do depends on you."

Mildred held her ground. "What a load. You live to brag and talk. Kill me and you're back to expressing glee to your own reflection in the mirror. I'm sure the locals don't exactly comprehend the full import of what you've got set up here."

"A parry of ego, eh, Dr. Wyeth? I can handle being alone. I've been alone before. I kind of like it."

Mildred got to her feet, realizing part of one breast was exposed by the low-cut blue dress. She lingered as she pushed herself up, allowing Jamaisvous a long look at her cleavage.

"There's always room for discussion, Silas…and nobody likes being alone," she said in her huskiest voice.

"Please, don't come any closer. I hate heroes, especially misguided, oversexed ones. I daresay none of us wants any more shooting in here, what with such delicate and irreplaceable equipment lying about," Jamaisvous said. He waved an impatient hand at Doc. "Go ahead, Theophilus! We can't get started until you're encased inside."

"I beg you, Dr. Jamaisvous, do not hurt my friends," he implored.

"That's entirely up to them, isn't it? Now go. Fly."

Doc did as ordered, stepping into the gateway and closing the door with a soft click.

Mildred, her racing heartbeat belying the fine sheen of sweat on her face and forehead, stepped over briskly, not caring if she was shot, and began to pound on the blue armaglass of the gateway chamber with both fists. From within, if he skewed his eyes, Doc could make out her faint, shadowy outline.

"Doc! Don't do it! Doc!" she screamed, even as the tendrils of mist began to form and collect inside the chamber like a damp embrace from an old friend. "He's using you! Using you as a test subject, you crazy old fart! He doesn't care if you live or die! Doc!"

There was an incredibly bright light from inside the sheltered chamber, filtered by the colored armaglass but still as bright as the noonday sun. All of the secondary lights and comp banks in the room dimmed in intensity as the light within the mat-trans unit reached blinding levels. Mildred closed her eyes and still was blinded, finally having to turn her back to the light to save her overloaded visual receptors.

Then, he was gone again. There was no fading or even the sudden violent changes in the air and gravitation fabric as the last time he'd been taken by time trawl.

He just ceased to be.

Doc Tanner...wasn't.

"The chron jump is now in progress," Jamaisvous announced calmly. "First stop—tomorrow."

Mocsin, Montana, 2095

DOC TANNER STARED UP toward the voice that had just threatened to kill him, his eyes falling on a kind of stepped pyramid, approximately twelve feet high, wide at the bottom and tapering off to a smaller, flat top, upon which rested a wide, high-backed wing chair draped in the stars and stripes of an American flag.

Sitting in the chair and on the flag was a man, dressed in a dingy robe of purple silk, with a dirty white fur collar. Purple silken pajamas could be glimpsed beneath the folds of the half-open robe. The man was wearing black knee-length riding boots whose sheen caught the reflection of many candles. He was fat, but not grotesque, although the potential for obesity of an incapacitating manner was present in his fleshy face and build. A white scarf, brighter and cleaner than the fur collar of the gown, was wrapped around his throat.

Short, white hair topped the man's head, which craned down as he peered intently at the kneeling figure of Doc Tanner with mild curiosity. The room was silent as he stared Doc down. Pausing only to take out and light up a ridiculously large cigar with an odor even more cloying and sweet that the burning pots of incense, he finally decided to speak.

"Who the fuck are you?" the fat man asked, blowing out a plume of smoke.

"Tanner. Dr. Theophilus Algernon Tanner," Doc replied, getting enough of a whiff to note the cigar wasn't made of tobacco, but could be traced instead to the cannabis plant.

The revelation made the baron's ears perk up. "Doctor? Medical doc?" Teague asked eagerly, looking past Doc to his right-hand man, Cort Strasser. Strasser made no overt movement to indicate yea or nay, allowing the kneeling man as much rope as required to hang himself.

"No, my friend. Philosophy. Philosophy and..." Tanner discovered the years of scientific training he'd taken had vanished from his mind, vanished to such a degree he was having trouble even recalling what his second major in university might have been.

"Sounds like a bullshitter to me. He come into Mocsin with tribute?"

"Nothing on him, Baron, except for these." The bearded sec man reached into a canvas shoulder bag and held out a pair of perfect metal spheres, each about the size of a baseball. Strasser took the offered globes and walked up the steps to the top of Teague's bizarre indoor pyramid. The overweight baron had ordered the pyramid built as his throne, having been advised that a pyramid was a power object, and by sitting atop one he could harness the latent energies and become a stronger leader.

At first Baron Teague had been hesitant, but after discussing the matter with his closest advisers, including Cort Strasser, he decided a pyramid was just what he needed.

With almost superhuman effort Strasser had managed to keep from erupting into gales of laughter at the sight of his boss perched atop the pretentious construct, and word quickly escaped into Mocsin that the good baron was becoming loonier and loonier each day. It was an assumption Strasser had done nothing to suppress.

Cort Strasser had his own plans for Mocsin and for the ville's leader.

"Balls," Teague said confidently, rolling one of the spheres between two fleshy hands.

"That's right," Strasser agreed, ever the vigilant yes-man. "Balls."

Teague didn't appear to be impressed. He gave a great sigh that seemed to start low in the pit of his doughy stomach and then come hurtling out of his open mouth. Strasser and the other sec men in the room knew the signs. Their boss was bored. "So, this old fart's no peddler or trader, since he offers nothing of value in the way of hard goods, correct?"

"Correct," Strasser replied.

"And he's too dried up to be worth fucking or selling his ass," Teague continued. "So a thriving career as a male gaudy seems to be out."

"Right."

Teague leaned forward ever so slightly and fixed Doc with a contemptuous stare. "My question is, what do you have to offer me, old man?"

"First, uh, my good fellow," Doc began, trying to

summon the courage to ignore the men with high-powered weapons surrounding him and fixate instead on the unarmed baron.

"Baron," Teague corrected in a frosty tone.

"My good, um, Baron," Doc said nervously, but without pause, "I am not old. Haggard, yes, I will accept that description. But old, never."

"Seems like you're in a powerful world of denial, old man," Strasser said, and the other men in the room chuckled. Teague didn't acknowledge the crack, another sign of Strasser's continually growing power, since a year ago the baron would have slapped his second-in-command down either verbally or physically for daring to comment during one of his interrogations.

Doc pressed on, keeping his chin high as he looked up at the seated baron of Mocsin. "Second, I am a teacher, a man of learning who wishes to share his knowledge."

"Teacher?" A wash of confusion passed over Teague's ruddy face. "Teach what?"

"The sciences," Doc replied.

"Tech?" the baron asked with the first active look of interest he'd shown since Doc's arrival.

Now it was Doc's turn to be confused. "Beg pardon?"

"Tech. Hardware. Machines," Teague replied impatiently. "You a fixer? I can always use a fixer. Or a techie. Know anything about engines? Comps? What's your field?"

Doc shook his head sadly. "No, mechanical apparatuses are not my forte. 'Tech' is not my calling."

Teague shook his head, already bored again. The siren call of the addict was starting to whisper in his ear, and he grew weary of discussing job descriptions with Doc Tanner. The glowing pipe, the oversized joint of happyweed, both were waiting for him and Teague wanted to feel the burning sensation between his lips and teeth.

But not until business was done. Baron Jordan Teague hadn't backslid so much as to reveal his addiction openly to his underlings. At least, not yet.

"We have no use of theory here, Doctor," he finally said. "I need men who can produce results. You sound like a user, a taker, a man with nothing to offer."

"Begging your pardon, Baron Teague...?" Strasser said in a polite tone.

Teague matched it, answering as if they were seated together at a banquet table passing a basket of biscuits instead of deciding Doc's fate. "Yes, Cort?" he asked.

Strasser stepped up beside Doc and placed a friendly arm around the man's skinny shoulders. "I think you've got Doc all wrong. He *does* serve a purpose."

Teague wiped his mouth on the sleeve of his purple robe. He needed a fix, and soon. "Enlighten me, please, Cort, for I sure as hell don't see it."

Strasser pulled back the friendly arm and used it to slap Doc on the back...hard. "He's a fun guy, a clown. He can help keep us entertained. He tells great stories. Recites Shakespeare! Why, I bet he even sings and dances once you get a few beers in him.''

Doc stayed on his feet, gritting his fine teeth against the pain now throbbing between his bony shoulder blades. ''I am no man's monkey, Mr. Strasser.''

''That's what you think.'' Strasser jerked a thumb in a downward motion. ''Let me have him, Baron. I'll find a use for old Doc here. Train him up good and when you least expect it, I'll drag his sorry ass out for a show.''

Teague nodded, the bored mask back on his fleshy face. The drugs were in his left robe pocket and it took all of his self-control to stop from pulling them out and lighting up. ''He's yours, Cort. You found him, you're responsible for him. Now leave me, all of you. I need time alone to think and meditate upon my current affairs of state.''

Strasser bowed. ''Yes, my lord.''

''UNHAND ME, SIR!'' Doc yelled at the sec man.

The bearded man obliged, pushing Doc into the filthy basement room. The walls were a mix of earth and heavy stone; the floor damp and muddy. The room was barren, no furniture or windows, only the single wooden door with the tiny window cut in the upper section for viewing.

''You just don't get it, do you, old man? I think you need a lesson in manners.''

Strasser slapped Doc across the face with the back of his hand, sending him stumbling sideways into the wall. While Doc was no coward, he wasn't a seasoned fighter either, and the events that had seen him taken from the end of the year 2000 and dropped nearly one hundred years into this future hellhole had robbed him of almost all his strength.

Doc raised an arm, managing to block a second punch. He felt his entire shoulder go numb from the force of the blow. Strasser gave a nasty snort of laughter and feinted with his right fist, taking advantage of his victim's hapless avoidance to easily kick out with a booted foot, catching his prisoner in the kneecap.

Doc screamed in pain and went down on the earthen floor.

"Strip him," Strasser ordered and the two sec men bent down to comply, pulling away the well-worn clothing, the grimy long underwear.

"You animal."

Strasser laughed, and his amusement was as false and cold as his smile. "No, you're the animal here, Doc, and I'm going to enjoy proving it. I hope you can get it up, because I've got a special job for you. One you're gonna like."

"Get it...up?" Doc asked, confused by the slang.

The second sec man laughed, pointing at Doc's genitals. "Even if he does pop a boner, I don't think it's going to amount to much!"

Strasser strode over with his hand on his hips and looked down. "Doc, you've just been appointed

Mocsin's ambassador of swine, and as such, your number-one duty is to service all the female members of your entourage. You might as well save your strength—you're going to need it all for your harem.''

The sec men gathered around and laughed heartily at Strasser's edict.

Doc looked horrified. ''Bestiality?'' he said, a shudder of revulsion running down from his nape to the back of his thighs.

Strasser laughed again, slapping Doc on the back. ''See? Quips like that are what make you the top funny fellow in Deathlands. 'Bestiality,' he says. That's a mighty fancy word for fucking, old man, and that's what you are to me now, Mocsin's very own piggy-humper.''

Doc wasn't smiling. The joke was taking a nasty turn. ''I'll not lie with swine,'' he declared as firmly as he could, but to his own ears the declaration came out in a breathy quaver of a voice.

Strasser kept the pasted-on smile. He reached out and poked a heavy finger in the center of Doc's scrawny chest, catching him right at the top of the breastbone with each painful jab. ''You'll do whatever the hell I tell you to do, and come back asking for more, you crazy old loon! Take pride in your new position, and thank me for not chilling you right now.''

''Frankly, sir, I would rather be dead,'' Doc said.

''That can be arranged. Bring him.''

Too exhausted to really care anymore, Doc offered

little resistance as he was taken through the halls of Baron Teague's manse and out a back door to a waiting wag. The ride to the compound where the pigs were kept was short, and soon Doc found himself standing in front of a wide wooden gate looking at the dozens of muddy sows within.

"Toss him into the pit. I'll be standing on the observation platform above. And he stays until he's shown his love and affection to the pig of his choice."

Doc gave out a bellow of protest, which was clamped down to a whimpering sound, like a whipped dog, after Strasser smashed the butt of a shotgun into Doc's gut. Soon he found himself standing among the terrible-smelling pigs.

"And Doc, don't take too long, or I might see if you prefer porking piggies of the same sex. Being a pig-fucker is bad enough, but a homo pig-fucker is even worse," Strasser yelled down from above, much to the amusement of his lackeys.

The long hour spent in the pen seemed like the most painful nightmare Doc had been forced to endure since being taken away from his wife and children, and as it was, only by focusing on their faces and voices and memories was he able to detach himself from the current situation he was being forced to participate in and do the requested deed.

Never in his life had he felt so degraded and alone.

Chapter Sixteen

In Puerto Rico, within the confines of a modified mat-trans gateway designed not only for simultaneous matter transfer but also for quantum leaps into the past or future, the gaunt figure known to friends and family as Dr. Theophilus Algernon Tanner ceased to exist.

The man, Doc Tanner...wasn't.

Yet, he was, and there he stood, his knees unbowed, in the center of a mat-trans chamber. "Most curious," he murmured to himself. "I usually return to these unearthly carrels horizontal and sick of mind and body, not erect and invigorated." Other than the queer sensation of tingling flesh, as if he were covered in a layer of squirming insects, Doc felt wide-eyed and alert.

His eyes searched the colors of the tinted armaglass walls and saw they were an unfamiliar brown. No sign of blue was to be seen anywhere around him. He touched a wall and received a slight electric shock. Looking at his hand and arm, Doc noted a faint halo of light that seemed to dance around his entire body, like a glistening silver cloak of silk.

"I wonder where this might be?" he said softly, debating whether to cross the small room and open the waiting door or remain standing until he had more opportunity to assess his situation. He regretted the absence of his trusty Le Mat now more than ever, and cursed himself for a fool for having left it behind in Puerto Rico. He could stand there as long as he liked, but eventually would need to cross the threshold and see what waited outside.

If events held to the norm, outside would be an anteroom leading to the control center for the mat-trans gateway he now resided in. Some blinking lights, a few soft noises of comps talking to themselves in binary clicks and Doc would be all alone. He hoped. Squatters in redoubts were rarely the friendly sort.

All of this was true, if events held to the norm.

Pausing cost Doc any element of surprise. While he stood woolgathering, the heavy armaglass chamber door swung open.

"He who hesitates is lost," flitted through his brain. If Ryan were here, he'd undoubtedly remark that such an expression sounded like something the Trader would say. Doc had met the Trader, and spent many a day traveling in his company. Despite the origins of the phrase, the Trader would have agreed with the words, or at the very least, the sentiment.

Doc held his ebony swordstick in both of his elegant hands, long fingers wrapped around his lone possession in a manner indicating there would be no taking of the cane unless he were unconscious or dead, the latter being most likely. One of his age-spotted hands was at the base of the silver lion's head atop the stick, and the other was lower, ready to unsheathe the hidden blade within—readying himself, for what, he did not know—but he wanted to be as prepared as a man facing the unknown could be.

He peered out through the open door and into the anteroom and spotted three figures, all dressed identically in formfitting white bodysuits.

The suits were the only thing the trio shared in common. The man standing slightly in the lead was Caucasian, with a high forehead and thin lips. A pair of steely blue-gray eyes were sunk above high, almost regal cheekbones. It was a cruel face, Doc decided. Next to him was an older man, with dark brown coloring similar to Mildred's, although Mildred had never sported shoulders as wide as the ones atop this man's torso. He had a long, heavy-jawed face adorned with a thick black mustache and a frowning, suspicious expression.

The third member of the white bodysuit club was one of the most striking examples of feminine beauty Doc could remember ever seeing, rivaling Krysty for pulchritude. Her honey-blond hair was a tousled mane of wavy thickness atop the most delicate of features, and like Krysty she had eyes of deepest emerald. A graceful swanlike neck led to a slender body of curves, accented even more by the hug of the white clothing she wore.

None of them appeared to be armed with the usual plethora of weapons he was used to seeing on denizens of Deathlands, a fact that allowed Doc to release the deep gulp of air he'd taken by reflex when the door to the chamber had opened. As Doc exhaled, he noted they didn't seem to be intent on inflicting or creating any immediate harm. For now, they merely gawked. Doc could handle gawkers. He decided to turn on the charm and allowed himself to grin nervously, revealing his perfect white teeth.

"By the Three Kennedys! Something tells me I'm not in Omaha," he said by way of greeting.

Hearing the booming basso profundo voice echoing from within the chamber, a fourth man joined the others, also dressed in the tight-fitting white bodysuit, which Doc couldn't help but note was nowhere near as flattering as it looked on the other three. The new arrival was in a wheelchair and didn't appear at all happy to be so confined, the arm movements he used to wheel himself over impatient and quick.

The man in the wheelchair was much older than the other three, with decades on Doc's own elderly appearance. A pair of thick-lensed glasses were perched on his long nose, and a small mechanical hearing aid was attached to the right earpiece. The man's appearance and manner vividly reminded Doc of a perpetually annoyed old chemistry professor he'd been forced to suffer under during a long fall semester of his stay at Harvard.

Armed with blasters or not, Doc realized he was rapidly becoming outnumbered. He took a cautious half step back, quickly turning the lion's head on the swordstick with a twist of a wrist, rewarded by the appearance of a half-foot of glittering, razored steel from the stick's sheath.

At the same instant, the halo of light scurrying around his lean body exuded curling, crackling strings of pure energy, and the skin-crawling sensation was replaced with a much more uncomfortable jabbing feeling, as if ten thousand tiny needles were all being shoved into the upper epidermis of his skin at once.

"It's cycling again!" a voice cried out. "We've got to seal the chamber! We don't know the wavelengths of that radiation! It could be fatal, or could contaminate the redoubt if it's not contained!"

By this time, Doc had no idea who was speaking, since his vision was starting to break down into streaks of multicolored light, followed by a sodden darkness all too familiar to anyone who'd previously traveled on the mat-trans express.

SILVER ARMAGLASS.

Silver, the color of betrayal. He knew the mat-trans chamber from a previous visit, and now, here he was again. Doc had felt the sting of betrayal that dark day, the cold flush of having one's trust rejected because of suspicion or fear radiating out from his helpless body.

"What's that panel of numbers and letters by the side of the door?" a woman's voice asked him, mere moments before the event that he knew was soon to occur.

"Control codes," Doc heard himself reply. "Sadly, at the time of what is called skydark, all of the relevant documentation and comp disks have been wiped clean or destroyed or have quite simply vanished. So we have no way at all of understanding what any combination might do."

"Makes me nervous, Doc," the woman said. "Going into this strange-looking room and closing the door to wake up somewhere else. Makes me claustrophobic."

Doc watched himself give the woman his most reassuring smile. "Nonsense, my dear," he told her. "As long as I am at your side, no harm shall come to you."

He had turned to look down at the attractive woman standing outside of the mat-trans chamber next to him, one of her hands curled tightly in his own. She was around average height, five foot six or so with the lean build of a woman used to moving. Her golden shoulder-length hair was streaked with the first tints of the eventual waterfall of gray to come. Against the blond hair, her deeply tanned face and neck looked even darker than they truly were, but the sun had been kind and her face remained relatively wrinkle-free, despite her age of forty-three and continual exposure to the elements.

Another blonde. Doc hadn't felt an attraction to any woman since Lori Quint's untimely demise, but this one was different. Where Lori had been headstrong and pumped with the self-aggrandizement of youth, this woman was mature and cautious. Doc liked that, liked the white flash of her smile and the calm assessment in her dark eyes.

Susan "Sukie" Smith, originally from Rice Falls,

Wisconsin, had a past as tragic as his own, maybe even more so in terms of loss and heartache. Now, she was on her way out west seeking her sister in hopes of reclaiming the last remnants of her scattered and mostly dead family.

She wore a divided blue skirt with a few patches over well-worn riding boots, along with a dingy white blouse and a jacket that matched the blue in the skirt. A necklace of rough-cut turquoise and pewter around her long slender neck completed the ensemble.

When they'd first met, she had the advantage on Doc with an autopistol and a hankering to fire, only to come forward after they'd talked to collapse before him in a tumble of unconscious limbs and bright red blood. He later learned the wound had been given to her by a man who she hired as a guide. In return for her injury, she'd chilled the man with his own blade, and had been going it alone until encountering Doc.

The spark of attraction had been there between the two, and Doc had delighted in engaging in a sprawl of days of consensual lovemaking and leisurely travel in some of the most beautiful country he'd ever seen. Now, Sukie was at his side in front of the mat-trans chamber, along with all the other members of Ryan Cawdor's group of survivalists. There had been no hesitation in letting her accompany them—if the woman was good enough for Doc, there would be no disputing her place in the group of friends. Although hardened by the harshness of her life, she was friendly enough, although still sticking close to Doc.

Like most people at first, she was attempting to grasp the complexities of the matter-transfer process. Doc had explained the process to her as best as he could, promising her that he'd spent more time than he cared to tell within the various six-sided armaglass chambers jumping to and fro and he was still in one piece.

So, she'd agreed, and entered with the rest of them, Krysty, Jak, Dean, J.B., Mildred, the Trader and Abe—both of whom were traveling with the companions at the time—and Doc himself, who felt slightly guilty since none of them actually liked jumping, and he was the one who usually came out on the other end suffering the most. Yet he still had to put on a brave face for his lady. Outside in the ruin of the anteroom next to the chamber, Ryan had waited until all were safe and seated inside before stepping into the booth himself and closing the door.

Once closed, the door triggered the auto mechanism of the mat-trans and the incredible process, so familiar to everyone, began once more.

Familiar to all but Sukie Smith, who sat stiffly next to Doc, her face a twist of worry as the metal disks began to hum like a thousand stirred bees and the swirling mists fell around their shoulders like a gentle cloak, gray-white mists that started high before falling to the floor and wrapping around each form inside the chamber.

Doc had promised that no harm would come to

her, as long as he was alive to be her champion, and Sukie had smiled weakly in return.

The humming grew louder and the light of the chamber became brighter and Doc closed his eyes, hoping he wouldn't dream, and if he did, that Sukie would be in whatever mental confabulation his slumbering mind conjured.

"No."

A simple word, said very clearly and distinctly came from the woman at his side.

The transitional phase of the mat-trans jump was almost complete, and Doc had to struggle to open his eyes to focus on what he'd heard and the implications of the single spoken syllable. Across from Doc and Sukie, Ryan saw what was happening, even as he battled to keep his own eye open. J.B., his vision dulled by the removal of his specs, also tried to react, but found his body numb and impossibly slow to respond to the mental commands he was issuing.

Sukie Smith, who'd buried a quartet of husbands during her rough struggle to survive in Deathlands, who'd endured all the hell an attractive woman faced in a lawless land of cruel men and still managed to retain the capacity to love, who'd encountered a curious older man with a lilt in his voice and the flowery speeches of a true romantic and for a week of her hard life bought into the fantasy of being swept off her feet, now stared into the unfathomable face of the unknown and was frightened to death.

Fear pumping into her lithe body, she was already up into a crouch and lurching clumsily toward the closed mat-trans chamber door, her mouth working soundlessly with only a few words escaping to the ears of those sitting around her, and all could hear and make sense of only two: "Doc" and "sorry" and "sorry" and "Doc." They were spoken over and over like a tape on auto-loop, even as her very atoms were scattered to the four winds on a subatomic level.

The future Doc Tanner watched all of this from outside the gateway, saw the door open a crack, saw the world erupt, saw Sukie die from the other side.

This time, when he felt the tugging of the temporal leash trawling him to yet another locale, he was more than relieved.

DOC OPENED HIS EYES and realized he was slumped on his feet against the side of a wooden wall. His legs were tingling with needles of pain, and he could barely stand. Flakes of chipped white paint stuck to his jacket and the side of his face as he leaned for support, his presence hidden away by the shelter of an empty doorway, and struggled to fight back grief for Sukie, grief and guilt that were already intermingling with new emotions brought on by what he was now viewing from the span of a single muddy street away.

He gave an audible gasp when he first saw himself, his wife, his children.

"So young," he whispered to himself. "Too young."

There was no stopping the tears now, and his vision blurred and the scene ran like melting paint. The out-of-body experience was taking a great toll physically, but mentally he felt numb. Dead.

He wanted to run to them, to grab up Rachel in his arms and spin her in a circle and never stop holding her, spin her as she laughed and laughed, like she always did—like she always had—until she squealed for him to stop.

But he knew there would be no such reunion, for how could he confront himself? The Theo Tanner walking down that wooden sidewalk with his wife and children had no clue, no concept of the disaster soon to befall, and even if he was forewarned, how would it change the future?

Then, with the clarity of old, the acute mental sharpness he'd once possessed, he recalled words he'd once read on a monitor screen during his captivity with Operation Chronos, words that had haunted him greatly with their implication then, and even more so now as each syllable came rushing back with the fury of a hurricane:

> Temporal anomalies are not clearly understood, nor easily explained. Evidence is limited as experiments have not proceeded far or fast. Most experts hypothesize that time is multistranded. There is at any one second millions upon millions of time possibilities, an infinite choice of parallel futures, any or all of which will persist. Thus, it is believed that the classic example of a person traveling back into the past to alter his

own present is false. He will alter only one of the parallel streams, but his own present will not change. He could be killed in the past, but his own time stream will not be sullied by the disturbance. But in one universe, he will cease to exist. That is all that is known.

"That is all that is known," Doc whispered.

Then, he knew what he had to do. Whether or not the theorists at Chronos were correct in their extrapolation and understanding of how the time stream worked, he still had to warn himself. However, before he could reach his family, he felt his teeth begin to hum, a hum that stretched through his skull and nasal cavity.

The chronal transport process was beginning once more.

Doc took a single step forward and felt his metabolism start to slow, freezing into place as if his very bones were made of ice, and his skin frosted on. He tried to call out, cursing himself now for playing coy and not immediately going up the steps to his own front door and grabbing his young face in his hands and screaming: "It's over, Theo! Everything falls apart! The center cannot hold! For I am you and you are me and right now, in this reality, we are both separate entities and by God, you must do all in your power to prevent this Dickens-like apparition that has appeared on your doorstep from coming to pass!"

He had done none of these things. Hesitation had cost him dearly once more. When the trawl of the mat-trans unit finished locking and sucked him away from that plane of existence, he welcomed the nightmares to come. He hoped for them to never end as eternal punishment—the dark dangerous visions of the dead.

Chapter Seventeen

"We've got seven seconds," J.B. said tightly, his voice even as it measured out the unstoppable countdown he'd started when setting the fuse on the grenade. His eyes were wide behind the lenses of his wire-rim spectacles as he continued to list the numbers backward to the eventual zero and its explosive conclusion. "Six, five."

"Let's gamble these ugly bastards haven't learned to count. On two from J.B., everyone go flat," Ryan said, tensing his body in preparation as he spoke loudly over the verbal countdown.

"Four, three," J.B. continued softly, continuing to count even as Ryan had given the order. "Two—"

Jorge, Soto, J.B., Ryan, Krysty and Dean dived to their knees and stomachs like dropped stones. Seeing their prey suddenly collapse into horizontal positions, the waiting trio of *chupacabras,* who had activated the weird bioengineered hypnotic spines along their backs the moment they had been spotted, interpreted the movements as a sign of submission, and sprang forward with their wings open to hungrily attack.

As such, all of the horrid mutations were facing the brunt of the explosion when it came rushing upward in a hot spray of dust and debris. Miraculously none of the companions were shaken from the stairs, but there were multiple creaks and groans from the stressed metal of the framework they all hung onto.

"They weren't below. Got above us somehow," Jorge said softly as the dust settled.

"The vents," Ryan said, coughing. "The bastards are probably spread all over the redoubt."

"Then we need to seal this entire complex," Soto said, limping from an injury sustained earlier during the fighting.

"If we live long enough to get to the door," Jorge replied pessimistically.

"Oh, we'll live that long, no problem," J.B. snarled. "I've got to have a long talk with our prissy friend back at the fortress before I can take time enough to die."

J.B.'S THREAT WAS PROVED to be true. There were a few more sporadic attacks from random *chupacabras,* but now all in the group were prepared to deal with the creatures and their methods of murder. Soto used his rusty revolver to take down one, while Jorge's long blaster was good for two more. At one point, Soto looked incredibly sad, remarking to all, "I find it hard to believe my people spent so much time frightened of these creatures."

At the exit back into the cavern, J.B. took the last of the four grens and set the time for thirty seconds, tossing it inside as Ryan reversed the code and brought the massive vanadium steel door sliding down with a ring of finality.

Outside, the sun had come up.

Ryan sat at the wheel of the Jeep, turned the ignition key, and was rewarded with the thrum of the small wag's engine firing into life.

"Now, we settle accounts with Jamaisvous," he stated.

THE TRIP BACK to Old San Juan was speedy and uneventful, except for the discovery that the injuries inflicted upon Soto's foot were worse than he'd let on. He apologized profusely for being unable to accompany the others to El Morro, but Ryan would hear none of it, and insisted Jorge stay with his friend.

"There's enough of us here to take care of business," he told the two men.

When the group of companions reached the imposing fortress, all was quiet inside. No table had been set for breakfast, and other than the cook and her daughter, no sec men—or, for that matter, no Doc Tanner or Mildred Wyeth or Silas Jamaisvous—were to be found.

"Gateway," Jak suggested, and they traced their steps back along the path taken mere days before when Jamaisvous had led them up into the living quarters of the fortress.

"Halt, Cawdor!" a voice rang out.

The barrel-chested sec guard stood firm at the open hallway leading to the inner bowels of the fortress where Jamaisvous had installed his modified gateway and temporal laboratories. The hefty Tec 10 blaster was held ready, a silent deterrent backing up its master. There was nowhere to duck for safe cover in the hall, a tidy piece of extra security that the guard seemed well aware of from his position.

"Hold up," Ryan said to the others. "I don't think we're welcome."

"Where's Luis?" the sec man asked.

"He ate something that didn't agree with him," Ryan said blandly.

"Que?"

"Forget it."

The guard sneered. "Where is the rest of your merry band of *chupacabras* hunters?"

"They're back at home with their families," Krysty replied. "Glad to be alive and proud to have accomplished something to help their people instead of cowering up here in this fortress."

"They're all scared. Too frightened to come up here to El Morro. Frightened the *chupacabras* is going to come hopping out of a rathole and bite them on the ass!"

Ryan's visage managed to grow even more defiant. "So you say, but I didn't see you volunteering to go tramping around in El Yunque either."

"I was not assigned. My duties were here."

"Sure, much easier to let someone else take the risks, isn't it?" Dean said.

"You watch your mouth, boy, or I'll—"

"You'll what?" Ryan challenged. "Which one of the matching set are you, anyway?"

"Lopez. My brother is busy. You have no right to

be here. Unless you want to take this beyond words, I suggest you back up. Now.''

Ryan felt the anger flare inside his brain, but he kept it under control, leashed. ''Step aside, Lopez. I've got business with your boss.''

The guard frowned. ''Dr. Jamaisvous left strict orders not to be disturbed.''

''Your precious doctor has been playing you and your people for fools,'' Krysty said. ''We just got back from ground zero for *chupacabras.*''

Lopez looked at the long-limbed redhead with a confident smirk. ''*El chupacabras* doesn't exist. Old tales told to children to frighten them into bed.''

Ryan jerked up his bandaged hand to the fresh scabbing on his face. ''I didn't get these cuts shaving, Lopez. Nor did any of the rest of us. Every scab and bruise you see on us came from one of those mutie sons of bitches, and your master, the mighty Dr. Silas Jamaisvous is the one responsible for unleashing them on San Juan.''

Lopez wasn't convinced. ''You lie. How is this possible?''

''I'm not saying he did it on purpose—mebbe he screwed up somehow when he came to San Juan and took over this fortress. But I do know he's the one behind the *chupacabras* problem, and I want to discuss it with him. Now.''

''My brother has been as polite to you as possible. I think words are not going to convince you, Cawdor.'' On that note of menace, the second of the twin sec men, Lopez's brother, Garcia, stepped around the corner behind the group, his matching Tec 10 leveled and ready.

Ryan kept his cool on the surface. Things were going south triple fast, and every second they spent in pointless debate with Jamaisvous's watchdogs was a second more that could spell disaster for Doc and Mildred, neither of whom had been found in the upper levels of the living areas of the fortress.

Caught in the makings of a cross fire, Ryan had no choice. Trusting his comrades in arms to match his movements, he pulled the SIG-Sauer in a practiced fast draw the most hardened of the mythical old Western gunslingers would have been envious of and squeezed the trigger. A single 9 mm bullet blasted out of the end of the pistol, the explosive sound muffled to a large degree by the baffle silencer.

Lopez never even had a chance to use his rifle as the slug from the SIG-Sauer punched through his forehead, lifting the red headband from his hair, along with a bloody chunk of his bony scalp.

Even as Ryan was taking the most direct method of reasoning with the sec man blocking their path, J.B. was following through on his own end with the Uzi, lifting the half-hidden machine pistol from under his jacket and sending a string of steel-jacketed bullets in a wavy pattern across the midsection of the backup sec man. Two of the slugs struck true, into the sec man's muscled torso.

At such close range, neither bullet stayed in the body, but instead hurtled out the back of the falling figure with enough energy to strike the stone wall behind the sec man. One went into the wall and stayed, the other ricocheted off and buried itself in the stone floor.

Unlike his brother, Garcia was able to fire off a few shots from his Tec 10, but they went high and wild, sailing over Jak and Dean, plucking at their hair. They also passed over Krysty's red head, since she had used her full body weight to shove the two boys to the floor.

She hadn't worried about the use of her own pistol. If Ryan and J.B. had failed in their attempt to take down the twin sec men, the group of friends would have been chilled faster by the autofire than a succeeding hail of returned fire would have allowed anyway.

The firefight was over in a handful of seconds.

Ryan stood calmly, not looking back to see the status of those behind him, but keeping his eye on the fallen sec man in front of him. "Everybody okay?" he asked.

The voices of his friends and family chimed out in affirmative.

Stepping forward lightly, Ryan nudged Lopez with his toe, but it was obvious that the sec man wouldn't be moving ever again. On the other end, Garcia took a few more seconds to die, but no parting words of defiance came from his lips as he blew bloody bubbles of saliva. A spreading pool of red was on his chest and pouring out from his back where he lay in wet vermilion.

Ryan held on to the SIG-Sauer, having reloaded

the clip outside El Morro. "This is getting bloodier by the bastard minute. I want to find Doc and Mildred and get the hell out of this place in one piece."

"I agree, lover," Krysty said. "Seems sunny Puerto Rico has lost all of its appeal."

"WHAT WAS that noise?" Jamaisvous asked, having sent the sec man ahead before bringing Mildred out from the control room of the mat-trans unit. He paused, and sealed the gateway and comps behind him with unbreakable vanadium steel.

"What noise?" Mildred replied.

"Gunshots. I heard gunshots." Jamaisvous was moving now and gestured with the barrel of his weapon for her to step ahead of him. He kept the heavy Czech target pistol leveled at Mildred's head, the pleated braids of her hair clacking gently against the barrel of the blaster every time she took a breath. His right hand was now handcuffed to her left, and he used the handgun with the ease of the ambidextrous as he moved her along.

"Going somewhere, Silas?"

The man in the long white coat jerked Mildred closer, startled by the sound of Ryan's voice. "Cawdor. Back from chasing *chupacabras*?"

"Yeah." Ryan stepped forward, backed by J.B. and Jak. Krysty and Dean hovered as closely as they could, their weapons also ready if Ryan gave the word. "Your mutie buddies back at the redoubt send their regards."

"How nice. You'll have to thank them for me."

"You okay, Millie?" J.B. asked softly.

"Can't complain," she said. "Some piece of shit stole my pistol."

"Borrowed, Dr. Wyeth. Borrowed," Jamaisvous replied, tugging her arm back harshly and making her wince.

"Where's Doc?" Ryan asked, his voice tight with menace. Mildred started to answer, but Jamaisvous jammed the muzzle of the target pistol against her skull, which silenced her but drew forth a dangerous, almost imperceptible growl of anger from J.B.

"I honestly don't know. Quite a span of years for him to choose from, actually. I sent him forward and I sent him back and back again and forward, with this being the final stop. He should be arriving inside the chamber any moment now, but I imagine after four chron jumps he's not going to be feeling all that peppy, so I wouldn't count on an assist from the good Dr. Tanner anytime soon." Jamaisvous paused. "I was about to take Dr. Wyeth in search of some medical supplies, just in case he does make the trip in one coherent piece."

"Oh, yeah. Right. You're a real concerned guy, Silas." Ryan's blue eye was alert and watching, waiting to find a chink in the mad doctor's armor so he could take him out without hurting Mildred.

"Thanks, I'm sure. Hey, I make the effort. I want to be acknowledged, okay?"

"As what, an asshole?" Mildred asked.

"Shut your mouth," Jamaisvous whispered, his

face close to her own. "Shut your mouth or I'll shut it for you."

"Your play," Ryan said. "What do you want to do, here? Make the wrong move, and we'll chill you so fast you'll be dead before hitting the floor."

"I wouldn't want that, Cawdor. Not when I'm so close. So, in old-world vernacular, what say we play 'Let's make a deal.'"

Ryan smiled back wolfishly. "I don't negotiate with crazy sons of bitches like you, Silas. Always come out on the short end of the stick."

"Who's negotiating, Cawdor? Mildred lives, I live, we all live! Hell of a deal, I think, and best of all, we get to posture and preen and fight another day." As he spoke, Jamaisvous was slowly working his way backward to the heavy steel door leading to the mat-trans gateway and control room. "I've been working toward an agenda for the last two years, and your arrival only accelerated my plans. In fact your timing was perfect."

"What are you talking about?" Ryan asked.

"He lied, Ryan," Mildred said tightly. "He was never placed in cryo suspension. He's a time traveler, just like Michael Brother and Doc."

"Guilty as charged, Cawdor. And like your precious Doc Tanner, I want to go back home, but unlike him, I have the means and the wherewithal to carry though with the plan!"

His back now up against the door, Jamaisvous reached behind with the hand cuffed to Mildred's and keyed the entry buttons, and in reply, the door slid upward into the ceiling. Backing into the doorway of the room, he shoved Mildred forward and hit the lever that brought the door slamming back down.

The same door cut the chain linking the manacles, expediently freeing Mildred and Jamaisvous from each other without the worry of using the key.

The Armorer was at his lover's side in an instant, his usual poker face animated with concern. "You okay, Millie?" he asked.

"Fine. Have to get held hostage more often," she remarked. "Actually seems to have got a rise out of you."

"Have to admit one thing, lover," Krysty said to Ryan as she helped J.B. pull Mildred to her feet.

"What?" Ryan barked back as he glared at the door.

"Jamaisvous does have style."

"Fuck him and fuck his style," Ryan snorted, glaring at the reinforced metal door leading into the control chamber for the mat-trans chron unit. Despite his glowering, the door remained shut. Ryan had heard the sound of an auto lock being thrown from the other side, the bolt sliding solidly home once Jamaisvous had gone through.

Furious beyond reason, the one-eyed warrior pulled his SIG-Sauer from his holster and was about to unleash a hail of 9 mm bullets into the lock when Mildred screamed out shrilly for him to stop.

"What? He get to you?" Ryan snarled, his eye sweeping up and down the physician's body, taking in the new clothing Mildred was wearing. The blaster swiveled in his hand, the muzzle pointing from the door to Mildred's midsection. The one-eyed man's face was a study in barely contained scarlet rage, the flush of heat brightening the scar stretching down his cheek.

"Screw you, Ryan," Mildred retorted hotly. The handcuff was still attached to one of her wrists and the shiny metal caught the light in the room and cast off a series of quick reflections, accenting her words. "I yelled for you to put on the brakes because a stray bullet could end up blasting one of the mat-trans comps behind the door. The last thing we want right now is to have lead flying through some of the operating machinery. It's not worth risking our only way out of here for Jamaisvous."

"Isn't it?" the tall man said, barely repressing his anger as he spit his reply from behind clenched teeth. "Isn't it?"

"Easy, lover," Krysty said from behind Ryan. "There's Doc to think about, too—he might be in there."

Ryan didn't acknowledge Krysty's admonishment, choosing instead to glare at Mildred and hold her equally intent gaze for a span of five seconds before allowing himself to wind back his nerves a notch.

"Okay. Okay. You're right, Mildred. My anger got ahead of my brain," Ryan said tersely, discarding the matter and hoping the woman wouldn't press him. Mildred remained silent, and Ryan gratefully turned his attention to his longtime friend and partner.

"J.B.?"

"On it," the Armorer replied, pushing past with his lock picks already in hand. The smaller man knelt and examined the lock from behind his spectacles. He didn't move, as he studied the mechanism he was facing. "Shit," he finally announced, settling back on his haunches.

"What?" Ryan demanded. "This can't be any worse than fixing that mat-trans unit back in Greenland!"

J.B. threw up his hand and gestured at the mag lock. "Want to bet?"

Crater Lake, Oregon, 2096

DOC TANNER WAS playing with his balls.

At least, that's what Ryan Cawdor called the oddly perfect metal orbs his companion was manipulating with his fingertips. Both Doc and Ryan had thought the twin spheroids lost back in the inferno of Jordan Teague's manse during the fiery destruction of the pesthole known as Mocsin, but one of their companions had recovered the chunks of metal from the corpse of an overeager sec man and turned them over to Ryan for safekeeping.

Now, weeks after the fact, Ryan had remembered the balls weighing down the left-hand pocket of his long coat and gave them back to Doc. Upon their return, the man's lined face had lit up and his eyes watered with shining tears, making Ryan feel more than a bit embarrassed.

"Hell, Doc, they're only a few hunks of metal," Ryan had insisted.

Doc wasn't to be swayed. "Not to me, Ryan. Thank you. Thank you."

Now that he had them back in his hands, Doc was as happy as a child with a new toy. Everyone had queried Doc as to what the things were, but the odd-speaking man had been evasive. He preferred to call them his "spheres to the past, present and future." Ryan wasn't sure what Doc meant by that designation, but as far as he was concerned, the old man was welcome to call them whatever he wished, since he'd been right about the gateways: the matter-transfer units; the physics-breaking reality of the transfer of matter, both nonliving and organic; point A to point X and back to point Q without the worry of having to travel in a straight line to get there in the quickest possible fashion; a genuine way out of a situation minus the dangers of overland transport by animal or wag or foot.

Such high-concept science fiction was the last thing Ryan expected to find hidden in the heart of the secret underground military labyrinth he and his friends had stumbled into, deep in the dark hills of the lands once known collectively as Montana. All the talk of murderous fog with claws and teeth guarding over a great treasure meant nothing to the one-eyed man, since he considered himself by and large to be a stone-cold pragmatist.

It turned out that the treasure lurking high in the Darks was one of the original gateways, guarded by the scientifically created demon dog of hell itself, Cerberus. Ryan pondered the memories of the chill of the wind in that frosty piece of hell, the wet coldness like a damp shroud draped across his scarred face and decided if he had any choice, any choice at all, he'd never go back to that particular desolate chunk of death-strewed landscape. It was the land of the breathing fog, contracting and expanding, alive with cloudy gray tendrils of mist and muck that elongated away from the central mass, the towering mist with the strange pulsating light located inside the center. If a man got too close, tentacles would come slithering out, impossibly fast, and once they touched flesh, the fog became solid, pulling prey into the central body away from gaping human eyes.

Then came the smell of burning ozone, and the sparks, and the inhuman shrieking.

The fog was alive, somehow, and sentient.

There was no way of getting past the swaying mass safely. If one wanted to go forward, one had to figure out a way to punch a hole and go through the thick mist.

Until seeing it for himself those long months ago, Ryan had taken the descriptions of the fog he'd been given back in Mocsin as exaggeration. The one-eyed man had been confident that once he came face-to-face with…it, getting past would be a simple matter of running through or climbing around.

Now that he was standing in such near proximity to the storm cloud, Ryan realized with a mix of awe and fear that he was confronted with a primal force that functioned beyond his own understanding of natural laws and science.

"We could try some grenades," someone suggested.

"Might do," Ryan agreed. "No other trail. No way under it. Damn thing hangs over the edge of that sheer cliff. No way over it, and we can't go back with Strasser's men after us, that's for damn sure."

"And what's to stop the fog from reaching upward into the air as well?" Doc had added softly, his normal baritone pitched higher in a singsong tenor voice. "And pulling us down, down, down into the shimmering abyss?"

Ryan was quiet as he pondered the options. "Blow it," he ordered.

High-ex and incendiary grens were hurled into the gray mass. Noise and fire came whirling out, along with some minor bits of shrapnel made up of rocks and ice, and still the fog hovered, stopping at the bend of the trail, a huge wall of sheer mist.

"Fireblast," Ryan muttered.

"No, not fire, nor blast. Antimatter, Mr. Cawdor," Doc had replied, inspired by the epithet. "I believe that might do the trick. Implode, and the foul fiend will be undone—it will separate from its source."

"Implo gren. Turn that chiller inside out. Yeah," J.B. had agreed. "Good idea."

Two of the small bombs were hurled into the mass. Twin hollow booms came bursting out, followed by an elaborate sucking sensation as the grens imploded, pulling all surrounding matter inward into a vacuum of limitless, impossible smallness. The fog began to uncoil, the spectral tendrils now nothing more than dropped bits of string fluttering outward and dissipating; disappearing into frail streamers that crumbled in upon themselves.

Then the hellish fog was gone. In front of them, past the edge of the ravine, was the sanctuary they sought. Inside the nondescript building built flush against the mountain itself, and unknown to all of them but Doc, was the gateway, the path out of the Black Hills and into a new situation, a new part of Deathlands, a direct line on a one-way trip hundreds, perhaps even thousands, of miles away.

Ryan shook his mind free of the memory of that early discovery, and moved on to the next. Considering how his group of friends had already begun to grow acclimated to the process of matter transfer, coming across a sterile scientific stronghold like the Wizard Island Complex for Scientific Advancement was no big deal. The hidden secrets of Deathlands were beginning to be told, and with each new revelation came numbness, disbelief and finally, acceptance. It was hard to dispute the nose on your face.

"Pandora's box," Doc answered him in a whispered voice.

The words took Ryan out of his reverie. "Who's Pandora? She kin to the Emily you keep talking about?"

Doc sniffed. "No, Pandora has no ties to my own beloved Emily, and I should ask how you know her name, but I suspect I have begun my old habits of babbling in my sleep."

Ryan looked over and met Doc's blue eyes. "Might have heard tell of her that way, yeah."

"I shall endeavor to keep quiet from now on," the old man replied. "As for Miss Pandora and her box, well, it is better known as 'the gift of all.' The revenge of the gods upon all mankind. She was a laughing, beautiful creature set upon this mortal plain by Zeus, who also gave her a shining box filled with all things evil and harmful to man and bade her never to open it, while knowing the foolishness of such a decree."

"Yeah, most women are powerful nosy," Ryan agreed with a smirk.

"And, alas, her curiosity was unstoppable and she flung open the lid unleashing the terrors and plagues within and filled our world with all that is vile, unclean and dark. Still, good Pandora was able to slam the box closed in time to keep a single bit of good within."

Ryan scratched his arm and nodded. "Bit of good in everybody, I guess. Even Trader used to believe that, with the added homily that it paid to keep a watch on that bit of good by sleeping with one eye open at all times."

Doc fixed Ryan with a look. "What was kept in that casket of Pandora's was hope, Mr. Cawdor. Hope. And to this day hope remains mankind's sole comfort in misfortune."

"Is that what keeps your engine running, Doc?" the man with the eye patch asked. "Hope?"

Doc didn't reply, but Ryan saw his long fingers wrap around one of the two small gray globes and hoist it up.

"Hope, Ryan Cawdor, and a spirited game of catch," Doc said, his deep voice resonating as he underhanded the metallic orb to Ryan. "Catch."

Ryan caught and examined the spheroid with his bright blue eye. There was nothing unusual about the ball at least, as far as he could tell. The younger man was unsure why his new friend was so fascinated with the pair, so he decided to ask Doc again what the big deal was over twin hunks of metal.

"Oh, yes, yes, I have ignited your interest, yes," Doc said, losing the air of pomposity he'd been wearing and replacing it with the vocal inflections and smiling face of a young boy.

"Damn straight. First, I thought your little eggs were some kind of grens, but the way you keep tossing them around cured me of that assumption."

"These simple little objects, Mr. Cawdor. They were the first," Doc stated with a twinkle in his eye.

"The first what?" Ryan asked, baffled as usual by the gaunt man's predilection for understatement and riddles. Ryan's moods in talking with Doc ranged from amazement at the knowledge the man possessed about predark artifacts and history to sheer unadulterated rage at having to play Doc's twisted version of his own private guessing game.

"The first to make the trip, there and back again."

Doc said, waggling his bushy white eyebrows on the last three words.

"You mean to use the gateways?" Ryan asked.

Doc smiled broadly, revealing a frightening array of perfect white teeth.

"Ah, in a manner of speaking, yes. You are correct, sir. Like myself, these little balls were test subjects. Hurled back and forth, in and out. Unlike myself, they made the journey sane, whole, intact. No, uh, no added wrinkles. No moss on these rolling stones, no, sir."

Ryan glared at the man sitting across from him before getting to his feet and tossing back the metal ball. "There are times, Doc, when I just don't get you," he said disgustedly.

Doc shrugged, and idly switched the thrown sphere from one hand to another. "I know. There are times, friend Ryan, when I do not get myself."

LATER THAT EVENING, Ryan and Krysty headed toward the depths of the massive information storage and retrieval room located within the walls of the Wizard Island Complex for Scientific Advancement.

The leader of Wizard Island had called Doc Tanner by name when he first saw him, despite neither one of them ever having met.

Why this was so, Doc couldn't—or wouldn't—say.

So, Ryan had decided to take a trip to the island complex's library.

And that's where Doc had come upon them later,

as they huddled in front of a computer, ready to view the contents of a disc that came from an envelope with TT/CJ/Ce marked on the front. Now they were staring at a message on the screen: *Access denied. Refer to subcode CJ, all secs. Go to mainframe on limit/inject. Enter code now for reading.*

"It's *E,* then *M* and finally *Y,*" Doc said quietly from behind. "Spells 'emy.' Almost spells Emily, does it not? Ah, yes, the proper codes, I always lacked the proper codes. However, in this case, I can point you on the right path, since fate or a higher hand has decreed that you see a listing of all my fascinating past."

Knowing the voice, Ryan didn't even turn from the monitor screen as he quickly tapped in the three letters and pressed enter, and was rewarded with a series of glowing green letters that laid out all the cards on the felt of the playing table.

> Subject. Tanner, Theophilus Algernon. Doctor of Science, Harvard. Doctor of Philosophy, Oxford University, England. Birth date and location. South Strafford, Vermont. February 14, 1868. Married June 17, 1891. Wife, Emily Louise, née Chandler. Children, two. Rachel and Jolyon.

"Can't be the same man," Ryan murmured as he navigated a cursor light down to tool bar on the comp screen and clicked on a visual button. In response, a mug shot of a sad-looking man in his early thirties popped up in a window. The portrait was unmistakably their own Doc Tanner, a much younger version minus the complex map of age that now lined his face, but the bright blue eyes that still held a wink of childhood, and the strong white teeth being shown for the camera were one and the same.

Ryan clicked off the photo display and went back to the text of the file, reading farther down beyond the initial entry of biographical information. "No wonder they knew you when we showed up here, Doc. You were in their files, your pic, your bio—stored in here with all kinds of overlapping entries regarding time trawling and matter transfer," he whispered, as both he and Krysty read the secrets presented before their astonished eyes.

"And do you believe what you read, Ryan?" Doc replied.

"Yeah, I guess. Explains a lot. According to this, you were the only success in their entire time-trawling program."

"There are varying degrees of success, Ryan Cawdor," Doc said in a choked voice, before turning and exiting the library, running from the truths it housed.

"I'll go after him," Krysty said. "He sounded pretty upset."

Ryan held out a restraining arm. "Wait a sec, I'm about done here. We'll go together."

Going to the end of the document, Ryan and Krysty read the final entry:

Subject's refusal to become reconciled to temporal correction proved difficult. Several abortive attempts to bribe or cheat his way into the chron chambers were undeniable evidence of his overwhelming desire to travel back to his own time. Subject's constant attempts to rejoin "beloved Emily" and his own century became a considerable irritant. Dr. Tanner was taken by the appropriate responsible authorities and placed under restricted access and egress. When this proved to be an unsuccessful deterrent, subject was used in final-stage trawl and pushed along via temporal conduit to future setting, destination and chronological year, unknown.

"The arrogant bastards," Ryan muttered.

"There's a whole lot of names here, topped by some whitecoat named Herman Welles, who was apparently Doc's keeper during his years as a guest of this Operation Chronos," Krysty said.

"Ancient history, I guess," the raven-haired man retorted as he turned the comp console off, leaving the information disc inside the drive.

Outside the massive vault of the library, they found Doc waiting for them, his head hung low. The older man's eyes were red from crying, and he appeared even more downbeat than usual.

"You read it all?" Doc asked.

Ryan replied in the affirmative.

"I am so alone, my dear Ryan and Krysty. A mere speck of infinity, two centuries old, with my wife and children long dead. Yet in their world, they are all alive. And waiting. Waiting for me to return. So you see, I still cherish the hope that one day I will be able to go back to them if the right gateway is found. Now, if you will excuse me, I think time alone might do my weary soul some good.''

Doc turned and left the couple in the hallway. They watched his back as he slowly made his way down to the bend in the corner and disappeared from sight.

Chapter Eighteen

Within the main control room of El Morro's secured matter-transfer gateway complex, the heavy steel and armaglass door to the six-sided unit was hanging open on twin counterbalanced hinges, waiting to be closed in order to start yet another chron jump.

"Tanner!" Jamaisvous called out as he unlocked the single handcuff manacle left on his aching wrist. "You alive, Tanner?"

Of the temporal-skipping Doc Tanner there was no sign, save a few splatters of fresh red blood near the door to the chamber. Stepping over lightly to the gateway door, Jamaisvous rubbed a finger across one of the drips and it came back smeared with the crimson fluid.

"Still fresh. I'd say somebody's got a bloody nose," Jamaisvous said easily, the target pistol held loosely in one hand, ready for firing at the instant Doc might be stupid enough to reveal himself. Although he wasn't about to admit it, Jamaisvous was impressed. He'd expected Tanner to have been a mewling, puking wad of skin and bones hunched in the fetal position in the center of the gateway, already dead or wishing to be out of his misery. That the old man had instead possessed the stamina to stagger out of the gateway chamber and find a place to hide increased his respect for his fellow time traveler.

"I must thank you for allowing me to track and observe your vital signs during the trawls, Dr. Tanner," Jamaisvous continued as he scanned the room, eyeballing the banks of comps and debating whether there was enough room for a man to conceal himself behind them, his back pressed tight against the wall. Jamaisvous stepped closer, but saw nothing.

"Details of your resiliency were the final components required before I attempted my own return trip into the past, and I must say that your survival now tells me that with the proper usage of drugs I can make my own time jaunt without fear of being ripped apart in the temporal matrix once my molecules have been reassembled in the final stage."

Still peering warily at his surroundings, trying to deduce where Doc had gone to ground, Jamaisvous walked to the central comp console. Within the combination of control room, observation lounge and actual mat-trans gateway, there were a dozen places Tanner might have chosen to secure himself. Jamaisvous was loath to fire his weapon indiscriminately, not wishing to damage any of the sensitive operating gear in the room.

"You see, Tanner, it all boils down to takeoffs and landings," he said to the room, turning and speaking to all directions, since he didn't know where his audience of one was secluded. "In my experiences when trawling, we usually succeeded in picking up our living subjects, but where we consistently failed was in handing them off safely in one piece at the other end. Made for most messy landings."

Jamaisvous now wondered if Tanner hadn't just slunk off into a corner somewhere and died, like a wounded animal. However likely that possibility might be, he didn't want to take the chance, so he continued to speak as he stared at one of the comp monitors that had been tracking Doc's temporal processes.

"The same thing applied in our attempts to send back living matter to select times in the past. We'd break apart whatever living tissue we were sending down the line—monkeys, *chupacabras,* humans—it didn't matter, either way. We would disassemble them in the gateway using the same process designed for safely traveling from one locale to another, shoot their atoms into a quantum field, steer it to the precise instant in the past and bring them back to their corporeal forms—only during rematerialization they never held their shape."

Jamaisvous paused, then smacked one fist into his other open hand with a smack. "Pow! Instant disruption. It would have made for a most effective weapon if we could have taken the time to channel the stream somehow and direct it, but I digress."

Taking his eyes from the monitor screen and back to the control room, Jamaisvous typed in commands one-handed, pausing either to check what the screen revealed or to push the compact mouse control located next to the comp keyboard. Despite his unease of where Doc might be lurking, and over whether

Ryan and his band of thugs would come busting down the door with blasters blazing, the gray-haired man smiled at the readouts the comp was presenting to him in a rush of numerals and codes.

"Takeoffs and landings. There are no mat-trans chambers in the past, and we can only guess if they exist in the future, and believe you me, those of us who knew what was coming down early in the year 2001 weren't counting on the future's hospitality," Jamaisvous said with a chuckle. "So, more tests were needed, but we ran out of time...thanks to you. *If* you'd agreed to go back like a good little boy, and *if* we could have delivered you safely, all of this might have been moot and you'd be considered one of the architects of a brave new world."

Jamaisvous touched a key on the panel of the comp and nodded as the screen flickered and changed. "At least, in a perfect world," he added softly. "Only, if."

The stone walls of the room remained silent.

"I imagine you're not feeling so hot, Tanner. That's to be understood," he said, continuing to speak even as he dropped his guard, stepping closer to the comp. "I honestly did doubt you'd make it back alive, although I hoped there was something about your stubbornness that carried you through safely from past to present to future. Now I know. Even if you did make it you'd arrive here in pieces, but from what this screen is saying to me my adjustments to the quantum phase interface and time-trawl bubble matrix were a success. I appreciate your willingness to lend a hand, so let's deal. You stay tucked away in your shell until I'm out of here, and I won't blow your brains all over the room. Then you can enjoy this brave new world as much as you like."

As a response, Jamaisvous felt a white-hot needle pierce deeply into his upper thigh. He shrieked in stunned surprise, staggering back in time to see the tip of Doc's swordstick pull free from his flesh. The blade had been thrust outward from beneath the desk where the comp system rested, beneath the desk in the alcove where Doc had been hiding.

Doc had been forced to crawl into the nook, knowing Jamaisvous would undoubtedly want to check any temporal readings from his journey, and while there he'd listened and waited.

Doc had struck blind, aiming his jab by the sound of his foe's voice, but the angle was awkward and the old man wasn't up to delivering any kind of real force behind the assault. He'd hoped to land his rapier into the soft gut of the long-winded lord of El Morro, but the blow landed low.

Still, the blade sunk deep, and the sharp bite was ample to send Jamaisvous spiraling backward, the blaster sailing away from his outstretched hand as he fell against an empty swivel chair and completely lost his footing, flipping over the piece of wheeled furniture and crashing to the heavy stone floor, his lab coat tangled around his body.

"I have read Huxley's book, Jamaisvous, and found it lacking. And you, sir, are entirely too much in love with the sound of your own voice,'' Doc said, his rich baritone a cracked whisper of its usual self, like the unearthly dry rustling of fall leaves as stiff October winds whipped through gathered piles. A mad sepulchral whisper was what came out of Doc as he hunched his way out of hiding, crawling stiffly from his lair like some crazed angular spider.

The lower half of his face was a smear of vermilion where the final chron jump had caused something in his septum to burst in protest, and when combined with his high forehead, his long silver-white hair coiling about his shoulders and the glistening white of his perfect teeth shining like pearls within the red smear coating his lower face, he looked utterly, irreversibly, mad.

Jamaisvous had been shocked into a frightened silence, and he scrambled to his footing as quickly as possible, logic replaced by blind terror. The only sound he made came from the numerous phlegmy intakes of air his body was requiring as it struggled to control the flight response.

An expression of complete and total hate transformed Doc Tanner's bloody visage as he wrapped spindly fingers around one of Jamaisvous's feet and pulled the stunned overlord of Chronos closer.

''You...were...*there!*'' Tanner hissed in a spray of pink saliva, his words coming faster, the sentences breaking down into one long stream of slurred accusations as for a brief and shining moment his mind became clear and Jamaisvous's face shimmered into stark clarity and focus—but only in a memory, in a view Doc had snatched as he was hurled into the gateway by Welles and his security team, a glimpse of a solitary figure standing slightly back and watching the struggle to shoot the most unwilling subject into the future.

"You were there," Doc repeated, trying to bring his foe down through fading brute strength. "Lurking in the shadows, observing when I was trawled from that pit of filth, another hundred years of my life stolen away in a single heartbeat! You were there, snickering when I was sent screaming into this future hellhole of a world, taken from the arms of my wife, my children, you were there, you arrogant son of a bitch, you were there!"

"Of course I was there, you quote-spouting hayseed!" Jamaisvous gasped in response, finally finding his voice as he stomped down with his injured leg, trying to free himself from Doc's iron grip. "If I were not, how could I know anything of how Operation Chronos was designed? Sure, I read the manual, but hell's bells, man! I could never hope to master it without some prior knowledge!"

"If you knew so much, why did you need me?" Doc asked as he continued to hang on, dragged across the floor as Jamaisvous moved closer to the dormant mat-trans chamber.

"Even with what I knew then—and combined with what I know now—it's not enough! Not near enough, damn your eyes! We never fully understood how the matter-conversion array could be realigned for temporal transport! It was a working theory, goddammit! A *fluke!* And so were you!"

"I do not accept such simple explanations, then or now."

"Perhaps if you had been less inclined to sabotage and violence, and instead focused on doing as you were asked, you would have been returned to your wife and family. Instead, you made dealing with you a most unpleasant experience, and finally, tragically, they decided to cut their losses and get rid of you in a manner that best suited their immediate needs. They'd been peeping into the future and a few, a select few, saw what was coming."

"Armageddon."

"Yes. I suspected but never really knew for sure. Word had gone out among the power elite, and the puppet masters can rarely keep a silent tongue in their empty heads. You were supposed to be trawled backward in an attempt to alter the future time line. Too bad you were too damn arrogant to stick to the bargain."

Doc felt his heart ache with agony. Every word out of Jamaisvous's mouth was a reminder of what he had lost.

No, not lost.

What had been taken from him, boldly snatched away even as he had been snatched like a flailing rag doll and tossed into the unforgiving winds of a cyclone.

"You are the reason for your eventual downfall, Tanner, not I."

And then, Tanner's remorse and grief were transformed into a new mass of emotions, and the driving one pulsing through his brain and heart was hate. He pulled on the captured foot harder, trying to twist it into a painful position.

Jamaisvous swayed on his feet, stomping down again and again on Doc's forearm and wrist to release the insanely tight grip the man had on his ankle. Freeing himself, the self-appointed lord of El Morro Fortress stumbled toward the mat-trans chamber, ready to flee and abdicate his domain. He looked around, his eyes narrowed to slits as he tried to find the lost blaster, but he didn't see it. What he did see was Dr. Tanner determinedly crawling toward him.

"You just don't get it, do you?" Jamaisvous snarled. "You never did." And then he lashed out at the crawling figure, using his good leg as support to raise his other, bleeding leg in a kick and driving home the point of his polished dress shoe right into Doc's chin, snapping the man's head back and causing his upper body to go high before slamming down painfully face-first to the hard floor.

"Sorry to chat and run, but I really must make this important date," Jamaisvous said in a breathy voice, and followed up the statement with a peal of hysterical laughter. "For, 'I'm late! I'm late! For a very important date!' So late! Too late!"

Nearly unconscious, Doc still managed to drag himself up to watch as Jamaisvous entered the mat-trans chamber and pulled closed the armaglass door. Now, even as the cycle began, and the burst of light erupted within the room and the peals of fog came slithering out from the shimmering metal disks that broke down the molecules of whatever, whoever was inside, Tanner made it up to his side, using one arm to prop himself in a secure position while his other hand splayed awkwardly on the desktop next to him.

His fingers felt, searching until they came across the plastic surface of the keyboard. Doc pulled it toward himself, twisting his hand in the mire of cables behind the monitor linking the comp, pulled it hard, using what was left of his fading strength along with his body weight.

Then, with a final Herculean effort, Doc yanked down, bringing the central processing unit and monitor onto the hard floor, where they both erupted on impact into a mass of sparks, impacting at precisely the same moment that the long figure standing inside the mat-trans unit ceased to exist…at least, at this particular location at this particular time.

Chapter Nineteen

"Shit."

"What?" Krysty asked. The Armorer was almost always a study of grace under pressure. For him to allow himself the luxury of a curse meant he'd hit an unexpected block.

"Shit, shit, shit. This will take a moment," J.B. replied, fishing through his jacket pockets for the needed implement as he continued to speak. "This is a mag lock. Not the hardest kind to navigate past, but they can be triple-damn annoying minus the proper tool. I need an electric wand to reverse the polarity. Once that's taken care of, we'll be on him in no time."

"You got one of those wands?" Dean asked.

"Please," J.B. said, sounding offended.

"Sorry."

"No time, indeed. No time is what I fear the most, John," Mildred murmured, lost in her own inner thoughts. "I never should have allowed Doc to participate in Jamaisvous's mad experiments."

"I imagine you didn't have much of a choice. Doc's his own man. Always has been," Ryan said. "He'd be willing to try anything to get back to his wife and kids."

J.B. twisted the end of the cylinder-shaped handle of the wand he was manipulating and pushed at the locked door. "Wrong frequency," he said to himself and took out a second device, working with it and trying to keep focused.

"How much longer?" Mildred asked.

"Ease up, man's workin' on it," Ryan said.

"What, now you're preaching patience to me, Ryan?" Mildred retorted.

Ryan grinned. "Guess so."

"Got it," J.B. announced. The Armorer had brought forth the necessary tool on the third try and had inserted it into the join between latch and door. Using both hands he twisted it back and forth, and was now rewarded with a loud *ka-thak*, indicating the sliding sec door was loose in the frame.

Ryan gestured with his chin and Jak stepped up to cover him as he slid the heavy door into the recessed area in the stone wall. "Anything?" he asked the albino, who was positioned better to look inside. Jak shook his head no.

The one-eyed man held up a hand and counted silently with his fingers. One…two…three, and he stepped inside, Jak and Krysty both backing him up.

Inside, the control room appeared immaculate at first glance, same as before until one looked closer and saw the disarray of a dropped file of sheets of paper, along with a splattering of blood on a comp keyboard and farther down on the floor itself, a prone Doc Tanner, who was still bleeding from the nose.

"Gaia, Doc. Are you okay?" Krysty asked as she and Dean both knelt next to the elder man.

"How do I look?" he asked weakly.

"Like hell," Dean said.

"Perfect. Exactly how I feel, my boy," Doc replied. "Is Jamaisvous...?"

"Yeah, he's gone," Krysty replied.

Inside the shining blue of the tinted armaglass chamber, the unique heavy vapor created during and after a jump was dissipating and only a few sparks of electrical energy were zipping about, lightning blasts among the thinning clouds. Even through the thick armaglass, Ryan could see the gateway was empty. Running over, he pulled open the door anyway, lifting up the latch and pushing it inward. The unholy arid smell of burned ozone mixed with wet cloth that was always left behind after a jump assaulted his nostrils.

Ryan felt his teeth grind in frustration as he realized another odor was mixed with the gateway's stench—the bitter smell of defeat. Jamaisvous was gone, long gone, the empty floor tiles creaking, mocking Ryan, as they cooled.

"Go after bastard," Jak spit, stepping up the steps into the chamber behind Ryan. "Use button: Last Destination. Follow him."

"Not a good idea," Mildred called from outside the gateway interior. She was standing next to a flashing comp monitor screen on the lower floor where the control readouts were downloading.

''Worked before,'' Jak insisted as he left the chamber.

''Won't work. Not this time.'' The stocky woman was leaning over one of the flat tables and staring at a monitor. Despite the uncertainty of the situation, J.B. shot her an approving look. Since she was still wearing the antique clothing provided by Jamaisvous, Mildred was displaying a generous sampling of cleavage in the low-cut dress.

Mildred didn't notice. Perhaps if she had, the whitecoat's words on dressing to attract your man would have come back to her.

Symbols and numerals flickered on the comp's monitor screen, creating row upon row of single-spaced coded information. ''I think Jamaisvous expected us to try and track his moves. If we go after him, there's no telling where we might end up.''

''Or when,'' Doc added disdainfully. He was now standing, leaning on Dean and on his swordstick, which Krysty had retrieved from where it had been thrown across the room.

''Exactly, or when. I'll have to try and shut down the system, reboot and keep my fingers crossed everything comes back on-line. Otherwise, we're either going to have to go native and share the island with the *chupacabras,* or else find a boat and sail back to Deathlands.''

''Doubt there's many of the *chupacabras* left,'' Krysty said. ''We found the nest. They were coming out of the redoubt in El Yunque.''

Mildred pointed a finger at a block of blinking

numbers in the upper right corner of the monitor. The numbers were in a constant state of motion, the numerals flickering as they changed back and forth. "He's using some sort of randomizer here. I don't know all the redoubt codes and destinations, but even if I did, we'd be rolling the dice with little chance of following him."

A beeping sound caught the woman's attention and she crossed over to the fallen CPU and monitor that Doc had broken. The screen was still functioning despite the large crack running down the face.

"What happened here?" she asked, kneeling as best she could, trying to avoid cutting her bare knees on the broken plastic and glass. "Doc?"

"Pulled it down...trying to get back to my feet."

"I think you might have done more than knock over a computer," she said, tilting her head for a better look at the comp. "This one was acting as the guidance system for Jamaisvous's destination. He didn't enter a code manually at the gateway. He was operating it from a preset in here. You took it offline at the same time he jumped out of here and it switched over to the back-up system, the same one running the randomizer."

"Meaning what, Millie?" J.B. asked.

"Meaning Jamaisvous is going to make his chron jump, but when or where I have no idea. I'd say wherever he ends up, it won't be where he thought he was going."

"What about us?" Dean asked. "We stuck here?"

"No. Like I said, I'll have to try and shut all this

down. Doc, you can help me. Once we reboot and bring it all back on-line, any presets should be erased."

"Do what you have to do, Mildred," Ryan said wearily. "When you think the system is safe, we'll try another jump."

"Any danger of our boy Silas popping back here?" Krysty asked. She was standing next to the open door of the gateway.

Mildred shook her head. "There's always a possibility, but I doubt he'd return here so soon. Besides, we keep the door open and he can't reuse this gateway anyway."

"If does, take care of him," Jak said, grinning. "Take care of him good."

A DAY PASSED before Mildred gave the word they could use the mat-trans chamber and be on their way. She'd changed back into her usual clothing, leaving the gaily colored dress and the shiny baubles behind. Her target pistol had been recovered from the control room undamaged. There would be little or no use for finery where she was going, and after Jamaisvous's treatment of Doc and betrayal of the others, including the poor locals who called Puerto Rico home, Mildred had no interest in hanging on to memories or souvenirs.

Save one.

Dean watched with interest as Mildred touched a small button on the front plate of a desktop comp. A drawer slid out of a recessed area when summoned.

In the drawer tray rested a single compact disc. The disc was silver and clean, with no identifying marks or words. The woman carefully removed the disc from the drawer between thumb and forefinger, taking care not to touch the shining surface, and placed it snugly within a waiting nondescript jewel box cover.

"What's on the disc, Mildred?" Dean inquired. The boy had seen both computer disks and CDs with recorded music during his education at the Brody School in Colorado, and knew they were used for information storage and retrieval.

"Got pretty good with comps at Brody's," the boy said casually, peering over Mildred's shoulder.

"So you've told me before," the woman replied.

"I liked the games—some of them were on discs like the one you've got. Smoking fun. In one, you beamed in a mat-trans and got to go round blasting hell out of muties in old redoubts and space stations on other planets. My fave weapon was the B.F.G."

Mildred bit. "Bee Eff Gee?"

"Big fucking gun," Dean said. "Totally bitching boss blaster."

"That's one thing that never has changed with computers," Mildred sighed, remembering her own weekend addictions to the role-playing fantasy worlds a good game could provide. She'd never been too fond of the violent ones, but instead liked the ones that featured puzzle-solving to advance.

"So, is that a game?" Dean asked.

"No, I'm afraid not. This disc contains Jamaisvous's listing of all the mat-trans units, both in and out of Deathlands,'' she replied. ''A greatest-hits catalog of the world's gateways. In his haste to make a retreat, he must have forgotten to take it with him. He's encrypted the list, and I don't have his password to access the codes, but in the future, with Doc's help, maybe I can circumvent his security tech and we'll have our personal guide to Deathlands and beyond.''

''Waste of time,'' Ryan said, stepping next to the duo. ''That just adds weight to your load.''

''You think?'' Mildred replied. ''You honestly think so?''

''Yeah,'' the one-eyed man replied without hesitation. ''Wouldn't have said so otherwise.''

Mildred held the disc high in one hand and pondered for a moment, before tucking it inside the lining of her denim jacket. ''No offense, Ryan, but I hope to make you eat those words someday.''

''Suit yourself,'' he said, and walked back over to where Krysty and Doc were standing together. The older man was trying to show her something on the comp, but between his own shaky memory and the redhead's lack of interest, neither seemed to be enjoying the demonstration.

''I knew the code, once upon a time,'' Doc said bitterly as he stared at the blue armaglass of the mat-trans unit. ''I knew it like my own address, knew it like the date of the births of my children. No longer.''

''What code is that?'' Krysty replied, having noticed Doc's intense frown as he glared at the gateway.

"The gateway code. The numbers that would enable me to return to my sweet Emily."

"You mean, you could have programmed any one of the mat-trans units to take you back?"

"Once, alas, yes. I could have, although let me add that some mat-trans chambers are more inclined to be taken for a temporal spin than others, but I could have attempted them all until I found the correct vehicle to allow my passage."

"How did you know the code, Doc?"

"I reached past Cerberus's yawning maw and down his heated throat and down farther even into his vile stomach and I pulled it out, dear girl."

"There's a lovely image," Krysty said.

Doc cocked an eyebrow, giving his lined face a quizzical, yet stern look. "Computers. When I was a younger man with a far keener intellect, I adapted to their encrypted uses in a most timely fashion while being held prisoner as a member of Operation Chronos. I never did learn to type worth a damn, I fear, since I kept looking at the keyboard, but I was a demon with that little track-ball thing. A rodent, I think they called it."

"A mouse, Doc," Dean said, stepping next to Krysty. The younger Cawdor had been listening to the conversation, but not wanting to be accused of eavesdropping he decided to join in with his full presence.

Doc gave the boy a quick toothy smile. "Yes, a

mouse! Well done, lad! Your knowledge is growing by leaps and bounds! Yes, Theo Tanner was greased lightning with a mouse.''

''I don't get it,'' Krysty said, running a hand through her flaming red hair. The prehensile locks responded in kind to her grooming, arranging themselves around her shoulders. Used to the way the redhead's hair acted and reacted like a living thing, neither Doc nor Dean commented.

''Get what, dear Krysty?'' Doc replied, looking blank for a second.

''The code, Doc. Did you forget or something?'' Dean asked.

''Or something. When I was sent forward into the future, my physical form suffered in transport. Overnight, I aged thirty years in body, if not in soul, and much of my earlier keenness was damaged as well. Short-term memory loss, young Dean. I remember more of the horrors, but less of the routine day-to-day details. As for the gateway code that I ripped out of the innards of that black project, now all my mind gives up is a fleeting number, here or there, with no order, rhyme or reason.''

''Well, hell Doc, if you had the code, why didn't you use it?'' Ryan asked bluntly.

''I tried, Ryan, God knows I tried my best,'' the old man replied in a whisper.

''Well, I was thinking,'' Ryan began. ''All this with Jamaisvous might have been avoided if I'd been quicker on the draw. I still can't believe you didn't want us to know you were going to try and trawl back to your wife and kids while we were gone, Doc."

"I feared you might try to stop me."

"No. Your choice. You would have had my vote no matter what you did."

"There are all kinds of support, Ryan," Doc said softly. "While you might not be conversant in the mathematics used in time trawling, I sleep easier knowing you are at my back."

Ryan smiled, the expression pulling back the ghastly scar on his right cheek, and clasped Doc firmly on the shoulder. "You've always been a stand-up guy, Doc. From the first time we met, I just knew you were going to drag my ass into all kinds of craziness. I thank you now for not proving me wrong."

Doc beamed. "My friend, I do believe I have been insulted, but I do not take it personally."

Across the room, Mildred made a final adjustment and switched off a comp monitor. "What do you think, Dean? About the disc?" Mildred asked.

"Me? Boy, I think being able to find our way around would be a hot pipe," Dean said, picturing a future when they could choose their destinations within the mat-trans units.

"Dean, that would be worth two hot pipes," Mildred replied with a grin.

J.B. stepped over and placed an arm around Mildred's shoulders, giving her a squeeze. "What's going on?" he asked. At the chamber, Ryan was waiting for the rest of the group to step inside, before closing the door and triggering a new jump to take them into another part of the world—or Deathlands.

"Nothing, John, just making a small investment in our future."

J.B. cocked his head, then nodded. "Sounds good."

Mildred kissed him on the cheek. "Doesn't it, though?"

Epilogue

"Heavens, sir, are you hurt?"

At the sound of the query, Dr. Silas Jamaisvous, or, rather, Torrence Silas Burr, as he'd been known in a previous life a long time ago, opened his cold pale eyes. Above him was a woman in her late twenties with a delicate heart-shaped face dressed in period clothing of what he associated with being late Victorian. She looked concerned, almost frantic, about the status of his well-being.

Jamaisvous didn't recognize the woman, so his first thought of being awakened from a lengthy bad dream was probably incorrect, although up until this instant of hearing the new voice, he'd been under the impression of plummeting downward from a great height with no visible sign of ground below. Since he'd been having the same nightmare of falling since he was a young boy, he'd assumed he was indeed sleeping.

But who was the woman?

The line of thought was doubly rammed home by the fact he was resting on a hard surface, not a mattress, and he could look down his prone body and see a slightly scuffed pair of black dress shoes, and for all his eccentricities, Jamaisvous wasn't inclined to wear shoes to bed.

He turned his attention back to the lady in the old-style dress standing over him. A gingham bonnet was tied tightly over her auburn hair, but a few wisps had escaped from the top and dangled coquettishly over her creamy white forehead. She looked so worried, so fragile, that Jamaisvous had to stop himself from reaching up and tucking the stray hairs back where they belonged...while offering up his own words of reassurance that everything would be all right.

"Can you hear me?" she asked. "Are you hurt?"

"No," he said from his supine position. "I fell, I think."

She shook her head in a manner indicating she knew exactly what he was talking about, which was good, for Jamaisvous was still attempting to find his footing—at least, in a figurative manner. He was glad she hadn't expressed any curiosity over how a man fell and ended up prostrate on his back. Until the queasy sensation in his stomach went away, he was quite content to remain flat on his back until he had to try to move his inclined body.

"This lot is a hazard," the woman scolded, her eyes raking over the empty area in which Jamaisvous was resting. "Fencing should be put in place if construction is going to be continually delayed, else children and adults alike shall continue to use it as the quickest route between two points!"

Jamaisvous merely listened to the tirade and took in a breath of oxygen, feeling the cool of the dusky air flow agreeably into his lungs. The air tasted good and clean, but there was no hint of salt, which even if his own eyes hadn't provided a series of essential clues, told him he was by no means still in Puerto Rico.

"Of course, I'd expect to find children playing their games here as opposed to a man dressed in the formal attire of a scientist, although I must say I am not familiar with the cut of ascot around your neck," the woman continued as she fetched a swallow's-eye blue kerchief from the sleeve of her dress. "Your nose is bleeding. Here, press this against your left nostril. If any blood gets on that white lab coat you will never be able to wash it out."

Jamaisvous took the proffered piece of cloth and wiped his nose, bringing back a bright smattering of blood. He then stuck out his tongue, running it along the exterior of his upper lip. The blood he tasted was indeed fresh.

"My ascot...?" he asked, finally comprehending the first half of the woman's statement.

"Around your neck," she said, and mimed tying a bow around her own graceful throat.

"Oh! My tie. Um, yes. New fashion. From Europe," he said dryly.

"Ah, that explains it!" she replied brightly, kneeling and offering a hand to help raise and support the bleeding Jamaisvous.

"Explains what?" he asked.

"Your attire, sir. And your accent."

Jamaisvous sat up slowly, letting his benefactor's arm do most of the support work. Directly in front of him was a weather-beaten wooden sign staked in the dirt. In black faded letters on white-painted weatherboard the sign read Opening Soon, A New Boutique of Bargains! and at the bottom was a name printed in block capitals: Mr. Wesley Keith Johnson, Esq.

"Might I ask your name, sir?"

"Silas," he replied, and suppressed the silly urge to add "Mariner," choosing instead to stay with "Jamaisvous. Dr. Silas Jamaisvous."

"Doctor? You are a physician?"

"No, madam, I'm a scientist."

"You must meet my husband. He should be home by now. He is a scientist, too!" the woman chatted, steadying him to his feet as he carefully stood.

Jamaisvous swayed like a child's kite in a gale-force wind and his injured leg folded when he tried to place his weight on the limb. Crusted blood could be seen on his pants where he'd suffered a previous wound, but only if one looked closely, and his new-found friend seemed more interested in his face and the obvious nosebleed.

"I appreciate your kindness. Tell me, dear. Who are you?" Jamaisvous asked, his voice gaining strength as he managed to finally stand erect without falling. A train of thought was on a runaway collision with an idea he was developing, and if what he suspected was true, then the gods of the cosmos were certainly having a belly laugh at his expense right now.

The young woman held out a hand gloved in white lace and said in a gracious tone, "My name is Emily, sir. Emily Tanner."

GOLD
EAGLE